Also by Richard Scarsbrook

Novels

The Indifference League
The Monkeyface Chronicles
Cheeseburger Subversive
Featherless Bipeds

Short Stories

Destiny's Telescope

Poetry

Six Weeks

Richard Scarsbrook

Canada Council for the Arts **Conseil des Arts du Canada**

The publisher gratefully acknowledges the support of the Canada Council for the Arts and the Ontario Arts Council for its publishing program. We acknowledge the financial support of the Government of Canada through the Canada Book Fund (CBF) for our publishing activities, and the Government of Ontario through the Ontario Media Development Corporation, an agency of the Ontario Ministry of Culture, and the Ontario Book Publishing Tax Credit Program.

LIBRARY AND ARCHIVES CANADA CATALOGUING IN PUBLICATION

Scarsbrook, Richard, author
Nothing Man and the Purple Zero / Richard Scarsbrook.

Issued in print and electronic formats.
ISBN 978-1-77086-311-8 (pbk.). – ISBN 978-1-77086-313-2 (mobi).--
ISBN 978-1-77086-312-5 (epub)

I. Title.

PS8587.C396N68 2013   JC813'.54   C2013-903674-1
C2013-903675-X

Cover art: Nick Craine
Interior text design: Tannice Goddard, Soul Oasis Networking

Printed and bound in Canada.
Manufactured by Friesens in Altona, Manitoba, Canada in August 2013.

This book is printed on 100% post-consumer waste recycled paper.

DANCING CAT BOOKS
AN IMPRINT OF CORMORANT BOOKS INC.
10 ST. MARY STREET, SUITE 615, TORONTO, ONTARIO, M4Y 1P9
www.dancingcatbooks.com
www.cormorantbooks.com

This book is for
all the unsung heroes,
everywhere.

Contents

"Some are born great,
some achieve greatness,
and some have greatness thrust upon them."

— William Shakespeare,
Twelfth Night
(Act II, Scene V)

Click the "Play" Button Now!

This is the internet video that started it all.

Real Live Superheroes! Nothing Man and the Purple Zero

Uploaded by ObserverX on October 28.

VIDEO DESCRIPTION:
Real Live Superheroes in Action! Mysterious crime fighters Nothing Man and the Purple Zero help foil a bank robbery in progress in Faireville, Ontario! Filmed live on the scene by Observer X, the Eyes and Ears of Faireville.

67,411 Views   25,431 Likes   2,129 Comments

Top Comments

For all the people who have been asking, "Is this fake?" or "Is this for real?" — I assure you, IT IS FOR REAL! The Faireville Police REALLY arrested the bank robbers! Nothing Man and the Purple Zero are THE REAL DEAL!!!!!!!
Posted by ObserverX on October 30

4,890 Likes   21 Dislikes

Gr8 superhero car, 4 sure! Might even B cooler than the Batmobile! Gr8 2 C a team like Batman and Robin out there fighting crime — for real!

Posted by DarkKnight234 on October 29

2,101 Likes   17 Dislikes

Those robbers had guns, but the "superheroes" didn't. Either they've got some serious combat training, like S.W.A.T. police or Navy S.E.A.L.s, or else they are totally insane, disarming dangerous criminals like that. Either way, I love 'em!

Posted by SuperGamer459 on October 29

1,986 Likes   12 Dislikes

Love those retro superhero outfits! Did they travel back through time? For the future of Mankind?

Posted by IamIronMan9999999 on October 28

451 Likes   14 Dislikes

Nothing Man – that "vanishing act" you do is SOOOOOOO cool! Also, you are tall, dark, and handsome. I LUV U! ☺

Posted by FunnGrrl21 on October 30

326 Likes   3 Dislikes

What kind of martial arts was the Purple Zero practising? It looks to me like a blend of Korean tae kwon do, Brazilian capoeira, and African Nguni stick fighting. So fast, so wild, so unpredictable!

Posted by FightBoy221 on October 28

321 Likes   9 Dislikes

So what are you waiting for? It's the internet video that everyone is talking about. You know you want to watch it, too! Click the "play" button now!

Greatness Thrust Upon Them

Maybe it was destiny. Perhaps the die was cast years ago. It is possible that their latent heroism was already inside them, that their imminent stardom was already in the cards. Could it be that their future was determined during that fateful incident at their grade eight graduation?

It is often those whom we least suspect who step forward and take charge in times of chaos and peril; maybe it was their destiny to become superheroes.

It was hot and sticky inside the Faireville Public School gymnasium on the evening of their grade eight graduation ceremony in June. Every student in their class of twenty-eight went home afterward with some kind of athletic, academic, or citizenship award; everyone except Bill Brown, Marty Apostrophes, and Elizabeth Murphy.

Bill Brown, whose report cards collectively contained the words "nice" and "average" more times than any other graduate in the school's history, won nothing, not even a School Letter Award, and there were nearly as many of those little trophies tucked away in the closets and basements and garages of Faireville as there were graduates of the school itself.

The only other boy who graduated without a prize of any kind was the flamboyant, over-indulged Marty Apostrophes, who had logged more hours on the bench in the principal's office than at his desk in the classroom. Nobody was surprised that Marty's particular gifts had gone unacknowledged.

The lone awardless girl in the graduating class was the well-meaning but slightly hyperactive Elizabeth Murphy. Murphy's Law states that, "If anything can go wrong, it will," and Elizabeth had earned a reputation for even her best-laid plans ending in embarrassing disaster. If (by some failure of accounting or some act of sympathy) Elizabeth had actually won a trophy or plaque of some sort, she probably would have just tripped and smashed it anyway.

Behind the lectern atop the gymnasium stage, Mr. Peershakker adjusted his small, round glasses, to help him read more easily from the yellowed notes he had used to conduct the grade eight graduation ceremony for each of his twenty-two years as principal of Faireville Public School. He cleared his throat, and, sounding like a scratchy recording of President Kennedy delivering his "Ask not what your country can do for you, ask what you can do for your country" speech, he began, "Proud parents, proud relatives, proud teachers …"

In the audience of soon-to-be-graduates, Marty Apostrophes was perched like a colourful talking parrot on the edge of his folding chair, adorned in a purple velvet dinner jacket, violet satin bow tie, red-wine-coloured tuxedo pants, and a frilly, fire-engine-red shirt. "Proud puppies," he squawked, mimicking Principal Peershakker's shrill, pseudo-British voice, "proud kittens, proud hamsters, proud goldfish, the proud ghosts of dead relatives …"

Many of the proud parents, proud relatives, and proud

teachers seated around Marty responded with a loud, collective "SHHHHHHHHH!"

"Graduates," Mr. Peershakker continued, undaunted, "this evening's ceremony represents a milestone for all of you. For the parents, it is a moment to congratulate yourselves on your fine parenting."

"Unless you're a crappy parent," Marty mused.

There was another collective "SHHHHHHHHH!"

"For the teachers, it is a moment to congratulate yourselves on your fine teaching."

"Unless you're a crappy teacher," added Marty, glaring with buggy eyes at Mr. Moreau, the science teacher, whom Marty felt had been particularly unfair to him during this past year.

Another "SHHHHHHHHH!" whirled around Marty, louder this time, like a rising wind.

"For the students," droned Mr. Peershakker, "it is a moment to congratulate yourselves on your fine learning."

Practically everyone in the gymnasium pursed their lips for another particularly hissy "SHHHHHHHHH!", but Marty said nothing this time, simply shrugged; he prided himself on being unpredictable.

"And now," Mr. Peershakker announced, with as much drama and enthusiasm as he could muster after delivering essentially the same speech for twenty-two consecutive years, "let us recognize the fine accomplishments of a fine group of fine young people."

From the back of the gymnasium, a loud voice guffawed, "Exact same speech as when I graduated! Same suit and tie, too!" The remark came from Malcolm Apostrophes, Marty's dad.

Even though he was probably correct about both the recycled speech and the durability of the principal's attire, his pronouncement drew disapproving huffs and annoyed glances from most of the other adults gathered within the humid space.

Someone rasped, "Grow up, would ja, Malcolm?"

Another grumbled, "The nut doesn't fall far from the tree, does it?"

Malcolm Apostrophes grinned and winked at their disapproval, and then raised an enthusiastic thumbs-up in his son's direction.

Perhaps Marty's flamboyant personality really was a genetic trait, and was therefore out of his control, as he often claimed it was; upon being ushered out to the principal's office after yet another incident of insolence, Marty would always proclaim, in his DRAMATIC VOICE, "I CAN'T *HELP* IT! IT'S JUST THE WAY I *AM*!"

Marty's DRAMATIC VOICE sounded like a cross between Darth Vader and Dudley Do-Right, and whenever he used it, the other kids in the classroom inevitably broke into conniptions of laughter, which incited sighs and head-shaking from the more composed teachers and retaliatory tantrums from those with shorter fuses.

The first trophies to be awarded on that fateful evening were the Male and Female Athlete of the Year Awards. Nobody in the gymnasium was surprised when the winners were announced.

Lance Goodfellow was already the star first-line centre for the Faireville Blue Flames Triple-A Junior Hockey Team, even though he was only thirteen years old. Because of his advanced skills, at the age of thirteen he had been given special permission to play in this competitive, full-contact league, despite the fact that most of the other players were eighteen years old, with the bruising physiques of full-grown men. He was the team's leading scorer, yet he was rarely ever checked or even touched by an opponent, because the rest of the Blue Flames were inclined to exact painful retribution on any opponent who even looked at their junior superstar aggressively.

Many of the Good Citizens of Faireville were already calling Lance "The Next Sidney Crosby," the way that people used to call Sidney Crosby "The Next Wayne Gretzky."

When Principal Peershakker handed the shimmering Male Athlete of the Year trophy over to Lance Goodfellow, Marty Apostrophes, in his DRAMATIC VOICE, began singing the lyrics to the *Captain America* theme song.

Marty's robust singing was drowned out by an even louder chorus of "SHHHHHHHHH!" from the assembled crowd, but from atop the stage, looking much like the muscle-rippled figure atop the trophy he held, Lance Goodfellow laughed; he found Marty Apostrophes to be unapologetically funny, even when Marty's jokes were at his own expense. Lance wasn't the type to hold a grudge over a joke.

The winner of the Female Athlete of the Year Award was no surprise, either. Virginia Sweet had legs like a gazelle, and could probably outrun one in the wild without even breaking a sweat; she had made it all the way to the national competition in her age group for the hundred-metre dash, and she was already being scouted for a future Olympic team. Virginia had won so many ribbons, trophies, and plaques at track-and-field meets that her bedroom resembled the display case at the Faireville Sporting Goods Emporium.

Many of the Good Citizens of Faireville were already calling Virginia "Our Next Gold Medallist."

As a tribute to Virginia's all-around perfection, Marty began lustily singing the theme song from the *Miss America Pageant*.

"THERE SHE IS …"

His singing was drowned out by a most heartfelt and anthemic chorus of "SHHHHHHHHH!"

Virginia rolled her eyes at Marty, and then again at the stylized, gold-painted figure atop her trophy.

Her legs are too short and her boobs are too big, Virginia mused. I could outrun the chick on this trophy running backwards. With a twenty-pound weight strapped to my back. While eating an avocado-and-brie focaccia and sipping a double-foam soy latte.

Then she bared her perfect, electroplated, white-picket-fence teeth in a stage smile, and held the trophy over her head for all the lesser beings to see. The applause was deafening.

After the clapping and cheering died down for the Male and Female Athletes of the Year, Principal Peershakker decided to save some time and also hand over the Overall Academic Achievement Awards to Lance and Virginia while they were up there on stage. After the applause eventually once again faded to an echo, he also gave the Valedictorian Plaque to Virginia and the Citizenship Award to Lance.

People hooted and whistled. Cameras flashed. Lance and Virginia acknowledged their admirers with thousand-watt smiles and royal waves.

"And now," announced Principal Peershakker, "the academic awards, for the top student in each individual subject!"

There was some polite applause. Everyone suspected that these awards would also be divided equally between Lance and Virginia. And that would be okay! Lance and Virginia were *superstars*, and they deserved to be awarded like superstars. The Science, Geography, and Music Awards went to Lance. The Mathematics, French, and Art Awards went to Virginia. And, since they were tied with 100 percent each in English class, the two superstars shared the English Award; they held the trophy between them, and they smiled once again for the machine-gun clattering of a hundred cameras.

When their parents were summoned to the stage to help them hold the trophies (since Lance and Virginia had run out of hands with which to hold their prizes), it looked like they were posing for their wedding photos. Of course, many of the Good Citizens of Faireville naturally assumed that Lance and Virginia would marry one day, as they would make a Perfect Couple; together they would produce genetically superior children, who would score lots of goals, run very fast, achieve A+ grades in every subject, and probably also save the planet in their spare time, just for fun, without even trying very hard.

◎

Hot tears trickled from the corners of Elizabeth Murphy's eyes, despite her best efforts to hold them back. She'd believed that she maybe had a chance of winning the Art Award. After trying *so* hard, for *so* many years, it would have been nice to be recognized for being good at *something*.

Elizabeth's father owned the local art supply shop, and he had once been a painter of some importance. If she had won the Art Award, her father would have been so proud of her. Elizabeth was constantly experimenting with her own sculptures, paintings, and multimedia creations in the workspace behind her dad's shop. She had even won a couple of blue ribbons at the Faireville Agricultural Fair and Exposition: one for an impressionistic painting of the red-and-black-streaked clay hills of the Faireville Badlands (where its famous natural gas fields had once been), and one for a sculpture, a Roman-style theatre mask painted silver and black, with catlike eye openings and a sly expression etched upon the mask's mouth. Nevertheless, Elizabeth's successes at the Faireville Fair didn't count toward her art class grade at school.

Mizz Greener was the grade eight art teacher at Faireville Public, but she was really a gym teacher, the sort of gym teacher who screamed slogans like "All it takes is all you've got!", "Failure is not an option!", and "Hustle, hit, and never quit!", while sitting on the sidelines in a folding chair, devouring salt-and-vinegar potato chips and chugging Coca-Cola from a two-litre bottle. Yes, Mizz Greener was really a gym teacher, so when she said "Jump!" she expected you to pull muscles doing it. "Gawd, Elizabeth," she would shriek. "You throw like a girl, not like an athlete! You can't throw to save your life!"

Mizz Greener got stuck teaching art because none of the other teachers wanted to do it, and Mizz Greener was *not* happy about it.

In art class, Mizz Greener gave marks for how perfectly a student replicated the example of the craft she had assigned in class, which was usually torn from a yellowing 1950s art magazine left behind by the previous art teacher, and then photocopied and distributed to the class (after which Mizz Greener would guzzle Coke and read *The Sporting News* or *Golf Digest* in the comfort of her desk chair).

The problem was that Elizabeth, as the daughter of a professional artist and a free spirit herself, always wanted to do something *different* in art class, rather than the same thing as everyone else; ever since kindergarten, Elizabeth had never been much interested in colouring inside the lines.

Virginia Sweet, on the other hand, was the sort of student who had coloured perfectly inside the lines since the moment she first held a crayon between her exquisitely manicured fingernails; her art class assignments always looked exactly like the picture on the photocopied page. Virginia was also the star player on every team that Mizz Greener coached, which perhaps gave her an additional advantage over Elizabeth when the winner of the Art Award was determined.

So, Virginia Sweet won the Art Award, and Elizabeth Murphy didn't.

Elizabeth swatted the tears from her face. Really, she scolded herself, *what were you expecting, Elizabeth?*

It would have been nice to see her father smile again, though.

Although Marty Apostrophes would never, *ever* shed tears over something as ridiculous as a little plastic trophy with gold spray paint on it, he caught himself sighing when the Science Award was handed over to Lance Goodfellow.

Marty liked science. A *lot*. Especially chemistry. And when Marty liked something, he poured *all* of his substantial energy into it. His Science Fair project, about chemical reactions, was *awesome*. It was *amazing*. And it totally proved what he set out to prove, which was supposed to be the *point* of a Science Fair project.

Because of the intense, eye-watering rotten-egg stench produced by one of his experiments, and the noxious, fire-alarm-triggering smoke produced by another, the school had to be closed for two days until the fumes cleared. This made Marty temporarily popular with his fellow students, but it didn't increase the value of Marty's stock with any of the teachers. By grade eight, Marty had earned a reputation as a troublemaker, and it was generally assumed that Marty had done a *spectacular* job making trouble at the Science Fair, when this time all he sincerely wanted to do was make good science. Nevertheless, despite his protestations, Marty's *awesome, amazing* Science Fair project was given a punitive grade of zero by Mr. Moreau.

Marty glared again at his now-former science teacher, who sat there in the front row of the audience, wearing his ever-present, bleached-white lab coat. *You're a fraud, Moreau*, Marty thought, while trying to burn holes in the back of the teacher's balding head with his hot, hateful stare. *You're a* textbook *scientist. You* talk *about science, but you never* do *it. You've never had a stain on that lab coat in your entire career.*

As if reading his mind, Moreau turned around in his seat and said, "Why, *Marty!* Are you *graduating* today? No summer school this year?"

Whatever, Marty told himself. *I'm the richest kid at this lame school; I could buy myself a room full of crappy plastic trophies if I wanted to. Hell, I could buy real gold ones if I felt like it.*

"SHHHHHHHHH!"

Did I say that out loud? Marty wondered. *I've got to stop doing that.*

"And now," Mr. Peershakker droned, "it's time for us to hand out the School Letter Awards, which are presented to each student who has achieved an average final grade of at least seventy percent and who has participated in at least one school sport and at least one extra-curricular activity during his or her grade eight year."

Marty Apostrophes was heard to quip, "It's the *Everyone Gets an Award* Award!"

Ironically, Marty was not called upon to receive one. Although he had played sporadically on the intramural volleyball team, and he had performed rather well on the debating squad, the zero he received for his school-closing Science Fair project was enough to bring Marty's average down to 69 percent.

As a solid B student, though, a bench-warmer for the touch football team, and the founding member of the School Beautification Club, Bill Brown *would* have received a School Letter Award, had it not been for his final mark of 65 in French, which brought his overall average down to 69.9 percent.

While any other student would have complained vociferously about losing out on an award over a measly *one-tenth of one percent*, Bill just accepted it. *The rules are the rules*, he figured.

Elizabeth Murphy also remained seated while nearly every other graduate traipsed onto the stage to receive their consolation prize. Despite her respectable overall average of 87 percent, and her enthusiastic involvement in *every* school club and committee, Elizabeth had never signed up for any sport, and was inclined to "feel ill" before practically every Phys. Ed. class, so Mizz Greener personally ensured that Elizabeth would not take home a school letter.

Behind the Staff Room door, when a kind-hearted teacher had suggested that Elizabeth, in light of her other efforts, be considered for a school letter anyway, Mizz Greener threw down her triple-pepperoni pizza slice and jumped up from her seat, hollering, "What kind of example would that be to the other kids? No pain, no gain!" She tugged her sweatshirt down over her expansive belly and bellowed, "Play hard or go home! Winners never quit, quitters never win! We might as well give an award to Marty Apostrophes while we're at it!"

"No way!" Mr. Moreau chimed in. "No freakin' *way*! My favourite lab coat *still* smells like rotten eggs. No *way* are we rewarding that kind of behaviour."

So, the kind-hearted teacher retreated, and hence there was no School Letter Award with Elizabeth's name engraved on it, either.

◎

Once all of the major awards had been divided evenly between Lance Goodfellow and Virginia Sweet, and once the School Letter Awards had been distributed to everyone else except Marty, Elizabeth, and Bill, there remained but one trophy to be awarded.

"The Unsung Hero Award," Mr. Peershakker announced from behind the lectern, "is a special award."

The gymnasium full of proud parents, proud relatives, proud teachers, and proud students collectively held their breath.

"It's special," Marty noted, "because someone other than Virginia or Lance might possibly win it."

This time, nobody shushed him. Everyone knew that Marty was right.

"It is a special award," the principal continued, "because it does not necessarily go to the student with the highest grade in any particular subject. It does not necessarily go to the student who can run the fastest or score the most goals. It does not necessarily go to the student who is gifted with musical or artistic talent. It does not necessarily go to the student who stands out in any one particular way, be it academically, athletically, or artistically."

"It should be called the *Not Necessarily* Award!"

The gymnasium reverberated once again with a hissing "*SHHHHHHHHHH!*", like steam being released from a pressure valve.

Did I say that out loud, too? Marty wondered.

Principal Peershakker cleared his throat and continued, "It goes to the student who always does the best that he or she can. It goes to the student who exemplifies kindness, goodness, and a positive attitude. It goes to the student who is always encouraging to others. It goes to the student who is always willing to lend a helping hand, without seeking any reward or affirmation."

Elizabeth Murphy turned around in her seat and whispered excitedly, "It's you, Bill! It's you! He's talking about *you*! You're the Unsung Hero, Bill."

How could the Unsung Hero *not* be Bill Brown?

Who always volunteered to put away the volleyballs and take down the net after gym class, when everyone else was running for the change room? Bill Brown.

Who, every day and in any weather, served as the unofficial crossing guard for the kindergarten kids when they toddled home at noon, while everyone else was eating their sandwiches and drinking their chocolate milk in the classroom? Bill Brown.

When Bill noticed all the garbage strewn around the schoolyard, he initiated the School Beautification Club. At first there were many enthusiastic participants, but by the time Earth Day had come and gone, there remained only one student still picking up garbage, washing windows, watering flowers, and raking up dead leaves. Who? Bill Brown.

When that freak ice storm hit, and several of the teachers' cars slid backward into the ditch beside the staff parking lot, who walked all the way home in the freezing rain, and then arrived back at school driving a tractor from his parents' farm, which he used to pull all of the cars out of the ditch? Bill Brown.

When a couple of kids were circling each other on the schoolyard, fists clenched, as others egged them on, shouting "Fight! Fight! Fight!", who was the one who always intervened and convinced the combatants that the conflict wasn't worth the consequences? Bill Brown.

How could the Unsung Hero *not* be Bill Brown?

Elizabeth also had a *personal* reason for believing that Bill Brown was the Unsung Hero: when she was in kindergarten, she had been a fan of the cartoon superhero She-Ra, and she loved to pedal her Big Wheel tricycle up and down the street, pumping her small fist in the air and shouting She-Ra's tag line, "the Princess of Power!"

Because she was missing both of her front teeth, though, it came out sounding like "the Pissah of Powah." Nearly a decade later, in grade eight, a few of the girls were *still* calling her "the Pisser of Power," until someone quietly reminded them that this incident happened in *kindergarten*, for goodness' sake, and perhaps it was time to grow up and move on. The girls stopped teasing her about it after that.

Who spoke up? Bill Brown, of course. He hardly ever said a word, but when he did, it always made a difference.

How could the Unsung Hero *not* be Bill Brown?

"The winner of this year's Unsung Hero Award," Mr. Peershakker said, "without saying a word to anyone, in *complete anonymity*, donated her *entire allowance* to various local charities."

Wow, thought Elizabeth, *Bill did that, too? Wait ... did he say "her"?*

Principal Peershakker's voice trembled with rare emotion. "The winner of this year's Unsung Hero Award is ..."

All the lungs in the gymnasium held their breath simultaneously.

"... *Virginia Sweet!*"

There was an eruption of applause. People leapt to their feet, regaling their salon-styled heroine with a standing ovation.

Marty Apostrophes remained seated, muttering incredulously, "Virginia's heroism is *unsung*?"

This time, nobody could hear Marty for the applause, so nobody shushed him.

Elizabeth Murphy wondered aloud, "How did they know she donated all of her allowance money if she did it *anonymously*?"

Nobody heard what Elizabeth said, either.

This time, the tears flowed freely from Elizabeth Murphy's eyes. The world was *so* unfair! How could the Unsung Hero *not* be Bill

Brown? She glanced over at Bill, to see how he was taking this disappointing news.

Bill was wearing one of his father's old brown suits, which was just *slightly* too big for him. He smiled and clapped along with everyone else. He hadn't expected to win any awards, so he wasn't disappointed. Bill seemed completely unaware of the injustice that had just been perpetrated, and this made Elizabeth feel even sadder.

"We would now ask *all* of our graduates to join us onstage to receive their graduation diplomas," Mr. Peershakker said, like a man who was looking forward to enjoying a nice glass of brandy in the quiet comfort of his own home.

So, the awardless Marty, Bill, and Elizabeth joined the rest of their classmates atop the tiny stage, pressing themselves into the only small space that remained, directly beside the principal's lectern.

For each of his twenty-two years as principal of Faireville Public School, Mr. Peershakker had concluded the grade eight graduation ceremony by quoting the same inspirational line: "As the great William Shakespeare wrote, in his play *Twelfth Night*, 'Be not afraid of greatness …'"

He paused for dramatic effect.

"'Some are *born* great …'"

He glanced over at Lance Goodfellow and Virginia Sweet, with their armloads of trophies.

"'Some *achieve* greatness …'"

His eyes swept across the students gathered in the middle of the stage, each clutching a Faireville Public School Letter Award.

"'And some …'"

Mr. Peershakker paused again, removing his round eyeglasses. He looked directly at Marty Apostrophes, and then at Elizabeth Murphy, and then finally at Bill Brown, his face uncharacteristically animated, his eyebrows arched dramatically upward, his eyes wide and bulging.

"'And some ...'"

He clutched his chest and stepped away from the lectern.

"'Some ... have greatness ... thrust ... upon them.'"

Mr. Peershakker lurched backward, teetering on his heels. Then he stumbled forward and toppled over the edge of the stage. With a dull thud he hit the floor face down, arms and legs splayed out at awkward angles.

While everyone else stood in awe, motionless, still processing what had just happened, Bill Brown leapt from the stage.

He was followed by Elizabeth and Marty. They knelt around their fallen principal.

"Sir, can you hear me?" Bill yelped, rolling Mr. Peershakker onto his back, loosening the principal's tie, and then gripping his wrist, feeling for a pulse. "Sir? Sir?"

"Mr. Peershakker?" Elizabeth cried out.

"Mr. P?" Marty said. "Say something, Mr. P."

"*Greatness thrust upon you*," he rasped.

Those were Oliver Peershakker's final words. His eyes fluttered and closed.

Bill Brown looked up and pointed at the nearest adult. "Call 911 and ask for an ambulance," he said. "Do it right now."

The nearest adult stood there frozen, in shock, wondering if maybe Bill was talking to someone else.

Elizabeth Murphy jumped to her feet, grabbed a cell phone from the hand of a slack-jawed onlooker, and called for an ambulance herself. Marty Apostrophes sprinted out of the gymnasium, down the hallway, and through the front doors of the school, so there would be someone out there to lead the emergency personnel to where Mr. Peershakker lay.

Then Bill Brown, who had earned his First Aid Training Certificate as a member of the Faireville Young Farmers Club, administered

CPR to the fallen principal, pumping his chest, inflating his lungs, until the paramedics arrived on the scene and pronounced Oliver Peershakker dead.

As Mr. Peershakker was strapped to a gurney and wheeled out through the panicked crowd, the voices in the gymnasium rose to a frenzied roar, and the heels of seldom-worn formal shoes clickity-clacked randomly back and forth across the hard tile floor, where Bill Brown remained on his knees, staring through the basketball back-board at the far end of the gym, muttering, "I tried. I tried."

Bill seemed to be somewhere just outside of his own body, and he didn't seem to notice when Elizabeth Murphy settled onto the floor beside him, wrapped her slender arms around his shoulders, and whispered, "I know you did, Bill. I know you did."

This tender gesture by Elizabeth will be erased from Bill's memory by the shock overtaking his brain and body, but Principal Peershakker's final words will echo in his mind, repeating like a mantra: *"Greatness thrust upon you. Greatness thrust upon you. Greatness thrust upon you."*

Maybe Mr. Peershakker's final words, spoken directly to Bill Brown, Elizabeth Murphy, and Marty Apostrophes, were merely coincidental. Perhaps those words didn't really mean anything special. Maybe, in the throes of death, Mr. Peershakker really didn't know who he was talking to.

But maybe he *did* know. And maybe those words really *did* mean something.

Perhaps the die *was* cast as early as the evening of their grade eight graduation.

Some are born great, some achieve greatness, and some have greatness thrust upon them.

Maybe it *was* their destiny to become Superheroes.

Chapter One

Dynamic Duos

B ill Brown watches Miss Womansfield, the grade twelve English teacher at Faireville District High School, as she glides across the front of the classroom, silhouetted by the smeared-chalk clouds suspended on the blackboard behind her. She always wears these billowing, loose-fitting cotton dresses, but Dale Bunion, who lives next door to Miss Womansfield, claims to have caught glimpses, over the fence from his bedroom window, of her lounging atop a chaise longue in a bikini. Dale says, to anyone who will listen, that their English teacher has a "killer little bod," and that she's "totally hot, like, *nuclear* hot." Bill Brown's eyes (along with the eyes of practically every other male student in the classroom) follow Miss Womansfield as she moves, straining to see the evidence beneath the drapery.

Many of the female students are as taken with Miss Womansfield as the guys are, but for mostly different reasons. She's an enigma, she's unique, she dares to be herself. She has the self-assurance of a much older woman, but a personal style and sense of fun similar to the young women she teaches. She's an English teacher, but she's equally comfortable discussing politics, B-grade horror movies, religion, vintage muscle cars, ethics, Iron Maiden lyrics, or just about anything else.

When most fashion-conscious women are strutting around in skin-tight spandex tights and plunging, revealing necklines, Miss Womansfield's form is revealed only as a shadow, when the afternoon sun shines through her translucent dresses. When most dark-haired women dye their hair blonde, perhaps believing that "blondes have more fun," Miss Womansfield has coloured her formerly honey-toned mane midnight black. (Dale Bunion claims of her new hair colour that "now the curtains match the carpet," but not even the most gullible student believes he could actually know this.)

From his seat beside Bill, Marty Apostrophes whispers, "Honestly, I don't see how she gets all the guys so steamed up. She dresses like a pilgrim girl from another century. She's no Marilyn Monroe. She's no Beyonce."

Bill just shrugs, while stealthily admiring the hints of his English teacher's form.

Miss Womansfield is famous for her in-class digressions. (She is also famous for legally changing her name from Mansfield to Womansfield after her divorce, but that is another story.) In class today, what begins as a lecture about the roles of Rosencrantz and Guildenstern in Shakespeare's *Hamlet* digresses into an animated discussion of famous duos throughout the history of popular culture.

"So," Miss Womansfield says, "in today's episode of *Hamlet*, the courtiers Rosencrantz and Guildenstern, supposed friends of Hamlet, have been hired by Hamlet's uncle, King Claudius, to spy on him. Rosencrantz and Guildenstern always appear as a pair. Why do you suppose that Shakespeare chose to have two characters perform their role in the play, instead of just a single character? Why do you suppose he wrote them as a duo?"

Bobby Bingham suggests, "Well, Rosencrantz and Guildenstern are huge ass-kissers, and their ass-kissing seems more extreme with two of them doing it."

He intends this response to get a cheap laugh from some of the other guys, but Miss Womansfield encourages him to continue. "Yes! Yes, Bobby! They *are* rather sycophantic characters, aren't they? And, two of them *kissing ass*, as you put it, does seem more blatantly fawning than merely one character doing it. Is that what you're saying?"

"Uh, sure," says Bobby. "Yeah."

Bobby leans forward, with his palms pressed against the edge of his desk, flexing the well-developed muscles in his arms and chest. Some of the girls at Faireville District High School (mostly the younger ones) think that Bobby is "man candy" and "a hottie with a body," but others would describe him as "arrogant" and "an asshole." Bobby only cares about the girls in the former category, and, just for them, he wears his trademark skin-tight black T-shirts, emblazoned with macho slogans like "Hockey Hero" and "Pump It Up!" *For the ladies*, Bobby thinks, as he flexes his triceps.

"And, by the way, Bobby," Miss Womansfield says, as if she's reading his mind, "if you ever want to sound smart for the ladies, you can always substitute the noun *sycophant* for *ass-kisser*. It's a much sexier word."

The way that Miss Womansfield says *sycophant* makes Bill Brown sigh. And the way that she says *sexier* causes his breath to catch in his throat.

As Bobby's line mate on the Faireville Blue Flames Triple-A Junior Hockey Team, Rick Rousseau decides to add something to the discussion, to support his buddy just like he would out there on the ice.

"Because Rosencrantz and Guildenstern are fawning, sycophantic characters," he says, "neither would have the character or courage to stand alone. They bolster each other's servile, parasitic personalities. Insincere characters are more blatant in their insincerity when surrounded by other insincere characters ..."

"Well done, Richard!" Miss Womansfield says.

"I thought you hated being called *Richard*," Bobby says.

"I'll let it slide this time."

"I'll bet you'd like to *let it slide* with Miss Womansfield, eh, *Richard?*" Bobby brays.

"Aw, Ricky's *blushing!*" says Dale Bunion, another of Rick's teammates from the Faireville Blue Flames.

Miss Womansfield makes a quick defensive play to save Rick from any further embarrassment; he hardly ever speaks in class, and she doesn't want this to be the last time.

"So," she says, thinking quickly, "can anyone think of any other examples from fiction in which two characters serve the needs of the story better than one? Any famous duos from popular culture … literature, film, television …"

And so today's digression begins.

Marilyn Agnes speaks up from the back of the room. "Bugs Bunny and Daffy Duck?" Marilyn says everything as if she is asking a question. "Beavis and Butt-Head? Ren and Stimpy? SpongeBob and Patrick?"

"Okay, *Scarilyn*," Bobby Bingham says. "We *get* it. You want to be an *animator* when you grow up."

The last part is true; Marilyn already draws a cartoon for the school newspaper, called *Punk Mouse and Rebel Kat,* which is very popular with the students (although Principal Tappin has tried to have it removed several times).

"You're the one who needs to grow up, Bobby," Kitty McMann says coolly.

Kitty sits in the extreme back left corner of the classroom, next to Marilyn. Her black vinyl tank top reveals the tattoo sleeves that cover her arms. Today her dyed-purple hair hangs loosely around her shoulders, but sometimes she gels it up into a tall, spiky Mohawk.

Normally, Bobby would mutter something like, "And you need to grow some *tits*, Kitty," or if the Rubenesque Marilyn had been the one to tell him to "grow up," he would have responded with something like, "And you need *stop* growing, chubby." But Bobby won't say anything to provoke Kitty McMann.

Once, while extremely drunk at a bonfire at Cedar Beach, Bobby Bingham attempted to put his hands up inside the front of Kitty McMann's tank top; he had assumed that girls with tattoos and purple hair *welcomed* this sort of attention. Bobby's assumption was incorrect. Petite Kitty knocked out the six-foot-four hockey enforcer with one well-placed roundhouse punch. The blood that gushed from Bobby's nose was copious.

"What? No snappy comeback?" Kitty taunts. When Bobby doesn't take the bait, Kitty continues. "By the way, Bobby, name-calling went out of fashion back in grade two. In case you missed the bulletin."

Bobby's fists clench. "Listen, Kitty ..."

Bill Brown grins; he enjoys seeing Bobby Bingham put in his place.

Miss Womansfield intervenes again. "Okay," she says, "these cartoon characters are good examples of fictional duos in which two characters serve the story better than one. Any other suggestions?"

"The Blues Brothers," says Susan "Strat" Sanderson.

"Predictable," mutters Bobby Bingham.

Bobby is not incorrect; everything in Strat's world is connected to music. Strat got her nickname from her robin's-egg-blue Fender Stratocaster electric guitar, which she plays in her own blues band, who were called the Wailing Pussies until Principal Tappin forbade them from playing in the school's annual talent contest, "Faireville High's Got Talent." So they changed their name to the Wailing She-Kats instead, and they won the show.

"Good," says Miss Womansfield. "The best car chase scene ever was in *The Blues Brothers*, in my humble opinion."

Bill Brown looks up from the latest issue of *Car and Driver*, which he's got hidden inside his English binder. He glances at Marty beside him, and whispers, "The best car chase ever was in *Bullitt*. A '68 Mustang GT with a 390 versus a '68 Charger with a 440 Magnum. Steve McQueen did a lot of his own stunt driving, too." Bill sighs. "Best. Car. Chase. *Ever.*"

"Did Steve McQueen have a partner or a sidekick in *Bullitt*, Bill?" Miss Womansfield asks.

Bill snaps his binder closed, concealing the *Car and Driver* magazine. *How did she hear me?* he wonders. *I was only whispering! She's got hearing like a predatory cat.*

Miss Womansfield has sprung at the opportunity to bring him into the discussion, because obtaining contributions from both Rick Rousseau and Bill Brown during the same class would be a *major* pedagogical victory.

Bill watches Miss Womansfield lean back against her desk, stretching and arching her back. *Her hearing is not the only thing about her that's catlike. Wow.* Bill stops breathing for a moment, and the blood rushes south, emptying from his brain and engorging another organ. *Oh no, oh no, oh no! Shit shit shit!*

"Uh, no," Bill manages, his cheeks flushing red. "Bullitt worked alone."

Bill hopes desperately that Miss Womansfield will move on to someone else, but she persists.

"Bill, do you think it would have served the story better if Bullitt had had a partner to reinforce his character?"

"No," Bill says. "Bullitt was a strong enough character to stand on his own."

He desperately hopes that nobody will notice that part of his own anatomy is standing on its own, too.

"Nice boner, buddy," a grinning Marty Apostrophes whispers from beside Bill. "Now you're blushing, too."

"Shut up, Marty," Bill hisses.

If Miss Womansfield's predatory-cat hearing has picked up on this exchange, she chooses to ignore it. Instead, she says, "Can you think of any fictional duos to add to our discussion, Bill?"

"Sorry," he says. "All of my heroes work alone, I guess."

Like Superman, thinks Elizabeth Murphy. She watches the lean, farm-labour-toned muscles in Bill's arms twitching as he shifts nervously in his plastic seat, and she listens to his voice, quiet and tentative, yet somehow also deep and resonant.

"Clark Kent and Superman!" Elizabeth yelps. She tries to make contact with Bill's dark, shy eyes as she says this, to communicate to him that she thinks that *he* is a Clark Kent waiting to transform into a Superman, but Bill is looking down at his lap at the moment. *He's so cute when he's shy like this*, Elizabeth thinks.

"That's not a duo, *Lezzy*," Virginia Sweet grunts from the front right corner of the room. "Clark Kent and Superman are the same guy, you ditz."

"Dual personality," Elizabeth says. "And don't call me 'Lezzy.'"

"I didn't. You must be hearing things. I called you *Lizzy*."

"Don't call me that, either. I go by *Beth* now," Elizabeth says.

On cue, Virginia's Minions, the little clique of girls who dress like Virginia, talk like Virginia, style their hair like Virginia, and follow Virginia around all day like obedient little lapdogs, croon, "*Ooooooh ...*"

"Like we care, you spaz," huffs Virginia.

"Virginia!" says Miss Womansfield, her vivacity slightly restrained. "Would you like an opportunity to contribute? Please, add your suggestions!"

Virginia rolls her eyes. "Barbie and Ken," she says.

One of the smart-asses in this class would have named the anatomically impossible fashion dolls anyway, and then glanced obviously toward Virginia and her boyfriend, Lance Goodfellow, who sits beside her. *But I beat them to it,* Virginia thinks. *Virginia wins again!* Jimmy "Zig Zag" Rogers pushes his dreadlocks out of his face with the sleeve of his tie-dyed jersey, revealing puffy, bloodshot eyes. Then he raises his hand.

Zig Zag was accused by Principal Tappin of repainting the banner above the stage at "Faireville High's Got Talent" to read "Faireville's

Talent Got High." Tappin threatened to take away his girlfriend Strat's first-prize trophy if Zig Zag didn't confess to the crime, but Zig Zag was careful to use paint that would easily wash off his hands afterward, so the charges were eventually dropped.

"Jimmy?" Miss Womansfield says.

"What, man?" Jimmy calls everyone "man."

"Your hand is up, Jimmy," she says. "Did you have a duo to add to our list?"

"Oh, yeah, man," Zig Zag says, in his slow, relaxed manner. "Shaggy and Scooby, man."

"Also predictable," says Bobby Bingham.

"We've got a lot of cartoon characters on the list now," Miss Womansfield says. "Any duos from other milieus to suggest?"

"Oh!" Bobby cries out. "I've got a duo for you! Farmer Bill and Farty Marty!"

"Hmm," Miss Womansfield says, "this is the first fictional duo with whom I am unfamiliar. Are they characters from a contemporary movie? A video game, maybe?"

"They're a *gay* duo," Bobby says. "They hide it well, but the evidence is there. Like Batman and Robin. Or Bert and Ernie."

Bill Brown closes his eyes and sighs. He thought that this rumour had finally faded away.

Calm, stoic Bill Brown had always considered himself to be a loner, an individual, a singularity. He was never looking for a sidekick, and he had certainly never intended on befriending a flamboyant, unpredictable entity like Marty Apostrophes. Nobody at their grade eight graduation would have predicted that Marty and Bill would become friends in high school, and no one at the assembly on the first day of grade nine saw it coming, either.

While Bill Brown hovered at the back of the Faireville District

High School's huge, echoing gymnasium, listening politely to Principal Tappin's intentionally intimidating "Welcome to Grade Nine (But Don't Goof Off or Screw Up)" speech, Marty distracted everyone by jittering around right in front of the stage in his wide-collared, sequin-encrusted orange shirt, his lemon yellow designer jeans, and his custom-designed high-top sneakers, which blinked with multi-coloured LED lights.

Wow, Bill thought, shaking his head, *this kid never misses an opportunity to make a spectacle of himself. He's going to get killed here.*

In the crowd of fresh, nervous grade niners, Bill Brown was statistically average and socially invisible, which was just the way he liked it. In his plaid jacket and work-worn Levi's, Bill didn't stand out any more than a pebble in a farm field. Marty, on the other hand, was about as subtle as a fireworks display.

Right from the beginning of his first week at Faireville District High School, Marty's spectacular personality got him noticed, and not necessarily in a positive way. While most of the kids at Faireville Public had been Marty's classmates since kindergarten, and had built up immunity to his wild, attention-seeking ways, not all of the students at FDHS were prepared to be as accommodating.

As Marty changed out of his gym clothes after their first high school Phys. Ed. class, Bobby Bingham snapped Marty's buttocks with a towel.

"What the hell!" Marty yelped, rubbing the already-swelling red welt on his behind. "Didn't locker room bullying go out of fashion in the fifties?"

"Ah, stop whining," Bobby said. "You look like the kind of guy who likes it in the ass."

"Say *what*?"

"Well, you play floor hockey like a fag, and you dress like a fag," Bobby said, "so I can only assume that you are a fag."

"No," countered Marty (with admirable confidence, considering the difference in size between himself and Bobby), "I don't dress like a 'fag.' I dress like a *rock star*. Like Mick Jagger, or David Bowie."

"Mick *Fagger* and David *Blow Me*? Who were *gay* together?"

"It was just a rumour that Bowie and Jagger were together that way," Marty said, in a serious tone. "It's an accusation that both have repeatedly denied."

"Deny whatever you want, *homo*."

"Sir," said Marty, in an exaggerated upper-class British accent, "you *wound* me!"

"I'm *gonna* wound you!" Bobby snarled.

Marty danced sideways to avoid the end of Bobby's towel snapping at him again, saying, "Look, *mon frère*, it's a free country. I've got the freedom to dress like a rock star if I want to, and you've got the freedom to dress like an auto mechanic if you want to. Isn't democracy *awesome*?"

"My *dad's* an auto mechanic," Bobby snarled, taking a step toward Marty.

"Well, good for him!" Marty said, dodging another towel snap. "My dad's an incorrigible, womanizing drunk! Inheriting a pile of money and not having to work for a living will do that to a guy. It's bad for a person's morals. Much better to be a working man, I think."

From behind Marty, another guy called out, "Hey, you little fruit! Are you making fun of working people?"

"No, no, I didn't mean it like that," Marty explained, while dodging the bite of another snapping towel. "I was being sincere! It's hard to tell with me sometimes."

"Fuck you, Richie Rich," someone said.

"Gay boy," another voice grumbled.

"OH, MY FRIENDS, MY FRIENDS!" Marty wailed, in his DRAMATIC VOICE. "DON'T YOU *LOVE* ME ANYMORE?"

In elementary school, Marty's DRAMATIC VOICE earned him

gales of laughter from the other kids, but in the high school locker room it just caused towels to snap at him from all directions.

"Ow! Ow!" Marty cried. "Stop it!"

"Are you gonna cry, fag?" some mocking Neanderthal whined.

From the back of the change room, Bill Brown stepped forward.

"Leave him alone."

Bill could hardly believe he was doing this. His heart was pounding in his throat. For a quiet, unassuming guy like Bill Brown, stepping out like this felt like an out-of-body experience. It always did.

"What?" Bobby Bingham taunted. "Are you a spoiled rich snot like him? Sticking up for your own?"

"My parents are farmers."

"So that's why you smell like cow shit."

"We don't have any cows," Bill said, trying not to take Bobby's bait.

"Maybe you smell like *him*, then, eh?" Bobby said. "Are you this little fag's gay lover or something?"

"No, I'm not."

"I think you are."

"I'm not."

"I think you are."

"He's not," Marty added.

Bobby snapped his towel at Marty again, aiming for his face this time.

"Ow! Gawd! Ow!" Marty cried, rubbing the spot under his eye where the wet towel hit him.

Bobby glared at Bill, and grumbled, "Bet that's what he says when you're doing him in the ass, eh? Bet you have nicknames for each other ... Farmer Bill and Farty Marty."

"Come on! Are you serious?" Bill said. "Are we in kindergarten? *Poo poo! Pee pee!*"

"Farmer Bill likes plowing Farty Marty," Bobby said. "In the *poo poo*. With his *pee pee*."

A couple of guys in the locker room snickered.

At this point, Bill was tempted to take a swing at Bobby, but he suspected that this was just what Bobby wanted: an opportunity to beat someone down, to make himself feel bigger than somebody else in front of an audience. So instead, Bill turned away from Bobby and looked at every other guy in the room, one at a time, directly in the eyes.

"Are the rest of you guys just going to sit there and let this happen?" said Bill.

Most of the others just looked away.

"If you're not part of the solution," Bill said, quoting Eldridge Cleaver, "you're part of the problem."

Silence.

Then, finally, someone said, "Drop it, Bobby."

"Yeah, man," someone else added, "leave him alone."

"Right," said Lance Goodfellow, in his authoritative voice. "It's over. It ends here."

And everyone would remember the day that heroic Lance Goodfellow saved weird Marty Apostrophes and his quiet, plaid-shirt-wearing buddy from a locker room beating.

But it wasn't over. And it didn't end there.

At 3:15 p.m., on the first Friday afternoon of the school year, while most of the rest of the students of FDHS raced from the building to go hang out at the Gasberg Mall, or to watch YouTube videos on their computers, or to drink beer or smoke weed in some-body's unoccupied basement, every hockey-playing boy at the school raced to the ice rink to audition for the Varsity Hockey Team.

Marty Apostrophes hovered outside the locker room door of the FDHS hockey rink, waiting for Bill Brown to arrive.

"You're late," Marty cursed, as Bill rushed around the corner into the concrete-block hallway.

"My watch says 3:15 p.m., sharp," Bill replied.

"Next time, we need to synchronize watches," Marty said, in an uncharacteristically serious tone.

"What is this, *Mission: Impossible?*"

Marty stepped aside to reveal a large, black duffel bag.

"Our secret weapons are packed inside this bag," Marty whispered. "Right after we toss them into the room, we'll jam this door shut, and the idiots can suffer in there for a while. I've already propped a board under the exit door handle on the rink side of the locker room, so they won't be able escape that way."

"Secret weapons?" Bill wondered.

"When we're finished," Marty cackled, "none of these douchebags will ever snap *me* with a towel again. And they'll think twice about calling us fags, too." He reached into the gym bag and pulled out a pair of plastic pop bottles, duct-taped together. One bottle was filled with a clear liquid, the other with thick, murky goo. "Remember my grade eight science fair project?"

"Who could forget?"

"Well, I've refined my formula since then. At 3:20, ten minutes before they're supposed to head out onto the rink, we'll pop the tops off the bottles, toss them into the room, and when the contents of the two bottles run out on the floor and mix together, well …"

"Well what?"

"A lot of smoke. And a lot of stink."

"It isn't poisonous, is it?" Bill worried. "I mean, I don't want to *kill* them!"

"No, no," Marty laughed, "the smoke created by the reaction is perfectly harmless. And it dissipates within a few minutes. It just smells *really* bad. Think rotten eggs, blended with sour milk and sewer gas … with just a *hint* of vomit."

"Aw, I don't know Marty. I'm not sure how this will stop Bobby Bingham from picking on you. Or me. It might make things worse. Maybe we should think this through a bit more before we —"

"IT'S 3:20!" Marty screamed, in his DRAMATIC VOICE. He kicked open the locker room door and hollered, "GO! GO! GO! START LOBBING BOMBS, SOLDIER! GO! GO! GO!"

With military precision, Marty and Bill each grabbed a pair of bottles, unscrewed the caps, and lobbed them one by one into the locker room. As Bill threw his tenth "secret weapon," he wondered, "Jeez, do you think just a couple of these would have been enough?"

"I DON'T DO ANYTHING HALF-ASSED," Marty bellowed. "ESPECIALLY NOT REVENGE!"

The swearing and screaming began inside the room.

"What the ... "

"Who farted ... oh ... oh my gawd!"

"I can't see! I can't see!"

"Awwww! Oh! It's terrible!"

"FEEL MY WRATH, CRETINS!" Marty cried (DRAMATI-CALLY, of course). "BILL! JAM THE DOOR CLOSED WITH A BOARD!"

"With what?"

"A board!"

"What board?"

"I don't know ... find one."

"*Find* one?" railed a disbelieving Bill. "You mean you didn't *bring* one?"

"I used it on the other door."

"You didn't bring one for *each door*?"

"Um, okay," Marty said, "a slight flaw in the plan. Let's just run away instead."

But it was too late. All of the hockey players came surging out of the locker room, coughing, swearing, gagging, rubbing their eyes, and shouting.

Bobby Bingham, dressed in all of his hockey gear but his helmet and gloves, click-clacked on his skate blades through the crowd of hacking, gasping hockey players. When he saw Marty, still gripping one of his twin-bottled bombs, Bobby grabbed him by the collar and raised his fist in the air. As tears and snot streamed down Bobby's face, he shrieked, "I am going to kill you, you dirty little faggot!"

With admirable fortitude, Marty looked up into the face of his nemesis and said, "Hey, Bobby, can I offer you a tissue?"

"I am going to kill you," Bobby reiterated.

"Let him go, Bobby," an authoritative voice echoed from just inside the locker room. Like a conquering hero, through the pungent chemical smoke, emerged — who else? — Lance Goodfellow.

"I'll let him go after I've beaten the shit out of him," Bobby snarled. "This is personal."

"Let him go."

Bobby did not let Marty go.

"Let him go, or you're off the team," Lance commanded.

"You're not the captain *yet*," Bobby challenged.

"I *will* be," Lance countered.

Bobby shoved Marty backward as he released his grip on Marty's collar. It was already a foregone conclusion that Lance Goodfellow would be the captain, the leading scorer, and the Most Valuable Player for the Faireville District High School Varsity Hockey Team.

Lance glared at Marty, and then at Bill, and then at Marty again, demanding, "What the *hell*, guys?"

"YOU GUYS *EARNED THIS* FOR SNAPPING ME WITH TOWELS YESTERDAY," Marty raged, using his DRAMATIC VOICE for maximum effect. "YOU *EARNED THIS* FOR MAKING FUN OF ME AND BILL!"

"What do you mean, we *all* earned this?" Lance said, remaining as improbably cool and reasonable as always. "Did we *all* snap you with towels yesterday, Marty? I seem to recall that some of us actually *stood up* for you. Have you been snapped with a towel since then?"

"Well, no, but ..."

"And did we *all* make fun of you, Marty?" Lance continued. "I don't think *all* of the guys trying out for the hockey team teased you. Do you think it's fair to punish *all* of us for the actions of a few, Marty?"

Bobby Bingham looked eagerly at Lance. "Can I punch him now? To teach him a lesson?"

"No, Bobby, you can't punch him now. Or ever. See, I went to elementary school with Marty, and I happen to know that he's pretty good with chemicals. He could do a lot worse than what he did today. The last thing we need, as a team, is you hitting him, and then Marty bombing us all in revenge, right before a crucial game or something."

It was a question of brute force versus chemical warfare. It was a situation in which there could be no winner.

Lance looked at Bobby with those cool, superhuman eyes, and then at Marty, and said, "So let's call a truce, okay, gentlemen?"

"Okay," said Marty, grudgingly.

"Okay," said Bobby, even more grudgingly.

"And get over the homophobia, Bobby," Lance said. "Some of your teammates could be gay, for all you know. Someone who could beat the crap out of *you* might be gay. So maybe you should tone it down a bit."

Lance gestured to the rest of the guys in their hockey gear. "Okay, boys, it looks like most of the smoke has cleared. Let's hit the ice."

Despite the fact that Lance was only in grade nine at the time, each one of those hockey players knew who he was, and even the grade twelve guys did as Lance instructed. They all filed back into the dressing room, silent except for a few sniffles and stifled coughs.

Then Lance turned to Bill. "How the hell did you get mixed up in this?"

"I don't know," Bill mumbled.

"I thought you should have won the Unsung Hero Award last year, Bill," Lance said. "I want you to know that."

"Thanks, Lance."

"And now you're throwing *stink bombs*?" Lance said. "You're better than this, Bill. Remind yourself of who you are."

Bill hung his head as Mr. Peershakker's final words rolled once again through his mind: *"Greatness thrust upon you. Greatness thrust upon you. Greatness thrust upon you. "*

"You two had better get out of here," Lance advised, "before Principal Tappin comes looking for the guys who stank up the locker room of his arena."

And, with that, Lance Goodfellow strode back into the locker room, heroically as always.

"That smug, pretentious goof!" Marty raged. "Who does he think he is, talking to us like that? And you *thanked* him?"

"He's right, Marty," Bill said calmly. "We *are* better than this."

Marty shrugged. "Still, that was pretty *awesome*, wasn't it? Bobby Butthead will think twice before he messes with *us* again."

"I suppose he will," Bill conceded.

"We should call ourselves the *Dynamic Duo!*"

"We should definitely *not* call ourselves that, Marty."

In Miss Womansfield's grade twelve English class, Bobby Bingham smirks in the direction of Marty and Bill, hoping for a reaction from at least one of them. "Farmer Bill and Farty Marty," he repeats.

Marty, showing remarkable restraint, just rolls his eyes and mutters, "Neanderthal."

Bill Brown sighs again.

Elizabeth Murphy wants to scream out loud. She wants to shout out that "Farmer Bill" Brown is *not* a fictional character; he is the most *real* person that she's ever met. And he is *not* gay; Elizabeth is observant enough to know that Bill is sexually attracted to females ... she has seen the physical evidence.

Elizabeth wants to bellow at the top of her lungs that Bill is her Unsung Hero, that Bill is Superman to her Lois Lane. But she has never said any of this to Bill himself, and to proclaim it now would just embarrass him more; so Elizabeth clenches her fists, closes her eyes, and holds her tongue.

While his girlfriend Virginia giggles quietly beside him, Lance Goodfellow says, "Let it go, Bobby. Seriously."

Sensing trouble, Miss Womansfield glances up at the clock on the classroom wall, while trying to think of an unobtrusive way to intervene.

"Okay," she says, "we've only got a minute or two left, so here is your assignment for next class: pair up with another student, choose one of the many fictional duos we've discussed today, and together you can compare and contrast the duo you've chosen with Rosencrantz and Guildenstern."

When all of the other students have paired up, Bill Brown, Marty Apostrophes, and Elizabeth Murphy are left over. Bill looks over at Elizabeth; maybe this time he should work with her instead of Marty, if only to put that annoying rumour to rest once and for all. Elizabeth catches his glance, and her heart races.

But then Marty says, "You and me, as always, eh, Bill? Who should we do? Leonard and Sheldon? Spock and Captain Kirk?"

Bill hesitates. "Maybe this time we should try working with someone else, you know, to try to ..."

Elizabeth holds her breath. She sits up straight, pulls back her shoulders, and pushes her breasts forward.

"Come on, man," Marty says to Bill, "I can't pass English without you! Oh, and also, I snuck the keys to the garage out of the vault, so I can finally sneak you out there to look at the classic car collection. If you still want to see it, that is."

"Really?" Bill says, his eyes widening.

"Really."

"Okay. Let's do Captain Kirk and Spock, then."

Elizabeth deflates. Bill has chosen a barn full of dusty old cars over her. She sighs emphatically.

She will still choose Superman and Lois Lane as the subjects of her class assignment, though. Bill Brown will be her Superman … eventually. He just needs more time to realize that she's his Lois Lane. *Patience, Elizabeth. Patience.*

She forces a smile and says, "Oh, well, I guess I'll work alone this time. I don't mind."

Miss Womansfield says, "You're a good sport, Elizabeth."

As the buzzer rings and everyone scrambles for the classroom door, Elizabeth overhears Marty say to Bill, "You know, instead of using Rosencrantz and Guildenstern, we could *really* impress Miss Womansfield by comparing Spock and Kirk to Hamlet and Horatio instead. They're the real power couple in *Hamlet.*"

Bill is incredulous. "Did you actually *read* the play?"

"Oh, I'm full of surprises," Marty says. "'Goodnight sweet prince. And flights of angels sing thee to thy rest.'"

Elizabeth watches them walk away together. She is sure that Bill is as straight as a laser beam, but … could the rumours about Marty be true? Did Elizabeth just see Marty look at Bill the same way that she looks at him?

That could complicate things, she thinks.

Chapter Two

Behind the Gates

B ill stands before the grand entrance gate of the Apostrophes Estate. The Baroque-style fence that surrounds the fifty-acre property reminds Bill of something one might see surrounding a Transylvanian vampire's castle, with twelve-foot-tall cast iron bars tipped with spikes and gargoyles snarling down from atop stone pillars.

An intercom speaker is built into the pillar beside the massive iron gate. Bill pushes the black button, and it buzzes with an anemic wheeze.

He waits, shifts his weight from one foot to the other, and then swaps the books he's carrying from his right hand to his left, and then back again. Between school and his evening farm chores, Bill stopped by the Faireville Public Library and checked out some books to help them with their report comparing Rosencrantz and Guildenstern to Captain Kirk and Spock: *Star Trek 101*, *I Am Spock*, and a strange little volume called *Captain Kirk's Guide to Women*. He would have also borrowed *Study Notes for Hamlet*, but somebody else (probably another student in Miss Womansfield's English class) had already nabbed it.

Bill pushes the intercom button again and waits. The home that Marty shares with his father (and a half-dozen domestic employees) is indeed an *estate*. Through the dense wall of shrubbery that stands behind the iron fence, Bill can see glimpses of the imposing stone buildings: the servants' quarters, the coach house, the stables, the greenhouse, the pool house, and the massive, turreted, Neo-Gothic mansion itself. Local legend has it that the Apostrophes Estate was not always so protected, so secluded; at one time it was Faireville's social and cultural centre.

When the mansion was originally built by Manfred Apostrophes, Marty's great-grandfather, there was no fence at all. The tall, elaborately carved front doors were left unlocked during the day, and the good citizens of Faireville were allowed to enter the foyer, the ballroom, and the dining hall at their leisure. Of course, nobody ever went inside without permission, but it made the townspeople feel included and respected that they had an "open invitation" to the home of Faireville's wealthiest residents.

As the owner of Apostrophes Munitions, Manfred had made his fortune manufacturing hundreds of millions of the bullets and shells fired by Allied soldiers in the First World War. Since there had been a lot of former soldiers hobbling around on crutches in Faireville at the time, and the names of many local boys on the Memorial Cenotaph in Victoria Square, Manfred Apostrophes figured that keeping the mansion open to the public was the least he could do to acknowledge the wartime sacrifices from which he had so greatly profited.

Manfred Apostrophes also loved to dress up in elaborate outfits, and so he threw lavishly decorated and copiously supplied costume balls on every possible occasion (New Year's Eve, Mardi Gras, Chinese New Year, Valentine's Day, the First Day of Spring, Groundhog Day, Swedish National Day, and so on), to which everyone in Faireville was always invited, regardless of their age, profession, or social standing. Bill supposes that, if there is a gene for flamboyance and attention seeking, Marty definitely inherited it from his great-grandfather.

But then the Depression came, and people became bolder about coming to the mansion to be fed, to seek paid work, and to beg for money for clothing and shelter for their families. Manfred Apostrophes' philanthropic largesse couldn't quite keep up with the needs of the good citizens of Faireville without erasing his company's profits completely, so that's when the iron fence went up. Bill assumes that this was probably also the point when local sentiment turned against the Apostrophes family.

If the First World War had made Manfred Apostrophes the richest man in Faireville, then the Second World War elevated him into the ranks of the wealthiest in the country. Of the billions of bullets fired in that terrible conflict, enough were supplied by Apostrophes Munitions for Marty's great-grandfather to build a glass-domed, heated indoor pool (where nobody ever swam), stables for his collection of race-bred horses (which nobody ever rode), and a large, elaborately decorated addition for the Prime Minister to stay in when he visited (which he never did). Manfred Apostrophes also built servants' quarters to house all of the employees required to maintain it all.

All of the costume balls were cancelled, even the one on Halloween; yet Manfred Apostrophes was often glimpsed roaming the grounds of the estate festooned in lavender satin, peacock feathers, and long, carpet-like capes. Meanwhile, more armless and legless veterans hobbled and wheeled themselves around town, and the names of many more local boys who were killed in action were added to the Cenotaph in Victoria Square.

By the time Manfred's son, Marshall, Marty's grandfather, took over as president of the company, Apostrophes Munitions had enough money in the bank for the next three generations of the family to live comfortably on the interest alone, and thanks to the wars in Korea and Vietnam, Marshall Apostrophes accumulated enough extra capital to add two of his own architectural signatures to the Apostrophes Estate.

The first building constructed during Marshall Apostrophes'

tenure as the family patriarch was a tribute to the family's heritage: the Apostrophes Munitions Museum, which looks like a one-tenth scale model of the Apostrophes mansion. It houses and displays pristine, fully functional examples of every rifle, shotgun, handgun, and cannon to ever fire an Apostrophes Munitions bullet or shell during any war or conflict.

Whenever anyone enters the museum, an audio recording of Marshall Apostrophes crackles to life. "APOSTROPHES MUNITIONS!" he boldy declares. "PROUDLY PROTECTING THE GOOD FROM THE EVIL SINCE NINETEEN-OH-SEVEN!" The voice sounds eerily like Marty's own DRAMATIC VOICE, but an octave higher in pitch, and without even a trace of irony in its bravado; kind of like Darth Vader after inhaling a balloon full of helium.

The second building erected by Marty's grandfather was more personal: an enormous carriage house–style garage, built to house Marshall Apostrophes' collection of rare and exotic automobiles. The Carriage House comes complete with its own gas pump, maintenance pit, and an auto mechanic named Bloombottom (whom Bill is pretty sure is still on the Apostrophes Estate's payroll, despite Bloombottom's advancing age).

Marty's father, Malcolm, hasn't added anything to the grounds of the estate, other than installing security cameras on all of the buildings and having privacy hedges planted around the mansion itself. The cameras went up after the Apostrophes Munitions Museum was robbed one night, and the still-at-large thieves made off with most of the newer rifles and handguns in the collection; Marty's dad also made the unpopular decision to close the museum to the public after that.

The privacy hedges were put in after the mansion was repeatedly pelted at night with rotten tomatoes and eggs. Apparently, some of the hard-working, down-to-earth citizens of Faireville didn't take kindly to anyone living among them in such luxury without working for it.

Bill pushes the intercom button a third time and sighs. Has Marty forgotten about their homework assignment? *Again?* Bill shakes his head; he's got to be up at 5:00 a.m. tomorrow to deliver the last load of cucumbers of the season to the Krispy Green Pickle Factory before he goes to school. He can't afford to be up all night while Marty goofs off. Nevertheless, Bill already knows from past experience that the evening will go something like this:

- Bill will enter the Apostrophes mansion with all of the books and other resources that he and Marty will need to complete their assignment.
- Marty will spend the first hour of their work session hunting for pens and paper, or finishing the video game he's been playing, or just generally flitting about in a distracted state.
- When they finally sit down at the massive, ancient oak table in the stadium-like, crystal chandelier–lit formal dining room, Marty will decide that it's time for a break, and he will ask their cook, Mildred, to prepare a snack. When Mildred asks, "And what would be to Master Apostrophes' liking this evening?", Marty will request some impossibly complicated dish like Shredded Quail Confit with Seven-Year-Old Cheddar and French Dijon Mustard on Sea-Salted Rye Melba Toasts.
- An hour later, after Mildred has somehow prepared and served the impossible snack and cleared away the dishes, Marty will decide that they should move from the dining room to somewhere "more comfortable and casual," which usually means the den.
- The den is adorned with the stuffed heads of lions and bears and antelopes shot with Apostrophes Munitions bullets by Marty's grandfather and great-grandfather; it has been retrofitted by Marty's father with a home theatre screen larger than the one at the

Cineplex in Gasberg, along with a sound system powerful enough to be heard on Mars, a pool table, a pinball machine, and several vintage arcade-style video game consoles. Marty will talk Bill into playing "just one game of pinball" or watching "just one video" or listening to "just a couple of tunes" before they begin working on their assignment.

- After playing a dozen games of Pac Man — or watching a movie or two, or listening to three or four albums by the bands that Marty's into this week — the butler, Von Kruugen, will enter the den to pronounce that, "The grounds are being closed and secured for the night, Master Apostrophes." This will mean that it's time for Bill to go home.

- Back in Bill's tiny, cluttered bedroom, inside the small, cluttered farmhouse that Bill shares with his parents and six younger siblings, Bill will work all night to finish the assignment for Miss Womansfield's English class. He will type the last words as the sky begins to glow crimson in the east, and, of course, he will put both his and Marty's names on the finished product.

- Without having slept at all, Bill will put on his boots, his cap, and his overalls, and he will trudge out into the cool, dewy early morning to start the tractor and tow a trailer full of freshly picked cucumbers to the pickle factory.

- Bill will inevitably earn a B+ on the assignment (he's sure he could earn A grades if he wasn't so tired all the time), and Marty will also earn a B+ for having done absolutely nothing.

Bill pushes the buzzer button on the intercom again. He huffs, taps the toe of his boot on the ground, and stares up at the full moon that has slowly risen into the clear, starry sky.

Maybe this time he should have accepted Elizabeth Murphy's offer to work with her. Elizabeth is an A+ student, and she's especially smart in English class, always hyper-analyzing everything she reads and then expounding about it at great length in class. Maybe it would be nice to be paired up with someone like Elizabeth for a change. Maybe *she* would do all the work, and put *Bill's* name on it.

Bill noticed the way Elizabeth looked at him when she mentioned Superman and Lois Lane in English class, but he was careful to make sure that she didn't notice that he had noticed. Bill Brown can get a stalled tractor running again, and he can unclog the flue in the grain elevator when it jams, but Bill has no idea what to do when a female looks at him with eyes like deep, dark pools.

On other occasions, Bill has also noticed Elizabeth's breasts straining against the stiff material of her paint-speckled coveralls, and he's detected the curves of her hips and the tapers of her thighs moving inside her bulky garments as she walks. He's collected all of these hints and glimpses, and he suspects that Elizabeth Murphy is hiding a rather attractive figure beneath those utilitarian threads. Alas, romancing a woman is nothing like rebuilding a carburetor or sharpening the blades on a field mower, so the Mystery of How to Approach Elizabeth Murphy remains unsolved.

And her hair! Some of the more catty girls (the ones who call her Lizzy when she wants to be called Beth, the ones who used to call her "The Pisser of Power") enjoy making fun of Elizabeth's untamed, product-free hair, but Bill longs to reach out over the chasm that separates their desks, to touch that thick, wheat-blonde mane; he imagines that it feels as soft as spun silk, that it smells like summer wildflowers.

Bill shakes his head. He hasn't got time for daydreaming. There is always so much to do. Bill's father is fond of saying, "The Lord loves a working man"; Bill supposes he's glad that *someone* appreciates him.

He punches the intercom button again.

"Come on, Marty," he grumbles. "I haven't got all night."

The speaker crackles with Marty's voice: "Jeez, dude! Chill out! Patience is a virtue, you know."

The electric lock hums, and the iron gate swings open, screeching out a high, operatic note. Bill is walking along the cobblestone pathway toward the towering Apostrophes mansion when he is intercepted halfway by Marty.

"I got 'em!" Marty cheers, jangling a ring of keys in Bill's face. "I got 'em! The keys to the Carriage House!"

"Ah, Marty," Bill sighs, wincing at the thought of the alarm blaring at 5:00 tomorrow morning, "we don't have time for that. We've got work to do."

"Whaddya mean, '*We don't have time for that*'? You're Mr. Car! Mr. Automotive! You *obsess* about cars! You read those car magazines *all day!*" He puts on his DRAMATIC VOICE, slapping the back of his hand against his forehead like Scarlett O'Hara in *Gone with the Wind*, and he cries, "YOU LOVE *CARS* MORE THAN YOU LOVE *ME!*"

This makes Bill laugh. Marty always finds a way.

Marty turns onto the path to the Carriage House, and Bill follows.

"Seriously, Marty," Bill says. "Let's finish our English assignment first, okay? We don't have time to goof off."

"Bill, my friend," Marty says, in a Television-Medical-Drama-Doctor sort of voice, "you need to find *more* time to goof off."

"You goof off enough for both of us. Seriously, the assignment is due tomorrow."

"The assignment is already finished," Marty says evenly.

"What? *Seriously*, Marty."

"*Seriously*," he says, mocking Bill. "It's finished. My dad helped me write it. Abigail is typing it for me right now."

(Abigail is Marty's dad's Personal Assistant.)

"Come on," Bill says. "You're kidding me."

"I'm not kidding you. It turns out that my dad was a huge fan of the original *Star Trek* series. Captain Kirk was, like, his *role model* when he was a kid. Which explains a few things about Dad, I suppose. And Abigail's got a Master's Degree in English; the only person with more knowledge about *Hamlet* was maybe Shakespeare himself."

Bill is speechless. Marty never fails to surprise him.

"So," Marty says, jangling the keys in Bill's face again, "do you finally want to go see my grandfather's car collection, or not?"

"Definitely," Bill says. "Definitely."

The Apostrophes Carriage House is rumoured to contain showroom-condition models of some of the rarest cars in automotive history. Many vintage auto magazines and TV shows have tried to get permission to bring their cameras inside, but no outsider has ever been allowed in. Bill's heart throbs just like it did when he was thinking about Elizabeth Murphy. (Okay, maybe it wasn't *just* his heart.)

"Hey, Marty," Bill says as they make their way toward the Carriage House, trying to sound as casual as possible, "what do you think of Elizabeth?"

"Elizabeth *Murphy*?" Marty shrugs. "I *don't* think about her."

"Do you think she's kind of ... pretty? In, you know, a *unique* sort of way?"

"Seriously? Calling her *unique* is being charitable. She's *weird*."

"People think *you're* weird, too."

"*Touché!*" Marty says. "And I'm more than happy to meet the expectations of my fans. But, listen, Bill, if *I'm* considered weird, then Elizabeth Murphy is from *Planet Nutso*."

"People don't understand Elizabeth," Bill says. "She doesn't care about being like anybody else. She doesn't even *try* to conform. Kind of like you. And me too, I guess."

"Billy, Billy, Billy," Marty teases, "aren't *you* philosophical tonight."

"Well, *philosophically speaking*, then ... do you think Elizabeth is pretty?"

"Why? Do you *like* her?"

Thankfully it is dark outside, so, even in the light of the full moon, Marty can't see that Bill is blushing.

Then, bluntly, Marty says, "I don't think she's your type, Bill. I really don't. Her dad is a wacky, lefty, pot-smoking, atheist artist, and your parents are decent, hard-working, law-abiding, God-fearing farmers. What could you and Elizabeth Murphy possibly have in common?"

Bill sighs. Maybe Marty is right. And yet, Bill still wants to run his fingers through Elizabeth's silky golden hair, and he still longs to inhale her summer wildflower scent.

Marty and Bill reach the entrance to the Carriage House. Marty turns the keys in the multiple locks and then throws open the door, shouting in his DRAMATIC VOICE, "*ANNND NOWWWW*, FOR YOUR *VIEWWWING* PLEASURE ... THE *FAAAAMOUS* AND *RARELY SEEEEEEEN* APOSTROPHES AUTO COLLECTION!"

As they step into the dark, echoey space, the phantom scent of summer wildflowers in Bill's nostrils is replaced by the smell of machine oil, gasoline, and Turtle Wax. Elizabeth Murphy's body is momentarily pushed to the margins of Bill Brown's mind, as the bodies of dozens of rare and beautiful cars are revealed by the fluorescent lights humming to life overhead.

"Wow," Bill rasps. "Wow."

"They're just cars," Marty says.

"They're more than *just cars*," Bill says, as he rushes from machine to machine like a toddler turned loose in a candy store. "They are ... *masterpieces*! These are *perfect* examples of some of the greatest cars ever built!"

"Whatever turns your crank," Marty says. But he is smiling; Marty rarely sees his serious, sober-minded friend this excited about anything.

"None of these start with a crank," Bill says. "They've all got electric starters."

He rushes toward the long row of gleaming, polished automotive specimens. The cars are packed into the Carriage House like sardines in a can, with just enough room to walk between them. Bill runs his hand over each machine's shimmering sheet-metal contours the way a lover might caress his sleeping mate.

"Wow," Bill exclaims, "a 1946 MG TC ... a '55 Corvette ... a 1963 Aston Martin DB5 ... James Bond's car, by the way."

"*Yesh, Munneypenny*," Marty says, doing a pretty good imitation of Sean Connery. "Pusshy Galore ... *I musht be dreaming!*"

Bill continues to gaze lovingly at the cars. "A 1949 Oldsmobile 88," he says, "and a 1938 Bugatti Type 57S Atlantic. Wow ... wow ... wow ... your grandfather really liked cars from the 1930s to the '60s ..."

"Just like you," Marty says.

"Just like me."

Bill pauses in front of a tiny, toylike car, which doesn't fit in with the rest of the incredible collection of prime vehicles. It is the one car in the entire room that nobody has bothered to polish; the pitted chrome letters on the tail of this weird, dusty little machine tell him that it is a Crosley Hotshot.

"This one's my favourite," Marty proclaims. "When I finally get my driver's licence, I'll ask if I can drive this one. It reminds me of the toy car that I used to pedal around the estate when I was little."

Bill remembers back when little Elizabeth Murphy used to pedal her Big Wheel tricycle up and down the street, pumping her small fist in the air and shouting, "the Pissah of Powah!" As a child, Bill had a toy International Harvester tractor, much like the one he now drives to the pickle factory each morning, except that the kindergarten version was much smaller and made of mostly plastic, and it was powered by Bill's feet instead of diesel fuel. And driving it felt like freedom, not like a burden.

Bill shakes off this negative thought, like he always does. *The Lord loves a working man,* he reminds himself. He continues fawning over the car collection.

"1930 Stutz Lancefield Coupe ... 1955 Buick Roadmaster ...

a 1957 Ford Thunderbird … you can tell it's a '57 by the porthole windows in the removable hardtop!"

"Fascinating," says Marty, who is about as enthralled by old cars as he is by watching golf tournaments on TV with his father (who doesn't do much else in life except play golf or watch golf on TV, while simultaneously drinking ludicrously expensive Scotch straight from the bottle).

"And … and … wow!" a love-struck Bill proclaims. "This Deuce Coupe is in *perfect* condition. It looks like it was never driven!"

"There was a car called a *douche* coupe?" Marty gasps in mock horror. "Did anyone ever buy one? Douchebags, I suppose. I'd rather drive a car called the Hotshot any day!"

"*Deuce*, Marty. *Deuce*. It's a nickname for the 1932 Ford Coupe. Like the Beach Boys song, 'Little Deuce Coupe,' or that song 'Blinded by the Light' by Manfred Mann." Bill begins singing, in muted tones, "'Blinded by the light, revved up like a deuce, another runner in the night.'"

"Oh," Marty says. "I thought it was 'Little *douche* coupe' and 'wrapped up like a douche.' Those songs make a lot more sense now! But, please, never, *ever* sing like that again, okay?"

Bill rolls his eyes. "I promise I'll leave the entertaining to you from now on. Anyway, my dad's got a Deuce parked in the back field. 'The first great car a working man could afford,' Dad says. His is mostly rust, though. And the engine is seized. And it's full of mice and bugs." Bill's voice drops. "He says he's going to restore it when he retires, but farmers *never* retire. They just keep working until they die; they never get to drive the cool cars."

Uh-oh, Marty thinks, *he's lapsing into one of his "I don't want to die a farmer but that's what my family expects from me" sulks*. Marty segues back into his DRAMATIC VOICE. "WELL FOLKS, IF YOU LIKED THE 'DAILY DRIVER' COLLECTION, YOU'RE GOING TO LLLLLLOVVVE THE 'EXOTIC CAR' ROOM!"

Bill's mouth drops open. "There's an *Exotic Car Room*?"

Marty shakes the keys in the air again. "Follow me," he says.

Marty opens the locks and unbolts the heavy, steel-reinforced garage door at the far end of the Carriage House. Inside the cool room are seven of the rarest, most beautiful machines that Bill has ever seen. These are not merely cars; they are mobile works of art.

The automobiles are parked in a circle, atop what appears to be a gigantic mechanical turntable, designed to rotate each car toward the exit door.

Bill recognizes the first car he sees: a 1937 Cord 812 Phaeton. He once saw a scale model of a Cord at an automotive museum that he visited with his father, but Bill has never seen a real one until now.

"One of the most beautiful machines ever built," Bill says, as he circles the gleaming black car. "So far ahead of its time … look at this Art Deco styling! Look at the hideaway headlights! It was the first North American car to have them. You open them with hand cranks on either side of the dashboard. And look at this beautiful, wrap-around chrome grille! They nicknamed it the 'Coffin Nose.' So intense. So masculine looking. Wow."

"Ah, interesting," a thoroughly uninterested Marty says, while roaming around the cavernous space for something that might amuse him.

"Look at these beautiful chrome side pipes," Bill continues. "It means that this one is equipped with a Schwitzer-Cummins supercharger, mounted on a Lycoming aircraft engine. With the supercharger running, it will produce almost two hundred horse-power, which was practically *unheard of* in 1937. This car set speed records at the Bonneville Salt Flats that stood for years."

Marty has no idea what any of this means, but he says "Awesome!" anyway. He knew that Bill would love this part of the Carriage House.

The convertible top of the Cord is folded down, so Bill peers inside the car. "Look at this!" he says. "The brushed aluminum, the recessed gauges — it's like the cockpit of a vintage airplane. And look at the horn ring ... a first for a North American car. The front-wheel drive and the covered gas cap were firsts, too. And look at ..."

But Marty isn't looking at the car at all. Inside an old wooden crate at the back of the room, he has found something that he considers more fun.

"Look at *this!*" Marty exclaims, holding up a long, black, duster-style driving coat. He puts it on. The sleeves hang right down to Marty's knuckles, and the coattails drag on the floor. "It's too big for me," Marty calls out to Bill, "but it would fit you perfectly!"

"No thanks, Marty," Bill answers from behind the Cord 812, "I don't feel like playing dress-up today." Then he mutters to himself, "Or ever."

Marty extracts a black leather helmet from the box, pulls it over his head, and tugs down the face shield, with its fitted nosepiece and built-in tinted goggles. Then he sees the long, black leather gauntlet gloves, and he tugs them over his forearms, extending the black fingertips in the air and rasping, in his DRAMATIC VOICE, "LUKE! *LUUUUUUUUUKE!* I AM YOUR *FATHER*, LUKE!"

"It's a driving outfit, Marty," Bill says, "from back in the days when driving in open-cockpit cars on dirt roads was usual. It protected the driver from the wind and dust."

But Marty's rapid-fire attention has already targeted something else inside the box. With wide-eyed enthusiasm (although Bill can't see Marty's eyes because of the tinted driving goggles), Marty tugs a faded purple sweater and an old-fashioned leather football helmet from the crate.

"Look at this!" he cheers. "This must be my grandfather's old football uniform. I recognize it from the picture in the trophy case at school."

In the 1940s, Marshall Apostrophes was the star running back for the Faireville District High School football team. His records for the most yards run and the most touchdowns scored in a single game have yet to be broken. Faireville won the county championship each of the four years that Marty's grandfather played. (Apparently, neither Marty's dad nor Marty himself have inherited their ancestor's athletic abilities.)

Marty tugs off the gauntlets and tosses them on the smooth concrete floor of the garage, followed by the driving helmet and the long, black duster; he's much more enthralled by the huge leather shoulder pads, the quilted, high-waisted football pants, and the stiff purple-and-white leather helmet that go with the jersey. He buckles up the protective gear, tugs the purple sweater over his head, and pulls the earflaps of the leather helmet over his elephantine ears (which Marty and Malcolm Apostrophes *did* inherit from old Marshall).

One strange thing about the football jersey is that it has a thick turtleneck collar, rather than the crew-cut neck opening that is usual on football sweaters. It was Marshall Apostrophes' fashion trademark that he always wore turtleneck sweaters, even in the heat of summer, even with suit jackets, even on his sports uniforms. Local legend has it that he favoured turtlenecks because they camouflaged his extraordinarily thin neck (a trait that Marty and his father *also* inherited).

Marty pulls the turtleneck up over his face. "Look at me! I'm Rudy from *Fat Albert*!"

"Who?"

"Rudy! From the *Fat Albert* show! The thin one, who always wore a turtleneck sweater. His was purple, too! You're sure not up on your classic seventies cartoons, are you?"

"I haven't got as much leisure time as you do, Marty."

"I look like a freakin' *monster* in these shoulder pads!" Marty says, pulling down the turtleneck and buckling the helmet's chin strap. He turns circles on the concrete floor like a fashion model on a runway. "And this gear even matches my purple sneakers!"

At least Marty only wears purple running shoes these days, rather than the velvet tuxedo pants that brought him so much grief in grade nine.

"That's nice, Marty," Bill says. "It looks like one of the numbers has fallen off the back of the sweater, though."

Bill's observation is correct. Marshall Apostrophes' number was 10, and everyone who ever attended Faireville District High School knows it, whether they are into sports or not; Marshall's retired number 10 has been hanging from a banner above the gymnasium stage for three-quarters of a century, and generations of students have stared up at it while trying to stay awake during speeches from the school's succession of principals.

The sweater on Marty's back is missing the number 1, though; only the zero remains.

"I'M THE PURPLE ZERO!" Marty shouts in his DRAMATIC VOICE. "I'M THE GREATEST ATHLETE OF MY TIME! OF *ANY* TIME! BETTER! STRONGER! FASTER!"

"And definitely *louder*," Bill says, circling again around the Cord 812, admiring the swooping curves of its fenders, the gleaming chrome hubcaps with the hand-drilled brake-cooling holes, the sensual, curved tail, the aggressive, forward-slanted nose.

"Look how sleek and low-slung the body is," Bill says, mostly to himself, since he knows that Marty is about as passionate about cars as he is about doing homework. "Most cars in this era still had running boards so you could climb up inside. The Hudson gets credit for its 'step-down' design, but Cord did it over a decade earlier."

Beneath the gleaming grille, Bill notices the small Cord emblem: beneath a knight's helmet, a simple shield adorned with three red hearts and three silver arrows. Everything on a coat of arms means something, and Bill wonders what the hearts and arrows are meant to signify.

One of the headlight pods is opened slightly, as if the car is winking at him, and the wrap-around grille grins at him like an old warrior longing for an adventure; it's as if the Cord Phaeton is begging him,

"Drive me, Bill. Drive me!"

The whole time that he and Marty have been inside the Carriage House, Bill has been carrying the books *Star Trek 101*, *I Am Spock*, and *Captain Kirk's Guide to Women*; he sets them down, nestled between the Cord's sweeping fender and the sleek chrome grille that runs alongside the car's cowl. With both hands free, Bill stands beside the driver's-side door and reaches into the cockpit to grip the slender, leather-wrapped steering wheel, in the ten and two o'clock positions, just like his father taught him.

A rough, deep voice scratches the air like 80-grit sandpaper. "DO *NOT* TOUCH THAT AUTOMOBILE! STEP AWAY FROM THE AUTOMOBILE *IMMEDIATELY!*"

At first, Bill thinks it's just Marty, using a new variation of his DRAMATIC VOICE, but when he looks up, he sees a tall, silver-haired man in mechanic's overalls glaring at him over the Cord's coffin nose hood.

"Stay RIGHT THERE," the man thunders, "while I call the police and report you for TRESPASSING!"

Chapter Three

The Eyes and Ears of Faireville

The heels of Elizabeth Murphy's tall rawhide work boots crunch in the roadside gravel as she strides purposefully back into town. Her wild mass of frizzy wheat-blonde hair bounces as she walks, and an ancient 35 mm film camera swings back and forth from a frayed strap around her neck. The oversized pockets of her paint-speckled orange jumpsuit are stuffed with an assortment of camera lenses, a mini video camera, pens of almost every colour, and a black-leather-bound Moleskine notebook.

Elizabeth walks with characteristic enthusiasm, as if the battery that powers her has been overcharged with energy. Of course, anyone who knows her (which is practically *everyone* in a small town like Faireville) knows that she does *everything* with unbridled enthusiasm; *Enthusiasm* is Elizabeth Murphy's middle name! (Or at least it should be.)

Not everyone in Faireville loves Elizabeth's energetic nature, though. During her four years at Faireville District High School, some of the other girls (usually in whispers to each other, but sometimes loudly and pointedly to Elizabeth herself) have suggested that Spazzy or Pesky or Klutzy should be her middle name. Her real middle name, actually, is Sweet Pea; her hippie parents didn't even officially name her until she was over a year old, and by then they were stuck on the temporary nickname they'd given their sweet-tempered baby. *Thank goodness nobody knows about that*, Elizabeth thinks. She would rather they start calling her "the Pisser of Power" again.

Elizabeth has been run out of the Student Council, the Glee Club, the Yearbook Club, and the Prom Committee, by other students who complain that she "takes over everything" and that "it turns into a disaster when Elizabeth is around." She *is* willing to admit that, *occasionally*, things haven't always gone exactly as she's planned.

For example, how could she have known that the caulking she used to put together the Plexiglas fish tank for the "Bon Voyage at Sea"–themed Junior Prom wouldn't hold the pressure of five hundred gallons of water? It took the school custodians days to mop up all the water, and apparently they are still finding expired goldfish under the gym stage and in the equipment room. One even turned up the next day inside the front of the gym teacher's track pants, still alive and wiggling; nobody had the nerve to ask how that could have possibly happened.

Elizabeth knows that she doesn't really fit in with the other girls at FDHS. While the rest of them wear painted-on designer-label jeans, stretchy miniskirts, or fine-anatomy-revealing yoga pants, Elizabeth prefers the comfort and utility of her brightly coloured coveralls. While many of her female classmates stumble around atop delicate high-heeled shoes, Elizabeth plods proudly forward in her practical, supportive work boots. While other girls trowel on their makeup like stucco, Elizabeth prefers to be fresh-faced and unpainted.

She also knows that she's not considered *hot*. She understands that nobody thinks she's *cool*. They just think she's *weird*, and they just want her to stay away from them, to prevent any of her residual weirdness from rubbing off on them. All of this used to really upset her, and she used to close her bedroom door and cry herself to sleep at night, but not anymore. This year, Elizabeth has decided to stay positive about life, *no matter what*.

The current reason for Elizabeth's enthusiasm is this: She's been out at the Faireville Memorial Arena, observing a Triple-A Junior Hockey game between the Faireville Blue Flames and their arch-rivals, the Gasberg Pipefitters. Normally, watching hockey is about as enjoyable to Elizabeth as suffering through a pukey, feverish bout of influenza, but this evening she's been snapping hundreds of pictures and scribbling down notes describing every play. She even brought along a miniature video camera to record the whole game, so she can review it later and make sure that her notes are complete and accurate.

This game will be the subject of the first article that Elizabeth will write as the official Junior Reporter for *The Faireville Gleaner*, and she wants the publisher, Mr. Gootenbourg, to be impressed with her journalistic prowess. She is grateful for his faith in her, and for the film and video cameras he's loaned her until she can afford to buy her own. He even gave her the Moleskine journal: "A real reporter's notebook," he said.

Elizabeth strides toward the town sign, which reads:

Welcome to
FAIREVILLE
Population 2,961
"The Victorian Era Boomtown"

Until recently, the town slogan was "The Cradle That Rocked the Natural Gas Industry," but then someone on the new town council made it their mission to change the slogan back to "The Victorian Era Boomtown." Opinions among the citizens of Faireville had been divided on the issue, and eventually the Mayor's office had to hold an Official Referendum on the issue, in which "The Victorian Era Boomtown" won by a vote of 31 to 29. Yes, they had a *referendum* on the issue.

"That's the sort of thing that passes for breaking news in this boring little town," she says to herself, rolling her eyes as she passes the sign. "Well, as Faireville's newest reporter, I'm going to make it my personal mission to change all of that."

The heels of Elizabeth's boots begin click-clacking instead of crunching as she steps from the gravel and onto the sidewalk where the downtown core begins.

"I am going to scour this town to find the big news, the news that people ignore, the news that people hide, the news that nobody sees."

The rhythm of her stride echoes from the walls of the immaculately maintained Victorian buildings, with their brick facades, their ginger-bread-lace trim, their tall, slender, painted wooden doors. As she walks beneath the glow of the streetlights, the lumpy shadow of Elizabeth's paraphernalia-laden coveralls stretches out before her.

"From this moment forward," Elizabeth triumphantly announces, "I am officially declaring myself *The Eyes and Ears of Faireville*."

A lone, elderly couple, apparently out for an evening stroll, look at her with raised eyebrows as they shuffle past her on the sidewalk.

"Yes," Elizabeth says, "I am talking to myself. I do that sometimes. Please don't be alarmed."

"Weirdo," the old lady mumbles.

"Pothead," the old man concurs.

"No," Elizabeth corrects them, while still speeding forward, "I'm *a journalist!*"

She passes Lynette's Little Edibles, the Tea Cozy, the Goode Faith Gift Shoppe, and then she waits patiently for the light to turn green at the only set of stoplights in town. Since all of the shops are closed at this hour, there is not a single car or another pedestrian to be seen. Elizabeth could strut right past the "Don't Walk" signal without any danger of injury or repercussion, but she waits at the intersection anyway; Elizabeth Murphy firmly believes in Following the Rules, in always trying to Do the Right Thing. She only bends the rules *some-times*, when her enthusiasm gets the best of her.

When the signal light tells her that it's okay to walk, she crosses the street and continues her brisk pace, slowing only when she approaches Burnoff Street. She peeks around the back corner of The Sergeant-at-Arms, a dilapidated old-school barroom with a reputation for serving minors and turning a blind eye to illegal back room transactions.

Like so many of the other streets in town, Burnoff Street was named after a natural-gas refining process from a century ago, when Faireville was still a boomtown and there was still some natural gas underground to be tapped. Burnoff Street is really more of an alley than a street, and it's been nicknamed "Burnout Street" by the locals, because it's where the members of Faireville's underground drug culture can often be found. Its shadows, crevices, dumpsters, and grease barrels provide convenient hiding places for the local drug dealers to deal and the local drug users to use.

Thankfully, there don't seem to be any users or dealers huddling in the shadows of Burnoff Street this evening, so Elizabeth is able to walk to her father's shop at the end of the sketchy lane without the usual shiver rippling through her heart. The cement block exterior of her dad's well-hidden storefront is splattered randomly with cracking blobs of dried primary-coloured paint, and above the shop's single window hangs a bright yellow sign, hand-lettered by her father in his characteristically free-flowing script:

Jack-O's
One-World, New-Age
Creative Supply Shop
Open most of the time
(Peace, brothers and sisters!)

Jack-o was Elizabeth's father's nickname in art school, and for many years it was what everyone called him. Sometime between the day she was born and the day her mother died, Elizabeth's dad adopted another moniker, Sebastien, because he believed that a famous contemporary abstract painter like himself should have a one-word name. By the time Elizabeth graduated from elementary school, though, her dad's artistic fame had failed to materialize, and he finally reverted back to the name on his birth certificate: Jack Murphy.

Elizabeth reaches for the daisy-shaped handle on the door to her father's store; daisies were her mother's favourite flowers.

A voice rasps behind her, "Hey, Lezzie Lizzy! Payin' a visit to Wacko Jack-o?"

Elizabeth spins around.

It's Chris Orff, a boy from the grade ten class. He's with his troll buddy, Davey Batterwall. Both of them are wearing grey T-shirts, with the logo for their basement heavy metal band, Fist Face, drawn in black permanent marker across their chests. Chris is the one doing the taunting; he is tossing a chunk of broken brick up in the air with one hand and then catching it in the other.

"Doin' lotsa lezzie lickin', Lizzie? Is Jack-o doin' lotsa jackin'?"

Two years ago, when Elizabeth was in grade ten herself, this sort of thing would have made her break down crying. She would have sputtered, "Stop calling me Lezzy Lizzie! I'm not a lesbian! Not that there is anything wrong with being a lesbian! And there is nothing wrong with my father, either!"

And then, of course, to make her cry even harder, her assailants would have responded with chants of "Lezzie Lizzie! Lezzie Lizzie! Wacko Jack-o! Wacko Jack-o! "

Last year, in grade eleven, she probably would have just thrown the insults back at them. Everyone knows the story of the time that Chris Orff's older brother Devin tied Chris's feet together and left him hanging upside down inside an abandoned well; Chris was so terrified that he wet his pants. It would have been easy to shout back at him, "Chrissy Pissy! Chrissy Pissy!", and then call his overweight sidekick "Davey Butterball" for good measure.

But then Chris probably would have thrown that brick at her, and then he and Davey would have picked her up and tossed her inside one of the dumpsters. Or, even worse, they would have returned later to spray-paint "LEZY LIZY" and "WAKO JAKO" all over her father's storefront; when Strat Sanderson's band the Wailing She-Kats beat Fist Face for the Best Band trophy at Faireville High's Got Talent, *someone* spray-painted "FIST FACE ROKS" and "SHE-KATS SUK KOK" across the Sandersons' garage door the next evening.

So, to avoid such repercussions, the more mature, dignified grade twelve version of Elizabeth simply says, "Hey, Chris, I go by Beth now, not Lizzy. So, if you want to be accurate, you should call me Lezzie *Beth*, not Lezzie *Lizzie*, okay?"

Chris looks puzzled for a moment; his atrocious spelling isn't the only reason that he's been assigned to the remedial classes at school. Then he taunts, "Lezzie Beth! Lezzie Beth!"

By the time Chris realizes that he has really only said her name twice, Elizabeth is already inside of her father's shop.

"That's right, Lezzie," Chris Orff mumbles, tossing the broken brick up in the air with his right hand, catching it with his left. "You go hide inside your crazy daddy's faggy art shop."

"'Cause some major shit is about to go down out here," Davey Batterwall adds, with bravado in his voice.

"Shut the hell up, Butterball," Chris barks, "why don't ya tell the whole world what we're up to, eh?" Then he pulls a cellphone out of his back pocket, speed-dials a number, and rasps into the phone, "Okay, bro. All clear."

Bamboo chimes tinkle as Elizabeth pushes the shop door closed behind her.

"Dad?" she calls out. "Dad? I'm back from my first news assignment!"

The floorboards creak under Elizabeth's boots as she manoeuvres around the obstacles in the overcrowded shop. The dusty space is crammed with display cases full of paintbrushes of all sizes and shapes, tubes of oil paint and watercolour flats, stacks of new canvases and watercolour rice papers, palettes and paint cans and big grey bags of sculpting clay, frames and easels, coat racks hanging with artists' smocks and coveralls.

Local rumour has it that the store used to also sell roach clips, bongs, and other drug-related paraphernalia, but this was before Elizabeth was born, and Elizabeth refuses to believe it. It would explain how Burnoff Street became known as Burnout Street, and why the local dealers and druggies still hang out back there, but Elizabeth would rather not think about any of that.

"Dad?" she calls out again. "Are you here?"

Displayed high on the back wall of the shop are two enormous paintings created by Jack Murphy when he preferred to be known as Sebastien. One is called *Birthglory*, which Elizabeth's father describes as "a rumination on the majestic beauty of natural birth," but she has overheard local "art critics" compare the painting to a close-up of a blood-filled mosquito after hitting a car windshield. The second painting, *Treegasm*, has been said to resemble the splattered guts of a green tobacco bug plastered to the sole of a dirty work boot.

There was a third painting in the series, called *Earthshine*, which her father managed to sell to a wealthy art collector in New York City for thirty thousand dollars; of course, that money was spent years ago.

"Dad?" Elizabeth calls out again.

He must be in the back room, in his "Creative Space." She cautiously pushes open the steel door between *Birthglory* and *Treegasm*.

Her father hangs suspended from the ceiling of his Creative Space, his wild beard and mass of prematurely white hair completely concealing his face.

"Dad? Dad?"

His body bobs slowly up and down on the bungee cords that secure him to the ceiling. In one hand he still grips an oversized paintbrush, from which he has been flinging paint at a canvas spread out on the paint-caked concrete floor.

A snore burbles from his lips.

While imitating the style of his artistic hero Jackson Pollock, Jack Murphy, the artist formerly known as Jack-o (and also as Sebastien), has fallen asleep. Again.

"Dad! Dad! Wake up and come down from there!"

"Huh? Wha? Oh, hello, Sweet Pea."

Elizabeth reaches up to help untangle her father from the home-made harness, which he has strung together using automotive bungee cords and old leather belts from the Salvation Army store.

When her dad is earthbound again, she asks him, "How was business today?"

"Oh, I sold a tube of burnt ochre and a watercolour set. But this new painting, Sweet Pea, it could fetch a lot of money, I think. I've really emptied my soul into this one. It could be my rebirth as an artist to be reckoned with. In fact, I think I'll call it *Rebirth*. No, wait, I'll call it *Reckoning*! Yessss … *Reckoning*! *The Reckoning*! Yesssssssss!"

"Sounds great, Dad. We sure could use the extra money."

They sure could.

Although Elizabeth would never complain about it, the profits from a tube of paint and a watercolour set will be barely enough to buy them a can of soup for dinner. The monthly "allowance" that her father gives her hardly covers the cost of her tampons, or replacing her bras and panties when they wear out. The others at school figure that she lopes around in her father's paint-speckled jumpsuits and work boots because she's trying to make some kind of radical fashion statement, but the truth is that Elizabeth could never afford to buy high-heeled shoes or yoga pants or miniskirts, not even if she secretly wanted to.

But Elizabeth never complains. Whining doesn't accomplish anything. Besides, things are looking up! Mr. Gootenbourg will pay her for each of the articles she writes as the new Junior Reporter at *The Faireville Gleaner*, and Elizabeth plans on writing a *lot* of articles. Maybe she will make enough money to buy herself a skirt, and perhaps one of those tight little tank tops. At the very least, she will make enough money to take her father to the Faireville Diner for burgers and strawberry milkshakes, which is one of the few things she can remember them doing together as a family back when her mother was still around.

Elizabeth smiles at her father. "You've worked hard today, Dad," she says. "Let's go home. I'll make you some soup."

Night has descended on Burnoff Street, and in the eerie quiet, a single streetlight at the end of the lane flickers, and the crackling sound seems as loud as gunshots. The shadows cast by the dumpsters and grease barrels are as dark as deep, cold water.

As she exits, Elizabeth locks the shop door. She pulls the corrugated aluminum security screen down to protect the single bay window and snaps the padlock in place. Her father is standing in one of the shadows, staring at the ground, maybe scanning for inspiration for his next great work of art.

"Hmmm," he says.

Elizabeth walks over to see what her father is studying. "What is it, Dad?"

He points to a spot on the broken tarmac, where a chunk of broken brick lies beside the shattered carcass of a security camera. Elizabeth's vision climbs up the rust-speckled, steel-plated door in front of them, up past the bricked-in window above the door, up high to the broken bracket that once held the surveillance camera.

"This is the emergency exit from the old Gasman's Trust and Loan building," Elizabeth's father says. "They built it back in the 1870s, after the bank was robbed several times, so that the tellers might have a chance to escape with the money before the thieves got to it. Instead, the bank manager at the time used it for 'secret meetings' with his 'lady friend' ... I think her name was Mistress Prunella or something ... but I'm digressing, aren't I?"

"What is the building used for now, Dad?"

"It's still a bank, of course!" Jack Murphy exclaims. "Jeez! Don't they teach you kids any local history in school?"

Elizabeth's heart begins to throb as she recalls the words she overheard earlier this evening, through the crack in the art shop door as she closed it:

"... *some major shit is about to go down out here,*" Davey Batterwall said.

"*Shut the hell up, Butterball,*" Chris Orff countered, "*why don't ya tell the whole world what we're up to, eh?*"

Then, just before the door clicked shut, Elizabeth heard Chris say, "*Okay, bro. All clear.*"

The Faireville Gleaner's battered 35 mm camera still hangs from its frayed strap around Elizabeth's neck. She tosses her mane of frizzy hair over her shoulder, raises the ancient camera to her eye, and begins snapping pictures of the empty camera bracket above the bank's escape door. Then she snaps several shots, from different distances and angles, of the broken security camera on the ground, and of the chunk of brick that she had seen Chris Orff tossing up in the air.

"Those will be pretty pictures," Elizabeth's father says, in an admiring tone of voice. "You've got a real artistic eye, Sweet Pea."

"I'm not being an *artist*, Dad," she says, "I'm being a *journalist*." She lowers the film camera, tugs the mini video camera out from one of the pockets of her paint-speckled orange jumpsuit, and begins filming. "This is a crime scene, Dad. And I'm the first reporter on the scene."

A slamming sound booms from behind the steel-plated door.

Elizabeth tugs her father away from the door by the sleeve and pushes him behind the nearest dumpster.

Then she crouches behind an oil barrel and raises the video camera.

The bank's escape door bursts open.

An alarm siren wails.

Two tall men sprint out onto Burnoff Street. Each man is dressed entirely in black and is wearing a balaclava over his face, and each is carrying a gym bag, stuffed with what Elizabeth assumes is stolen cash.

Elizabeth's heart is hammering in her chest, but her hands are steady as she captures everything with the video camera.

When she notices that both men are also carrying pistols, she wriggles further back into the shadow behind the oil barrel, but Elizabeth Murphy, Official Junior Reporter, doesn't stop filming.

Chapter Four

Drive the Car

Inside the Exotic Car Room of the Apostrophes Carriage House, the tall, silver-haired man in mechanic's overalls lunges over the hood of the Cord 812 at Bill Brown, croaking again in his 80-grit sandpaper voice, "Stay RIGHT THERE!"

Law-abiding Bill does exactly as he is told. He doesn't move a muscle, except to say, "Who ... who are you?"

"I am Jerome Bloombottom," the rough-voiced elder thunders, "and I am calling the police RIGHT NOW."

Marty steps out of the shadows on the other side of the Exotic Car Room and says to Bill, "Whatever you do, don't laugh at his name. The estate had to pay a four-thousand-dollar dental bill for the last guy that laughed at Bloombottom's name."

"I'm not laughing," says a mortified Bill.

"Master Apostrophes!" Bloombottom says, straightening himself and taking a step back from Bill and the Cord. "My apologies. I didn't see you there."

"No worries, Bloombottom."

"You do understand, though," the wrinkled-yet-imposing old man rumbles, "that in addition to my duty to keep all of the vehicles in your grandfather's auto collection in tip-top driveable condition, it is also my duty to *protect* the collection from intruders and miscreants, yes?"

"That's quite all right, Bloombottom," Marty says, mimicking the ancient mechanic's officious way of speaking. "We are neither intruders, nor are we miscreants."

"That, Master Apostrophes, " Bloombottom sniffs, "remains to be seen."

"And you can cut the 'Master Apostrophes' crap, okay?" Marty says. "Dad enjoys that snob stuff, but I don't. And Dad isn't here right now, is he?"

A slight smile cracks Bloombottom's stern facade. He looks at the football uniform Marty is wearing, raises one eyebrow, and says, "Well, I know that Halloween is coming, Marty, but I think you can do better than *that* for a costume."

"Don't mess with the Purple Zero, Jerome," Marty says.

"You may continue to call me *Bloombottom*, Marty. I may be your servant, but I am still your elder. Maybe your father doesn't expect you to show *him* any respect, but *I do*."

"Sorry, Bloombottom," Marty says.

Bill likes this Bloombottom guy already, and he extends his hand to him. "Pleased to meet you, sir. This is a very impressive collection of vehicles, and you have done an admirable job maintaining them. The cars in this room alone ..."

"Yes," Bloombottom says, "these cars are very special. In 1951, the Museum of Modern Art in New York City hosted an exhibition, titled simply, 'Eight Automobiles.' When Marty's grandfather Marshall — who was my employer at the time — attended the exhibition, he decided that we must add the same models to his own collection. Over the years, we managed to procure our own versions of each of those eight cars."

Bloombottom walks around the circle of vintage cars, and Bill follows him.

"All of the cars displayed here are the finest specimens of their kind," Bloombottom continues. "The only modifications I've made are to outfit each car with radial tires, so that they handle better on modern roads, and to outfit each machine with a push-button ignition. Marshall Apostrophes was too busy to bother with keys."

Bloombottom stops abruptly. Bill nearly runs into him.

"This 1941 Lincoln Continental, of course," Bloombottom says, "was not particularly difficult to obtain."

"This car was originally designed as a custom-bodied special for Edsel Ford, right?" Bill offers.

"You are correct," Bloombottom says.

"I notice that it's got a Borg-Warner overdrive on it," Bill says. "Not all of them did."

"Correct again," Bloombottom says, his frown unfurling a bit.

"Ass-kisser," Marty says from the background, while scratching at the itchy wool football sweater he's still wearing.

"And here is our 1938 Bentley," Bloombottom says, ignoring Marty, "and a 1951 Willys Military Jeep, which, strangely, was part of the 1951 exhibition, so we've got one, too. As you can see, our version has a rear-mounted Browning M2 machine gun, which the one at MOMA, of course, did not. I was going to remove it, but my employer didn't see the need; he was never the stickler for detail that I am." Bloombottom puffs out his chest a bit.

"Your restorations are all flawless, sir," Bill says.

"*Super* ass-kisser," Marty says.

"No need to call me 'sir.' We are kindred spirits, I think." Bloombottom continues weaving his way through the cars. "At the museum's exhibition, their Mercedes-Benz SS Tourer was mislabelled as a 1930, but the car on display was in fact a 1928 model, so that's what we have here. We purchased it from the estate of the late entertainer Al Jolson. And this *next* car ... well, it took us *years* to track down a suitable specimen, but this 1947 Cisitalia 202 GT is probably the finest example of its type. The body was designed by Pininfarina, of course."

"Who later went on to design bodies for Ferrari," Bill adds.

"Correct *again*," Bloombottom says, his staid countenance breaking into a tight smile for the first time.

"Super-*duper* ass-kisser!" Marty exclaims.

Bloombottom sighs, and continues, "And here is our 1937 Talbot-Lago, certainly the most difficult car of them all to obtain. Only sixteen were built. Figoni and Falaschi's *Goutte d'Eau* design is considered to be expressionist art by some. It's my favourite automobile in the entire collection."

Bill knows that *Goutte d'Eau* is French for "teardrop." He's paid more attention in French class in the four years since his award-losing performance in grade eight.

"It's very nice," Bill says.

"I see, however," Bloombottom intones, "that you are drawn to the Cord 812 Phaeton. The director of the Museum of Modern Art agreed with you; he called the Cord 'the outstanding American contribution to automobile design.'"

"It might be my favourite car of all time. I've never seen a real one until now."

There is a glint in Bloombottom's eyes as he glances over at the Cord. "It was the one vehicle that Marshall Apostrophes never got to drive before he passed away. Such a shame. It was possibly the fastest, best-handling car of its day. It was *built* to be driven. That car *deserves* to be driven."

Bill looks over at the Cord 812, which still seems to be begging him, *"Drive me, Bill. Drive me!"*

To distract himself from this weird phenomenon, Bill says, "Bloombottom, you said that the exhibition in 1951 was called 'Eight Automobiles,' but ..."

"But we've got only seven? Well, we also had the eighth car, a 1948 MG TC. Frankly, I think that the museum curators made a mistake picking it; I saw nothing revolutionary or beautiful about its design. So if Malcolm was going to crash and destroy one of the cars while driving drunk, it's just as well that it was the MG."

Suddenly, Marty is interested. "My dad *crashed* one of the cars?"

Bloombottom remains matter-of-fact. "That is why Malcolm is forbidden in his father's will from ever driving another car in the collection."

"Am I forbidden from driving the cars, too?" Marty wonders.

"Well, since you do not possess a driver's licence, Marty, the answer is, by law, yes. But you have not been forbidden by your deceased grandfather, if that's what you mean."

"That is freakin' awesome!" Marty says. "Start getting that Crosley Hotshot ready for me, Bloombottom."

Bloombottom snorts, "Of course! The one car that your grandfather purchased as a *joke*." Then he composes himself and says, "All of the automobiles in the collection, of course, are already in driveable condition, including the Crosley." He glances at Bill, and adds, "*And* the Cord 812 Phaeton."

Bill wonders, *Did Bloombottom just wink at me?*

"Only sixty-four of that model were ever produced," Bloombottom continues, shaking his head. "Such a rare *privilege* to drive one. Such a *shame* for it to just sit there, undriven."

Okay, he definitely winked at me that time.

"Well, I'm finished for the day," Bloombottom concludes, "so I think I'll head back to my quarters now. Marty, please lock up when you're finished here."

Without waiting for Marty to respond, the old mechanic turns on his heels and marches out of the Carriage House.

When Marty is sure that Bloombottom has left the building, he scampers over to Bill.

"You heard him,. Bill!" Marty says. "He just gave us permission to take the Cord out for a ride!"

"No, he didn't!" Bill protests. "He told you that your grandfather's will doesn't forbid you from driving it. But you don't have a driver's licence, Marty!"

"But *you* do," Marty says.

This is true. Bill got his beginner's permit on his sixteenth birthday, and his father took him into town to take his final driver's test on the day Bill turned eighteen. While most suburban parents are terrified of their offspring getting behind the wheel of a motor vehicle, Bill's father couldn't wait to have another licensed driver on the farm, to drive loads of apples and cucumbers and tomatoes and wheat to market, to run the pickup to Faireville Farm Supply to pick up feed and fertilizer, and so on.

"Bloombottom gave *you* permission to take the Cord out for a spin," Marty continues, taking a step closer to Bill and the gleaming black Cord 812. "What do you think he meant when he said, 'It was *built* to be driven. That car *deserves* to be driven.' He was telling *you* to *drive* it!"

"No, he wasn't, Marty."

"Yes, he was."

"No, he *wasn't*."

"Yes, he *was*. I saw him wink at you."

"He didn't wink at me. He was just blinking or something."

"He winked at you, Bill. I saw him."

Bill sighs. "You see what you want to see, Marty."

"Listen," Marty says, wearing a rare serious expression. "I've known Bloombottom since I was born. I understand his subtle expressions. He's impressed with how much you know about cars. He *wants* you to drive the Cord."

"No, *you* want me to drive the Cord."

"Well, that's true, I guess. But I want you to drive it because I know *you* want to drive it. You do, don't you?" Marty does a good impression of Bloombottom's sandpaper voice: "'Such a rare *privilege* to drive one. Such a *shame* for it to just sit there, undriven.'"

"It wouldn't be right," Bill says.

"What do you mean, it wouldn't be *right*?" Marty says. In exasperation, he slaps himself hard on the forehead; it doesn't hurt, because he's still wearing his grandfather's purple-and-white football helmet. "All you ever do is what other people *expect* you to do, Bill! You work your ass off on the goddamn farm because your parents *expect* you to! You work your freakin' ass off at school because that's what the teachers *expect* you to do! You're always doing all of these goddamn noble things all the time, because that's what you think the rest of the world *expects* you to do!"

Marty lowers his voice and says, "For a change, forget about everyone else's expectations and do something *you* want to do." He takes a step closer to Bill, the hulking shoulder pads beneath his purple zero sweater somehow lending him more authority. "Instead of worrying about doing what's *right*, do something that's *good*."

"Marty," Bill says, "I just don't think —"

"Drive the car, Bill."

"What if we get caught? What if —"

"Just drive the freakin' car, Bill. Drive it."

Bill looks over at the Cord 812, its grille smirking, its headlight cover winking, its shimmering body as curvaceous and alluring as a woman's. It still seems to be begging him, *"Drive me, Bill. Drive me!"*

"Drive the car, Bill," Marty says. "You know you want to. Drive it! Drive it."

"Okay!" Bill yelps. "Okay! I'll drive the car!"

"One condition, though," Marty says, holding up the long black driving coat in one hand, and the goggled helmet and gauntlets in the other. "You've got to wear these!"

So now, inside the cool, fluorescent-lit interior of the Exotic Car Room of the Apostrophes Estate's Carriage House, Bill Brown sits behind the slender, elegant steering wheel of the gleaming black 1937 Cord 812 Phaeton.

Marty Apostrophes pulls a lever on an electrical box attached to the stone wall, and, with a screech of steel gears, the enormous mechanical turntable beneath the seven cars begins to slowly rotate.

The grilles of the 1946 Cisitalia, the 1941 Lincoln Continental, the 1937 Talbot-Lago, and the 1951 Willys Military Jeep all grin through the open iron garage door before the Cord 812 finally peers through to the outside world.

Marty throws the switch down again, and the turntable grinds to a halt. Still wearing his grandfather's purple football uniform, Marty sprints toward the Cord and leaps over the door and into the car's open cockpit: quite an athletic feat for a self-proclaimed couch potato like Marty.

"Put your helmet on, and let's get rolling!" Marty cheers.

"Aw, do I have to wear the helmet?" Bill complains, even as he pulls goggles and face shield down over his nose.

"You look like a friggin' superhero, Bill!" Marty says. "Like *Batman*! The *Michael Keaton* version of Batman!"

"Really?" Bill says. "Not one of the cooler versions? Like Christian Bale, maybe?"

"Hey," Marty says, "there's nothing wrong with Michael Keaton. He's got a great-looking mouth. Women think so, anyway. Personally, I'm partial to the George Clooney version, but whatever."

"You're not going to make those gay rumours go away by swooning over George Clooney."

Behind the crossbar of the football helmet, Marty blushes. "Hey, I'm not *swooning* over him! I just think he's a great actor, that's all."

Bill grins. "At least you didn't compare me to Adam West."

"Oh, come on, Bill! Adam West had *man boobs!* He needed the Bat Utility Belt just to hold in his gut! You're in better shape than *that*. You're no George Clooney, though …"

Marty can't see Bill rolling his eyes behind the tinted goggles in his driving helmet.

Bill reaches his gauntlet-gloved right hand forward and pushes the ignition button. With a wheezing, metallic sound, the engine turns over. Bill holds his breath as the engine fires a few times. Then it stalls.

Bill sighs.

"Try again!" Marty says.

Bill tries again. The engine stalls again.

"Oh, well," Marty says. "There are plenty of other cars in here. Let's take one of the others out for a spin."

But Bill Brown doesn't want to drive any of the other cars. He wants to drive *this* one. He has already fallen in love with the Cord 812.

He jams his thumb against the ignition button one more time, and he squints his eyes and grits his teeth, just like Batman would. Without any hesitation this time, the supercharged V8 comes alive with a throaty, powerful rumble. It's as if Bill has willed the engine to run.

Bill taps his right foot against the accelerator pedal, just to hear that regal lion's roar again. Then he stabs the pedal down to the floor, and the V-8 screams like a charging warrior.

Bill feels his heart throbbing beneath the ancient black driving coat. He presses down the clutch pedal with his left foot, and his gloved fingers tremble slightly as they reach for the chrome-plated gear pre-selector box to the right of the steering column. Bill eases off of the clutch pedal, and the car surges forward in first gear, through the doorway of the Exotic Car Room. The rumbling exhaust note of the supercharged engine echoes from the walls behind the other vintage cars, lined up on either side of the passing Cord like soldiers awaiting the general's inspection.

"Awesome!" Marty cries out. "This is awesome!"

Bill shifts the car into second gear as it rolls out of the Carriage House and gurgles past the glass dome of the unused indoor pool, past the empty racehorse stables, past the stone-walled servants' quarters, and past the tall, Roman-style pillars and the elaborately carved front doors of the Apostrophes Mansion. The snarling gargoyles atop the imposing fence watch as Bill Brown steers the Cord 812 through the gate and out onto the road. The twin of the night's full moon gleams on the car's long, black coffin nose hood.

With his gloved left hand, Bill reaches to the side of the dashboard and cranks the handle labelled "RETRACTABLE HEADLIGHTS — TURN."

"Do the same thing on your side, Marty," he says. "We'll need to open the headlight pods."

"What?" Marty says. "You don't want to drive by the light of the moon, just like in the olden days?"

But he's just kidding; Marty opens the passenger-side headlight pod, and Bill flicks the chrome "LIGHTS" switch on the aircraft-like dashboard. The headlights don't add much to the already brightly moonlit road, but Bill doesn't want to get pulled over for driving at night without his lights on. Bill believes in Following the Rules.

"*Punch it, Chewie!*" Marty bellows.

"*You're* Chewbacca," Bill says. "*I'm* Han Solo."

Marty responds with a Chewbacca-like howl, but when Bill *does* punch it, the Cord's supercharged V8 responds with an enthusiastic roar of its own, drowning out Marty's voice.

As the car races forward, Bill shakes his head in disbelief. "It's so advanced for its time. It handles like a dream. And the front wheel drive is terrific … no pulling, no torque steer … wow."

Bill pushes in the clutch, clicks the pre-selector, and the Cord surges forward in third gear.

"How do you know how to shift it?" Marty shouts over the howl of the engine and the whine of the transmission and the screaming of the supercharger and the wind whistling all around them.

"I watched Jay Leno driving his Cord 812 on *Jay Leno's Garage*," Bill shouts back, never taking his eyes off the road. "But Jay's car was a four-door sedan, not a convertible … and his wasn't supercharged like this one!"

"This car is better than *Jay Leno's* car?"

"This car is pretty damn good!" Bill shouts.

"Let's see how fast this baby will go!" Marty cheers.

"We're already going the speed limit," Bill says.

"Forget about the friggin' *rules* for once, Bill! *Live* a little. *Punch* it!"

Bill squints and grits his teeth. *Fine,* he thinks. He downshifts, punches the accelerator, and the Cord 812 surges forward with a mighty howl.

"Jeez!" Marty shouts. "It's windy in here!"

He pulls the purple turtleneck up over his face, Rudy-style.

The power of the supercharged engine sucks Marty and Bill back into their seats. The scenery around them blurs as the needle on the huge speedometer climbs upward.

Grinning like the chrome grille of the Cord itself, Bill hollers it again: "This car is pretty damn good!"

The supercharged, V-8-powered machine is hurtling into Faireville at almost a hundred miles per hour when Marty and Bill hear the arresting shriek of a police cruiser's siren.

Chapter Five

Supercharged

The "Welcome to Faireville" sign rattles against its posts as the Cord 812 Phaeton roars past in a black blur of speed.

"No, no, no, no, no, no, no, no!" Bill laments. "Why did I let you talk me into this, Marty? Why, why, why, why, why?"

Bill lifts his foot from the accelerator pedal, and the exhaust pipes rumble as the Cord decelerates. The police siren gets louder as it gets closer. The Cord's tires crackle in the gravel as Bill steers it off the pavement and onto the side of the road.

"WHY ARE YOU SLOWING DOWN?" Marty hollers in his DRAMATIC VOICE. "YOU CAN OUTRUN THEM! PUNCH IT, CHEWIE! *PUNCH* IT!"

Behind the face shield of his black driving helmet, Bill shakes his head in defeat. "I'm already going to lose my licence, Marty. I don't want to go to jail for resisting arrest, too."

"PUNCH IT, CHEWIE!" Marty screams again. "*PUNCH* IT!"

"I've got a load of cucumbers to take in tomorrow morning," Bill sighs. "Not without a driver's licence. Gawd. My dad is going to kill me."

"NOT IF YOU DON'T GET CAUGHT! WE CAN GET OUT OF THIS! I'VE GOT A PLAN! *PUNCH* IT, CHEWIE!"

"You've got a plan?"

Marty looks through the grille of his ancient football helmet, through the tinted goggles on Bill's driving helmet, and right into his friend's eyes.

"I've got a plan," Marty says evenly. "We can get out of this. I'm the *king* of getting out of trouble. So punch it, Chewie. Punch it."

Bill hesitates; he has always thought of Marty as the king of getting *into* trouble.

"Trust me, Bill," Marty says.

Behind the black face shield, Bill Brown squints, takes a breath, and then says, "Okay, Marty. I trust you." And then he rasps through gritted teeth, "But *I'm* Han Solo. And *you're* Chewbacca."

And then Bill punches it. The tires spray gravel and dust, and then scream against the pavement as the Cord hits the road again.

The blare of the police siren is drowned out by the howl of the Cord's engine as it hurtles toward the only stoplights in town, which swing gently in the cool nighttime breeze, glowing red.

"If we stop, they will *definitely* catch us," Bill says. "Come on, lights. Turn green. Turn green."

"TURN GREEN, TURN GREEN, TURN GREEN!" Marty commands.

The lights remain glowing red. Bill glances left, then right, then he rockets the Cord through the intersection anyway.

"If I'm going to lose my license," Bill says, "I might as well *really* lose it."

Once again, the police siren gets louder and closer.

"So, what's this plan of yours?" Bill demands.

"TURN LEFT NOW!" Marty barks. "RIGHT NOW! RIGHT NOW!"

"*Right* now, or *left* now?"

"LEFT! LEFT! LEFT! ONTO BURNOFF STREET! NOW NOW NOW!"

Bill downshifts, hits the brakes hard, and cranks the steering wheel to the left, hand-over-hand-over-hand.

As the Cord careens into the narrow alleyway, Marty pokes a finger at the brushed aluminum dashboard and punches the switch for the lights. Bill cuts the engine, and the rumble of the supercharged V-8 is replaced with a shadowy silence.

With only inches of space between the car's fenders and the ragged brick walls on either side, the unlit, silent black car becomes almost invisible, wrapped in the darkness of Burnoff Street. Even moonlight is afraid to come to this part of town at night.

There is a flash of red light against the old brick walls, and then the siren's pitch shifts down a tone as the police car races past the alleyway where the Cord and its passengers hide in the darkness.

"My plan worked!" Marty cheers. "We lost them!"

It is only as the screech of the siren recedes that Bill and Marty hear the burglar alarm howling from deep inside the alleyway, and it is only as their eyes gradually adjust to the darkness that they see the outlines of two tall men standing directly in front of the car.

The two figures are dressed in black, with balaclavas pulled down over their faces. Each holds an overstuffed gym bag in his left hand, and each holds a pistol in his right hand; through the split windshield of the Cord 812, one gun is aimed at Marty, the other at Bill.

"Get this car outta here, muthahfuggahs!" one of the dark figures roars.

"You're blockin' our escape route!" the other grunts. "Move it! Move it! Now! Right now!"

"Don't shoot!" Bill says. "Don't shoot!"

"Then get this muthahfuggin' car outta here!" the first dark figure commands, adding as emphasis another, "Muthahfuggahs!"

"Yeah! Move it *now*, muthahfuggahs!" the second one shouts through his balaclava.

"Hey!" the first one grunts at the second one. "'Muthahfuggah' is *my* tag line, dude! Get your own muthahfuggin' slogan!"

"Right," says the second man in black, "'cause that line's *soooooo* original. It's never been used before by *anyone!*"

If Marty and Bill were not so distracted by the guns waving in their faces, they would notice the second robber rolling his eyes beneath the dark material covering his face.

"Move the car, muthahfuggahs!" the first one shrieks, waving his gun theatrically. "Move it! Now!"

With fingers trembling inside his black gauntlet, Bill pushes the ignition button. The engine turns over, with a wheezing, metallic sound, just like he had heard back in the Carriage House. The engine fires, sputters, and then stalls.

Bill tries again.

And again.

And again.

But the Cord's V-8 refuses to run.

The second black-clad figure strides toward the driver's-side door, with his gun still trained on Bill. "Let me try!" he barks. "Get outta the car, you mutha ..." He glances over at his partner in crime, and then rephrases. "You ... *idiot stick!*"

"*Idiot stick?*" the first bandit taunts. "Ooooh, nice one. You're definitely from the 'hood, bro!"

"At least it's *original,*" the second robber says, as he turns sideways to squeeze between the brick wall and the Cord's round fenders. "Open the door, *idiot stick!*" he hollers at Bill. "Now!"

Bill does as he is told; he throws the door open and leaps from the car, unintentionally smacking the sideways crook with the solid metal edge of the door. Right in the testicles.

"*AAAAAAIIIIIIIIIIIIEEEEEEEEEEEEEE!*" the injured criminal screams. When he reaches down to protectively cup his injured orbs, he accidentally slaps them again with the barrel of his pistol.

"*AAAAAAIIIIIIIIIIIEEEEEEEEEEEEE!*" he shrieks again, and the burst of pain causes his finger to clench. This instinctive reaction is terribly unfortunate for the robber, since his index finger is still curled around the trigger of his pistol.

The bullet blows off the little toe of his left foot, but instead of crying "Wee wee wee" all the way home, the debilitated bandit once again cries, "*AAAAAAIIIIIIIIIIIIEEEEEEEEEEEEE!*"

He drops his pistol and slumps backward against the fender of the Cord.

Criminal Number One spins and aims his gun at Bill. His voice trembles as he shouts, "What did you do to my man Cliff, muth-ahfuggah? What did you do to my man Cliff?"

"For gawd's sake, Devin!" Cliff yelps. "There's no point in us wearing *baklavas* if you say my *name!*"

"You just said *mine!*" Devin angrily counters. "And they're called *balaclavas*. Baklava is a Greek dessert."

"Ohhhhhh," Cliff moans. He slides from the fender onto the ground, gripping his crotch with both hands, choking back vomit, blood spurting onto the ground from the stump of his projectile-lacerated little toe.

Devin takes a step toward Bill, shaking the gun in his face. "What did this punk bastard *do* to you, Cliff?"

"Dammit, Devin! Stop saying my name!"

"What *did* he do to you?"

"It happened so fast! He musta disarmed me and shot me!"

"I ... I didn't do anything to him!" Bill stammers. "He ... he shot himself in the foot!"

Devin sighs and looks skyward, shaking his head slowly from side to side. "You shot *yourself?* In the *foot?* Boy, Cliff, you are some master criminal."

"Stop saying my name, Orff!"

"Aw, for gawd's sake, Cliff!" Devin Orff cries out. "Now you've said my *last* name! Why don't you give 'em my address and phone number, too? Why don't I tell 'em *your* last name, huh?" Devin does an exaggerated jig, singing, "*Cliff Boswink! Cliff Boswink! Cliff Boswink!*" like one child mocking another on a kindergarten playground.

Bill takes this moment of discord as an opportunity to scramble out of Devin Orff's line of fire; he doesn't want to accidentally lose his brains the same way Cliff Boswink has accidentally lost his little toe. Bill sprints for the nearest shadow, and in the long, black driving coat, the black leather helmet and face shield, and the black leather gauntlets and boots, Bill vanishes into the darkness like he's diving into a deep pool of murky water.

Devin Orff scans the area for Bill, aiming his gun every which way. "Where did he go? Where did he go?"

"He vanished into nothing, man!" Cliff Boswink says, his vision blurring from shock and blood loss.

"He couldn't have vanished into *nothing!*" Devin Orff growls, his sneer concealed beneath the balaclava that no longer protects his identity from anyone. He spins around in a circle, scanning the area once again. "Where are you, you little shit? Where are you hiding, *muthahfuggah?*"

"*Nothing man,*" Cliff burbles as he slides into unconsciousness. "*Nothing man. Nothing man.*"

Devin Orff cries out into the shadows of Burnoff Street, "You're *gonna* be *nothing*, man, if you don't come out from wherever you're hiding and get this muthahfuggin' car outta the way. Come out, *nothing man!* Come out before I start shooting! Come out, *nothing man!* Come out!"

Inside the cockpit of the Cord 812, Marty leaps to his feet and shouts in his DRAMATIC VOICE, "HE *IS* NOTHING MAN! AND HE WILL *NEVER* COME OUT! BECAUSE HE HAS *VANISHED* INTO *THIN AIR!* IT'S ONE OF HIS *MANY* SUPERPOWERS!"

Devin Orff turns to face Marty. "Are you retarded or something?"

"I AM THE *PURPLE ZERO!*" Marty wails. "WE *SPECIALIZE* IN FIGHTING DIRTY CRIMINALS LIKE YOU! WE *SPECIALIZE* IN MAKING THE STREETS OF FAIREVILLE SAFE! FOR PEOPLE! AND KITTENS! AND PUPPIES! AND EVEN COWS ... AND PIGS ... AND FROGS ... AND GRASSHOPPERS ... AND OTHER LIVING THINGS, TOO, I SUPPOSE!"

From his hiding place beneath a rickety loading dock platform, Bill realizes that Marty is buying him some time to move to a safer place, so Bill stealthily crawls through the alley's long shadows and wedges himself behind one of Burnoff Street's many garbage dumpsters. It's a pretty tight squeeze for the rugged farm boy.

"'Dirty criminals like me,' eh?" Devin says, levelling his gun at Marty.

Crap, thinks Marty; since he's standing up inside the open car, Marty realizes that he has made himself a very easy target, even for a terrible shot like Devin Orff.

"You wanna come down here and say that to my face?" Devin taunts. "What did you call yourself? The Friggin' *Zero?*"

"The *Purple* Zero," Marty says. With a lethal weapon pointed right at his face, Marty can't quite summon the bravado he needs to activate his DRAMATIC VOICE.

Devin Orff scans Marty's outfit: the purple football sweater pulled tight over the huge leather shoulder pads, its turtleneck collar pulled up over Marty's face. The quilted, high-waisted football pants. The purple-and-white leather helmet.

"Exactly *what* the hell are you wearing, you gayboy?" he says.

Marty is getting really sick of being called a "gayboy" and a "fag" and a "queer," and he would tell this goon just where to go ... if only this goon didn't happen to be holding a loaded gun.

"Come on down, here, muthahfuggah," Devin says, turning the pistol sideways like a true movie gangsta. "And put your hands up in the air where I can see them."

Since the passenger-side door is too close the wall to swing open, Marty climbs onto the dashboard and up over the windshield.

The narrow, sloped hood of the car has been waxed weekly for years by Bloombottom, and Marty's feet immediately slip out from under him on the slick, polished surface.

He flies from the nose of the Cord and crashes headlong into Devin. One of Marty's outstretched hands inadvertently knocks the pistol from the bank robber's hand.

Devin falls backward, and the back of his head splats in a thick, gooey mud puddle. Enraged, he throws Marty off of him.

Marty scrambles to his feet.

Devin charges, lobbing hard lefts and rights at Marty's face, as Marty dances from side to side to dodge the punches.

One fist glances off Marty's cheek, then Marty's foot lands in a pothole, and he stumbles backward just as another of Devin's meaty fists is about to score a debilitating direct hit.

Marty's right hand instinctively grabs at a wooden handrail as he falls, and, as he springs back to his feet, he realizes that it has broken off in his hand. He now holds a long, sharp stick, which he immediately swings wildly at his nemesis.

A surprised Devin takes a few steps backward, then grabs the stick in mid-air, wrenches it away from Marty, and thrusts its sharp end at Marty's chest.

"Stop that now!" thunders a resonant voice from behind Devin Orff.

Devin spins around and shouts, "Says who?"

Right behind Devin Orff, Bill Brown steps out of the shadows and into the dust-diffused beam of a streetlight, like an illusionist appearing out of nothing in the spotlight on a stage.

"Says *me*," he whispers, like the breeze before a storm.

Bill's clenched fist hovers above his shoulder. The muscles in his forearm twitch.

Then, his voice echoes from the walls of Burnoff Street like a distant roll of thunder: "Says *Nothing Man*."

Then, for the first time in his life, Bill Brown launches his fist at another person's face. He puts all of his strength behind it; all of the potential energy that his muscles have stored up from throwing hay bales and turning wrenches and hoeing weeds and carrying bushel baskets, all of that potential energy turns kinetic, and farm boy Bill Brown throws it all at bank robber Devin Orff.

There is a sound like the crack of a bat hitting a baseball. Then, the pointed stick hits the ground with a clatter, followed by Devin Orff, whose body pounds the broken pavement with a hollow-sounding thump. He rolls onto his back, out cold.

The force of Bill's punch has rolled Devin's balaclava up over his nose, revealing a crescent-moon-shaped scar, which runs from the corner of his mouth to the bottom of his chin. Even unconscious and disarmed, Devin Orff still manages to look threatening.

Bill says to Marty, "Let's get out of here."

"TO THE *PURPLEMOBILE!*" an adrenaline-charged Marty cries.

"We're not calling it that," Bill says.

From inside the bank, authoritative voices ring out into the alley: "*Police! Come out with your hands in the air!*"

"Out here, officers!" Bill shouts inside through the metal door, which swings back and forth on its broken hinges. Then he turns to Marty and says, "Let's go."

"TO THE *BLACK PHANTOM!*" Marty cheers.

"Just get in the car, Marty."

By the time the police run through the back door of the bank and into the alley called Burnoff Street, Bill and Marty are already roaring through Faireville's single set of stoplights (which, fortunately, are glowing green this time) and toward the Apostrophes Estate in the Cord 812 Phaeton (which, also fortunately, started on the first try).

Devin Orff and Cliff Boswink are unmasked by the police officers, and then, in handcuffs, they are escorted to Faireville Memorial Hospital to have their wounds treated; the sneering, grumbling Devin is ushered into the back seat of a police cruiser, while the mumbling, disoriented Cliff goes on a stretcher in the back of an ambulance.

Before the police catch up with either of them, though, Devin has a chance to remind Cliff, "Remember the story we rehearsed. Make sure you stick to the story."

"Okay, Devin," Cliff rasps, his face white and bloodless. "I'm sorry, Devin."

"You're the reason we got caught," Devin spits. "Make sure you're not the reason we go to jail. The cops will try to trick you into changing your story. Make *sure* that you *don't*."

"Okay, Devin," Cliff repeats. "I'm sorry, Devin."

"You should be, Cliff. You should be."

As soon as she is sure that the danger has passed, Elizabeth Murphy emerges from behind the dumpster where she's been hiding, her heart palpitating with adrenaline and excitement.

"I got it!" she cries out to one of the police officers who remained on the scene. "I got it all on video!"

"That's great," the officer says, "but I think we've already got everything we need. Those two idiots left their fingerprints all over everything. We've recovered both of their guns. One of them was still clutching a bag full of stolen cash!"

"But I've got it all on *video!*" Elizabeth protests.

"Well," the cop says, "so do we, actually. You've got whatever happened *outside* on video, but we've got a recording of what happened *inside*. Those geniuses broke the video cameras *out here*, but they didn't disable the ones *inside* the bank. What masterminds!"

"But I think you need to see what happened out here, also," Elizabeth protests. "I filmed the two ..."

Elizabeth is going to say, *"I filmed the two crime fighters who appeared out of nowhere and stopped those criminals in their tracks!"*, but the police officer interrupts her, raising her hand like she's halting traffic.

"What those two did *inside* the bank is what we'll use to convict them," the officer says. "The footage from the bank's security camera identifies them clearly." She laughs and shakes her head. "They didn't think to pull their face masks down until *after* they broke into the safe. Duh!" She pulls a notepad and pen from the pocket of her uniform. "But, listen, Mizz ..."

"Elizabeth Murphy. Reporter for *The Faireville Gleaner*."

"Okay, Elizabeth Murphy, reporter for *The Faireville Gleaner,* why don't you give me your contact information, and I'll give you a call if we need more evidence, okay?"

Elizabeth's shoulders drop, and she sighs and takes the pad and pen from the police officer.

The cop eventually joins the others, to help bag up the evidence and seal the doors to the bank with yellow tape, which reads "POLICE LINE — DO NOT CROSS." Soon they all drive away in their police cars, and an eerie peace descends on Burnoff Street.

Then Elizabeth notices a small, flat, rectangular object lying on the broken pavement, right where that mysterious, phantom-like car blocked the robbers' escape.

She picks it up.

"*Captain Kirk's Guide to Women,*" she mutters to herself. "Weird."

She tucks the small paperback into her bag with the video camera. She will investigate this clue later.

"Dad?" she calls out. "Dad? Are you still here?"

Jack Murphy, the artist also formerly known as Jack-o and Sebastien, stumbles out from behind the oil barrel where he has been hiding. Well, he hasn't been *hiding* so much as *napping*; Elizabeth's father has a tendency to fall sound asleep anywhere and anytime he is motionless for more than a minute or two.

"Wow, Sweet Pea," he says, "what happened out here?"

"It's a good story, Dad," Elizabeth says.

Then it occurs to her: maybe the police don't want her video, but Mr. Gootenbourg at *The Faireville Gleaner* will! This is breaking news! Elizabeth Murphy, Junior Reporter, has her first scoop! She will write a report about the robbery before the city newspaper even *hears* about it! This is *awesome*!

A beaming Elizabeth says, "You can read about it in tomorrow's newspaper."

⊚

After he has parked the Cord 812 Phaeton in its exact spot in the Apostrophes Carriage House, after he has stealthily walked home in the moonlit darkness, after he has tiptoed up the farmhouse stairs, avoiding all the creaky spots, after he has slipped past his snoring parents' open bedroom door, after he has slid under the covers of his bunk without waking any of his siblings, Bill Brown will lie awake, replaying the night's events in his mind, feeling the bruises darkening on his elbows and knees, and his fist throbbing where he socked that burglar in the jaw.

When exhaustion finally overtakes him, and he falls into a deep sleep, Bill will have a dream.

He will be a black falcon, soaring high over Faireville Bluffs. From the air, he will see a slender black cat, stretching and purring in a pool of moonlight. He will glide down to the nearest tree, landing on a high, exposed branch, which allows him to watch the black cat from a distance. And even though he is a falcon, and she is a cat, he will feel strangely fascinated by this creature, attracted to her, even. He will find it impossible to stop watching her.

By the time he decides to glide down to the ground to get closer, the cat will have scampered away somewhere else.

When the alarm buzzer screeches at 5:00 a.m. to wake Bill to deliver a load of cucumbers to the Krispy Green Pickle Factory, Bill will remember watching a running black cat through the eyes of a falcon, and watching a falling bank robber though the lenses of a pair of old driving goggles.

Bill's heart will race when he realizes that only one of these images was a dream.

Chapter Six

Viral

Once again, Elizabeth Murphy's boots clip-clop against the cool sidewalk as she strides toward the office of *The Faireville Gleaner*. Her frizzy wheat-blonde hair is even wilder than usual, and she's still wearing the same orange jumpsuit as yesterday, its pockets still stuffed with cameras, lenses, and other tools of the journalistic trade. Her backpack for school is flung over her right shoulder, and in her left hand is the article she's written about last night's caper. She grips the pages as if they are thousand-dollar bills.

"This story is a *scoop!*" she says to herself. "This story is an *exclusive*." The words sound delicious. "A scoop of delicious exclusive!" she says, laughing.

Normally, Elizabeth wouldn't find this quite so hilarious, but she hasn't slept since filming last night's foiled bank heist, so the world feels fuzzier and looks more comically surreal than usual. She stayed up all night writing her exclusive news story, and editing the raw footage into the most awesome video news report ever! She's included a link to her video in her article, so people can watch the story online after reading about it in the newspaper.

Despite the dark circles under her eyes, Elizabeth's expression is confident and enthusiastic; her battery is *supercharged* this morning!

She declares to herself, "I will single-handedly drag *The Faireville Gleaner* kicking and screaming into the digital future!" Her sleep-deprived brain also finds this term strangely entertaining, so she says it again. "The *digital future!*"

The sky is only beginning to glow faintly orange in the east, and the streets are still deserted, but Elizabeth knows that Mr. Gooten-bourg will already be sitting at his editorial desk. In addition to being *The Faireville Gleaner*'s Editor-in-Chief, Publisher, Copy Editor, Advertising Executive, Layout Editor, Office Secretary, Financial Con-troller, and Maintenance Director, Mr. Gootenbourg is also the Circulation Manager, which means that he has to wake up hours before sunrise to deliver a newspaper to every household in town, so that the Good Citizens of Faireville can flip to the lottery numbers on page three while they sip their morning coffees.

Elizabeth pushes through the door to the *Gleaner*'s office, inhal-ing the metallic odour of hot machine oil, the sawdust scent of fresh newsprint, and the alcohol-tinged smell of ink. *The Faireville Gleaner* is one of the few remaining independent newspapers in the country, and one of the only ones left with its own in-house print-ing press.

As she rushes toward Mr. Gootenbourg's desk, Elizabeth wonders if any reporter for a little local newspaper like *The Gleaner* has ever won the Pulitzer Prize for Journalism.

"Mr. Gootenbourg!" Elizabeth says, slapping her story down among the hundreds of other papers on the editor's desktop. "I've got an *exclusive* story for you! It's a *scoop*! It's *sensational!*"

Mr. Gootenbourg raises a finger in the air to halt Elizabeth, and then continues with the telephone conversation he's been having. He cradles the receiver of the phone between his shoulder and ear, while scribbling some notes on the back of a past-due electrical bill.

"Right, Ernie," he says, in his slow, deep, patient voice, "that's

'Buy two pints of sweet *cherries*, get the third pint free' ... Right, that's *cherries*, not strawberries ... sweet *cherries* ... Yep, I've got it, Ernie ... I was sure you said *strawberries* yesterday, though. Guess my hearing isn't what it used to be ... No harm done, Ernie. I'll print the correction tomorrow ... Yep, I've got it ... sweet *cherries*, not strawberries ... Yes, I wrote it down ... sweet *cherries* ... No, of course not ... no charge for the corrected ad ... That's okay, Ernie ... I'll also give you your next ad for free, how about that? Okay, Ernie. Bye now."

Mr. Gootenbourg hangs up the phone. Anyone else would sigh after an exchange like that, but he doesn't. Being the Editor-in-Chief, Publisher, Copy Editor, Advertising Executive, Layout Editor, Office Secretary, Financial Controller, Maintenance Director, and Circulation Manager of the local newspaper requires an extraordinary level of patience.

"Mr. Gootenbourg!" Elizabeth exclaims. "You have *got* to read the story I brought you!"

"Hello, Elizabeth," he says. "Is it about the hockey game last night? I heard it was a nail-biter."

"I brought that story, too," Elizabeth says, "but I've got another even *better* one! You had better take a look at it right away. It's a *scoop*, an *exclusive!*" Elizabeth *so* loves the sound of those words.

"We're the only paper in town," the editor observes, "so everything we print is a scoop, really."

"But this is a scoop on an *international* scale!" Elizabeth says. "It's *sensational!*"

"Hmm," says Mr. Gootenbourg, as he picks up Elizabeth's report about the attempted bank robbery. "Sensational like the sort of thing *The National Midnight Star* publishes? Is it sensational like, 'Monkey Boy Battles Aliens' or 'Elvis Marries Bigfoot'? Hmm?"

The old editor adjusts his rectangular reading glasses and strokes his thick, silver beard.

"That was Ernie over at the market, by the way," he says, in his slow, rumbling voice. "Apparently, he noticed a copywriting error in his advertisement in this morning's paper. We printed, 'Buy two pints of sweet *strawberries*, get the third pint free,' but what Ernie *wanted* us to print was, 'Buy two pints of sweet *cherries*, get the third pint free.' I was sure that he'd said 'sweet strawberries' yesterday when he phoned in his copy, but —"

"Yes, yes," Elizabeth pants, "I gathered all of that from your phone conversation. But —"

"That was very observant of you, Elizabeth. Being observant like that is a very useful tool for a reporter," he says. "But another important skill is *listening* when another person is speaking. And not interrupting. Such as you did when I was on the phone with Ernie, for example —"

"I'm sorry about that, but —"

"As I was saying, I was sure that Ernie had said 'sweet strawberries' yesterday when he phoned in his copy, but, you know what they say ... 'The customer is always right!' Ernie Smith has taken out a quarter-page advertisement for the Faireville Market in every issue of *The Gleaner* for the past thirty-three years, so I suppose that I can afford to give him a free ad in the next paper, in exchange for a mistake that may or may not have been my fault."

Mr. Gootenbourg inherited *The Faireville Gleaner* as a teenager, and he has managed it single-handedly ever since. Because running the newspaper took up so much of his time, Mr. Gootenbourg never married, and therefore never had any children; nevertheless, he has a fatherly way about him, a grandfatherly way, even.

Elizabeth's frantic heartbeat slows, and she sits down in the chair across the desk from the bearded editor.

Since his aging body has been slowing down lately, Mr. Gootenbourg decided that he could use a hand with some of the local news reporting, so Elizabeth is the first employee he has ever hired. He supposes that he can afford to be patient with her, too.

"Now, then," he says, adjusting his reading glasses again. "Let's have a look at this *exclusive story*, shall we?"

He raises the pages close to his face, and reads aloud, "*Real Live Superheroes in Faireville! Nothing Man and the Purple Zero!* By Beth Murphy, Junior Reporter." He looks over the page at Elizabeth. "Well. Doesn't *this* sound exciting! Do Elvis or Monkey Boy make an appearance?"

Elizabeth is about to protest, when Mr. Gootenbourg says, "I'm only kidding you, Elizabeth. A little journalist-to-journalist banter, that's all." Then he reads the article, silently, occasionally punctuating the air with a "Well!" or a "Hmmm."

Elizabeth drums her fingers on the desk, thinking, *He reads infuriatingly slowly for a newspaper editor!*

When Mr. Gootenbourg has finally finished reading, he places the pages on his desktop. Then he removes his reading glasses and sets them down atop Elizabeth's article. Then he slowly strokes his silver beard. "Well," he finally says.

"Well?" Elizabeth says, her heart racing again. "Well, *what*? What do you think? It's the scoop of the year, isn't it? *The Faireville Gleaner* hasn't published a story like this one in a long time, has it?"

"Well," the old editor says. He pauses for a moment. He wants to put this in exactly the right way. "You're right, Elizabeth. *The Gleaner* has not published a story like this one in a long time. Or *ever*, actually. And I'm afraid that it never will."

"What? *Why?*"

"Well," Mr. Gootenbourg says, "for one thing, you have broken a number of journalistic rules in this piece. For example, you should *never* call people who are accused of a crime 'criminals.' They are *alleged* criminals."

He is very careful to strongly emphasize the word "*alleged.*"

"And, until *alleged* criminals are specifically charged for their *alleged* crimes, you should *never* name names. Not only is it unprofessional, but it could make the newspaper liable for a defamation suit, which is something that neither our reputation nor our bank account can afford."

He lowers his voice to a raspy whisper.

"And, the last names of these *alleged* bank robbers are Orff and Boswink, correct? That is very troubling. *Very* troubling. For as long as Faireville has been incorporated as a town, the Orff and Boswink family names have been synonymous with criminal activity. Often rather *violent* criminal activity. Vandalism. Arson. Assault. Even murder. There are some frighteningly corrupt chromosomes in those gene pools, if you catch my drift. "

Now Mr. Gootenbourg strokes his beard in a very serious way.

"Do you think I want to arrive at the office one morning to find that it has been burned down in retaliation for mentioning the Orffs or the Boswinks in an unflattering way? Or, even worse, do you think I want to be *inside* the office when they douse it with gasoline and throw a match? With all of the newsprint in here, this place would blow up like a bomb!"

"I can take the names out of the article if you like!" Elizabeth says. "I can change anything you want! That's why *you're* the editor and *I'm* the reporter, right?"

"Well, Elizabeth," Mr. Gootenbourg continues, "there is also the problem of the *believability* of your story. There really are no *facts* to support your claim that these two figures that jumped out of that strange car are … as you so vividly and imaginatively put it … *superheroes.* Outside the comic page, there is really no evidence to support the existence of superheroes *at all.* So the very premise of your article is flawed."

"They sure *looked* and *acted* like superheroes," Elizabeth says.

"They could also have merely been two people out for a ride, who accidentally turned into the wrong alley at the wrong time."

"What about their *superhero costumes?*"

"Well," Mr. Gootenbourg says, in that consistently reassuring tone of his, "Halloween is this weekend. Maybe they were giving their costumes a test run before going out trick-or-treating in them. Or maybe they were escaped inmates from the Psychiatric Ward at Gasberg Hospital. Or maybe their mothers just dress them funny. The point is that we don't *know*, and we can't report *speculation* as *fact*."

"*Fox News* does," Elizabeth says.

Mr. Gootenbourg's eyes widen. "*The Faireville Gleaner* is not *Fox News!*"

Elizabeth's shoulders drop. "I can remove the superhero angle from the story, if you want me to."

"Well," Mr. Gootenbourg says again, regaining his slightly ruffled composure, "with all of those elements removed, there isn't much of a story left, is there?"

Elizabeth wants to be respectful, but now she has to protest!

"I witnessed two bank robbers getting stopped in their tracks by two unknown heroes! If that isn't news, *what is?*"

Mr. Gootenbourg resists the urge to sigh, and says, "I'll mention it in the Police Blotter section on page six, okay?"

"*Page six?*" Elizabeth gasps. "You're going to bury an amazing story like this one on *page six?*"

"Listen, Elizabeth," the old editor says, "I've been running this little newspaper for my entire adult life. I know what the people in this town want to read about. They buy *The Faireville Gleaner* so they can see pictures of their kids winning hockey tournaments, and so they can read about the money their Lions Club raised at their 53rd Annual Charity Bake Sale. They want to know which local country band is playing at The Sergeant-at-Arms on Friday night, and they want to be informed when the Faireville Market is having a three-for-the-price-of-two sale on sweet strawberries."

"It was sweet *cherries*, Mr. Gootenbourg."

"Yes, yes, right, right," he says, twiddling his beard with some fervour. "My point is this, Elizabeth: Since I've been running this little newspaper for my entire adult life, I also know what people *don't* want to read about in *The Faireville Gleaner*. They *don't* want to read about bank robberies and guns and violence in their safe, quiet, family-oriented little town. They *don't* want to read about weirdo vigilantes in funny outfits driving strange-looking cars. They've got the TV news and the internet and the big city newspapers for that sort of thing. They can read about Monkey Boy and Elvis somewhere else. Understand?"

Elizabeth feels like crying, but she forces herself to remain stalwart. Lois Lane wouldn't cry. "I guess so," she says.

"And, speaking of the *internet*," Mr. Gootenbourg continues, saying "internet" as if it's a vulgar curse word, "I note that in your article, you put a *web link* to a video you filmed of the incident in progress. A *web link*, Elizabeth? Really? The fact that people can read the news for free on the internet … even though half of it is unreliable and written by people who can't spell … is killing the sales of traditional newspapers. You haven't already uploaded this video, have you? I really, really hope that you haven't."

"Actually, sir, I already did."

"You didn't mention *The Faireville Gleaner* at any point in the video, did you?"

Initially, when Elizabeth had uploaded her video to a website called *NewsTube*, she had signed it, "Beth Murphy, Junior Reporter for *The Faireville Gleaner*," but at the last minute she chose an anonymous name instead: "Observer X." Maybe her instincts as an investigative journalist weren't so bad after all.

"No sir," she says, "I didn't mention the newspaper, or use my real name."

"Well, I'm grateful for that," Mr. Gootenbourg says, and he does sigh this time. "Fortunately, it's still early in the day. Remove the video as soon as possible, and hopefully there will be no harm done."

He sits back in his desk chair, still stroking his silver beard. Then he leans forward and scribbles something on a small, pink slip of paper.

"Sir?" Elizabeth tentatively asks. "Are you firing me?"

The old editor runs his long whiskers between his fingers again, and his cool grey eyes seem to look right through Elizabeth. Since his mouth is concealed by the ancient forest upon his face, Elizabeth can't see that he is smiling.

"No, Elizabeth," he says. "You are not fired. Let's say that you are on *probation* for now. Your report on last night's hockey game looks pretty good. Would you like to cover the Old Timers' Bonspiel over at the curling rink tonight?"

Frankly, Elizabeth would rather study the paint drying on one of her father's abstract canvases than watch a bunch of old guys throwing rocks down an ice sheet and sweeping and guffawing and chugging warm bottles of Labatt 50. But she *does* want to be a reporter, so she will do what she has to do.

"I guarantee you, it will be the most awesome report about a curling match that you will ever read, sir!"

"I'm sure it will be, Elizabeth," Mr. Gootenbourg says, handing the small slip of paper to her over his desktop. "Here is your first paycheque, by the way. Your hockey game coverage was well-written, thorough ... and *factual.*"

It's almost time for school to start for the day, so Elizabeth rises from her seat and practically skips for the door, with her first reporter's paycheque gripped firmly in her right hand.

"By the way, Elizabeth," Mr. Gootenbourg calls out behind her, "you didn't happen to mention your video to anyone, did you?"

"To just one friend, sir," she says, "and I promise that it will stay just between me and him."

Unfortunately, this promise was broken before it was even made, but Elizabeth doesn't realize it yet.

She only *meant* to email the link to the video to "one friend": Bill Brown. Her email read, "To Superman. From Lois Lane." It was a bold move, but she felt that she had to do *something* to get Bill to notice her.

Because Elizabeth's brain was foggy from sleep deprivation, when she typed Bill's name into her email program, her fingers misfired on the keyboard, and she spelled his last name "Bon" instead of "Brown."

This error somehow automatically loaded her old invitation list from the disastrous, goldfish-flooded "Bon Voyage at Sea" Junior Prom, which included the email addresses of every junior at Faireville District High School at the time; of course, like Elizabeth, they were all seniors now.

With one click on the "Send" button, a bleary-eyed Elizabeth, who meant only to deliver a cute, flirty email to the Man of her Dreams, sent practically every senior student at Faireville District High School a link to her video of last night's bank robbery.

And practically every senior at Faireville District High School has forwarded, or soon will forward, the link to practically everyone they know.

And almost everyone who received an email from Faireville this morning will forward the incredible video on to everyone on their own email lists.

And by early afternoon, the video called *Real Live Superheroes! Nothing Man and the Purple Zero!*, uploaded by Observer X on October 28, will have been viewed 67,411 times.

And by late afternoon, dozens of other video-based websites will have copied the video, and people will be viewing the exploits of Nothing Man and the Purple Zero all over the world. And, at that point, even if Elizabeth deletes her video from the *NewsTube* website, it will still be available on dozens of other sites that are beyond her control.

And, less than twenty-four hours after Elizabeth uploaded it, *Real Live Superheroes! Nothing Man and the Purple Zero!* will have officially gone viral.

Ironically, Bill Brown, the lone intended recipient of the video link, will be practically the only senior at Faireville District High School who hasn't seen the video by the time he gets to school. Bill is up early, delivering their farm's last load of cucumbers of the season to the Krispy Green Pickle Factory, and he will not have time to check his email.

But Elizabeth doesn't know about any of this yet.

"Don't worry, Mr. Gootenbourg," she says, as she leaves the office of *The Faireville Gleaner*, "your Junior Reporter has got everything under control."

Chapter Seven

Criminal Masterminds

As Elizabeth rushes away from the newspaper office and toward the high school, she runs right past the Official Headquarters of the Faireville Police Force. If she paused to peek through the police station's dusty front window, she would see Devin Orff, one of the *alleged* bank robbers that she captured on video the night before, captured for real inside the police station's small single holding cell. She also would see the other *alleged* robber, Cliff Boswink, being rolled in a wheelchair into the hallway leading to the interrogation room at the rear of the station.

In a time when practically every other small town in the province has replaced their local constables with a detachment of the Ontario Provincial Police, the Faireville Police Force has somehow soldiered on. Despite arguments that the OPP would cost the townspeople fewer tax dollars, and that they've got better training, better equipment, and more elaborate crime-fighting resources, members of the Faireville Town Council voted unanimously to keep the town police on the payroll anyway.

"They know us, and we know them," one councillor argued.

"They're our own people," echoed another. "We can trust them."

So, just as Faireville is one of the last small towns in the province that still has its own independent local newspaper, it is also one of the last to have its own local police force.

While most of the police stations of the modern, city-based detachments of the OPP resemble those seen on TV shows like *The Shield* and *Law and Order*, and their crime labs look something like the ones on *CSI* and *Criminal Minds*, the Official Headquarters of the Faireville Police Force resembles a set from *The Andy Griffith Show*, which was filmed in the 1960s, but seems to take place in "simpler times," like maybe the 1930s.

Many comparisons have been made between *The Andy Griffith Show*'s fictional small town of Mayberry and the real town of Faireville; locals tend to compare the two places fondly and favourably, while outsiders snigger that Faireville is much like Mayberry in its steadfast resistance to progress, in its refusal to become "modern."

Much like Sheriff Andy Griffith's police station, the Official Headquarters of the Faireville Police Force has just one big desk near the front door, upon which the police chief and all five officers take turns completing their paperwork. Beside the desk are three flagpoles, from which hang the Canadian Maple Leaf, the Red Ensign of Ontario, and the Faireville Coat of Arms. Slightly askew on the painted brick wall behind the desk there is a sun-blanched street map of Faireville, so old that the Cardboard Acres subdivision was still farmland when the map was printed.

The only real difference between Andy Griffith's workspace and this one is the outdated desktop computer, which crashes an average of three times per week; the constables of the Faireville Police Force use it as little as possible, instead opting to do their crime-fighting research on their kids' computers at home.

Also just like on *The Andy Griffith Show*, there is a single holding cell with thick iron bars across the front, like the kind used to contain ferocious lions inside circus trailers. The jail cell in fictional Mayberry was usually occupied by a charming-and-lovable fictional local drunk named Otis Campbell, but the jail cell in Faireville currently contains a snarling Devin Orff, who at the moment is neither charming nor lovable. He sits atop a plain wooden bench, which has been worn down over the years by the backsides of generations of vandals, miscreants, and thieves, including many of his own Orff family relations.

"When can I get the hell outta here, *muthahfuggah*?" Devin demands of the officer who currently sits behind the single desk.

"*What* did you just say to me?" the officer says, rising from the desk. The officer happens to be Carl Crane, Chief of the Faireville Police Force.

"Hey, hey," Devin says, "it's not actually a bad word. I said '*fuggah*,' not 'fucker.'"

Police Chief Crane sits back down and twiddles the tips of his impressive silver moustache between his thumb and index finger. "Why don't you try again *without* that part."

"Okay. Um … when might I be released from this cell, sir?"

"That's 'Chief Crane' to you, boy. As soon as they're finished questioning your buddy, they'll interrogate you. And then you'll be free to go … to the Detention Centre in Gasberg, I imagine."

"Don't worry, *Chief Crane*," Devin says, "I'll be out of here before the end of your shift."

"Don't count on it, kid," the chief mutters.

Devin rises from the bench and begins pacing back and forth inside the small cell. "Hey, Chief, I'm starving. Can you go out and get me a burger? Mustard, no onions, extra pickles. And ketchup, too, but only if it's *Heinz* ketchup."

"You want fries with that, sir?" says the silver-moustached cop, who puts his feet up on the desk and settles back into his chair. "Want me to toss you the keys to your cell, too?"

"Stop harassing me," Devin says.

"What?"

"STOP HARASSING ME, POLICE CHIEF CRANE!" Devin

shrieks, as if he's being poked in the eye with a branding iron. Devin knows that this routine doesn't always work, but it once got his father out of a Drunk and Disorderly charge, so Devin figures that it's worth a try now. "PLEASE STOP, POLICE CHIEF CRANE! YOU'RE HURTING ME!"

The chief sighs, and flips *The Faireville Gleaner* open in front of him. "You might as well end the performance, buddy, 'cause there's nobody else around to hear it. So, just sit down and shut up, okay? And maybe if you're a good boy, I'll get you something to eat after I've finished reading my paper."

Devin sits down, and grumbles, "Did we at least get mentioned in the newspaper?"

Chief Crane snorts. "When was the last time you read any actual news in *The Faireville Gleaner*, buddy? But, hey, I see that the Faireville Market's got a three-for-the-price-of-two sale on sweet strawberries ... I should mosey on over after my shift and get me some."

Devin leans back against the cool cell wall, stroking the crescent-moon-shaped scar that runs from the corner of his mouth to the bottom of his chin. He does this whenever he is angry or agitated, which is most of the time.

Devin Orff earned this particular scar (not the biggest one on his body, but definitely the most visible) when he was in grade eight. It happened in the Faireville Badlands, the pumped-dry former gas fields that nobody seemed to own or care much about, much like the kids who hang out there. Some goof, who wasn't part of Devin's gang, challenged him to jump his dirt bike over the tallest hill in the Badlands. So Devin did it; he couldn't back down from a challenge in front of his minions, and risk losing his dictatorship.

Devin botched the landing, and he was launched over the handlebars into the hard, lifeless clay. Devin can't remember the exact details of what happened next; he had lost blood and probably had a serious concussion. But he remembers that he scrambled to his feet, knowing that he would have to save face, to show his toadies that he was still the boss.

Devin ordered his Dobermans, Slash and Chopper, to attack the drooling little mutt of some skinny subdivision kid that he'd never seen before. *That* would show everyone who was still the boss.

But when the dogfight was over, the little mutt was still alive, and both Dobermans limped away, whimpering and bleeding profusely.

That was the worst day of Devin Orff's life. He destroyed his Suzuki RM 250, which his dad had stolen for him from some rich kid who'd left it out in the open one night. He lost both of his Dobermans, which his father took behind the trailer and shot, rather than paying the veterinarian to patch them up; "Ain't payin' to keep these two *pussies* alive!" his father spat. But worst of all, Devin Orff was humiliated in front of his gang. The only one who still hung around with him after that was Cliff Boswink.

Good ol' Cliff, Devin thinks to himself, as he sits inside the tiny holding cell in the Official Headquarters of the Faireville Police Force, stroking his crescent-moon-shaped scar. *That asshole had better stick to the story I gave him, or he's gonna be on my Bullet List.*

Devin keeps track of everyone whom he believes ever wronged him. Sometimes he lies awake at night, reciting each of their names, followed by, "I've got a bullet with your name on it."

And whoever those two freaks were who blocked our escape last night, Devin rages to himself, stroking his scar with renewed vigour, *they are DEFINITELY on the Bullet List. Right at the top.*

At the back of the police station, behind the holding cell, is the Interrogation Room, where any similarity between Faireville and Mayberry ends; the Interrogation Room is definitely more like *Law and Order* than *The Andy Griffith Show*.

The walls are painted a flat, sterile white, and they are completely bare, except for a large, rectangular mirror built into one wall. The claustrophobic room is lit to a glaring intensity by the bank of buzzing fluorescent lights overhead. There are no windows, not even built into the frame of the double-locked door.

Behind the single, rectangular metal table in the centre of the room sits *alleged* bank robber Cliff Boswink. He's perched uncomfortably in a hospital-issued wheelchair, with his bandaged, four-toed left foot jacked up in the air on an aluminum footrest.

The two officers who were questioning him have just left the room. Cliff heard the locks click after they closed the door.

As if that was necessary, he thinks. *It's not like I can run away.*

Cliff checks his hair in the mirror, and then digs into his right nostril with his right index finger, probing for a particularly itchy, stubborn, deep-seated booger nugget, which has been evading his excavations all morning.

Inside the soundproof room on the other side of the one-way mirror, the two police officers are conferring with the Crown Prosecutor, who will try to put Cliff in jail, and the Defence Attorney, who has been assigned the unenviable task of trying to keep Cliff *out* of jail.

"Good Lord!" the Prosecutor exclaims, staring with bugged-out eyes at the one-way mirror. "Do you think we should send in a mining team to help him dig those mineral resources from his nose?"

"Ten bucks says that my client gets what he's after in the next five minutes," the Defence Attorney offers.

Just seconds after the Crown Prosecutor accepts the bet, a content-looking Cliff produces a green-tinged gold nugget on his finger, which he promptly wipes underneath the interrogation table.

The Crown Prosecutor sighs, pulls his wallet out of his back pocket, and removes a ten-dollar bill, which he hands to the Defence Attorney.

"Okay, now let's get back to business," the Prosecutor says. "This kid confessed to the crime, and he said that the other one had nothing

to do with it. We all heard it. It seems like an open-and-closed case
to me. Let's charge this one, and we'll let the other one go."

The Defence Attorney scratches his chin. "I don't know, Atticus.
It all seemed awfully ... *rehearsed* to me. I think that this kid is
protecting the other one, for *some* reason. It just doesn't seem like
this kid would have been the ... *mastermind* of the operation. He
shot himself in the foot, remember?"

They all glance at the one-way mirror, to see that Cliff is once
again mining his nose for whatever irritants remain inside.

"Seriously, guys," the Defence Attorney reiterates, "do you really
believe that *this* kid is the *master criminal* responsible for this whole
escapade?"

One of the police officers says, "We asked him the same questions
three different times, in three different ways."

"His confession was consistent every time," says the other cop.
"As far as I'm concerned, we're finished here. He planned the crime,
he executed it, and he forced the other kid to help him."

"Your client said so himself, Carl," the Crown Prosecutor says.
"Three times."

The Defence Attorney taps his finger on his chin, and then says,
"I've still got a funny feeling about this. Go in and interrogate him
one more time, okay? If he sticks with his story, we'll let the other
kid go, and we'll charge this one. And I'll take all of you guys out
for lunch, okay?"

"I'm getting a steak sandwich," the first cop says. "And dessert,
too."

"Me, too," says the second.

"And if his story doesn't change the *fourth* time through," the
Crown Prosecutor says, "I want my ten bucks back, too."

"It's a deal," the Defence Attorney says.

The two police officers shrug, and they head back into the
Interrogation Room. The short, slim male cop sits down on one

of the folding metal chairs. The tall, muscular female officer locks the door behind her, and remains standing behind her partner.

"Okay, Mr. Boswink," the seated constable says, removing a digital recorder from the front pocket of his uniform shirt and placing it on the table between him and Cliff. "This is your last chance to make sure that we know everything that we need to know about the crime in which you were allegedly involved."

Cliff hears Devin's voice in his head: *"Remember the story we rehearsed. Make sure you stick to the story."* Cliff will not let his best friend down this time. He will *not* shoot himself in the foot again (metaphorically, this time).

"It's like I told you before, dude," Cliff says. "I planned *everything*. The whole caper was *my* idea. I had the *real* gun, with *real* bullets in it. Devin had nothing to do with —"

"For the record," the seated officer says into the recorder, "the accused is referring to his alleged partner in crime, Devin Orff."

"That's the thing, man!" Cliff says, trying to sound more agitated than he really is. "Devin had nothing to do with it! I *forced* him to come along! My gun was real, with real bullets in it! Bullets made by Apostrophes Munitions, by the way."

"It was good of you to support a local business with your bullet purchase," the male cop says.

"Winchester and Remington bullets are a lot cheaper," the female cop adds.

"But you've got to go into Gasberg to buy those," Cliff says. "You can buy Apostrophes bullets right here in town, at Faireville Hardware and Propane. And their slogan is 'The Best Bullets Money Can Buy.'"

"That's true," says the female cop, nodding. "And besides, the amount you would have saved on the cheaper bullets would have just been spent on the gas to drive to the city, anyway. Good thinking, kid."

"Thanks," Cliff says.

The male cop glances over his shoulder at the female cop.

"So I respect a smart shopper," she says, pursing her lips. "Shut up!"

"I didn't say anything!" the male cop protests.

"Anyway," Cliff continues, "like I said, I was responsible for *every aspect* of the robbery. Devin's gun wasn't even *real*. His gun was a *toy* gun! Only the *boss* gets a real gun. You can check them if you want to. My gun was a Smith and Wesson .38. Devin's gun was made by Mattel Toys or something. We spray-painted it black so it would look more real."

"We already checked the weapons," the standing officer says, crossing her muscular arms, "and the evidence supports your story."

In reality, Devin Orff was supposed to get the *real* gun, but in their panic to flee from the bank, Devin accidentally grabbed the plastic gun from the bag. Maybe if that mix-up had never occurred, Cliff Boswink would still have ten toes (although it would have robbed him of his future petty-criminal nickname, "Clifford Nine-Toes").

"By the way," the standing cop says, "we ran a check on the serial number on your gun, and it turns out that it was stolen from the Apostrophes Munitions Museum a couple of years ago. You wouldn't happen to know anything about *that*, would you?"

Cliff's face is already pale, from the pressure of being interrogated, plus the throbbing pain where his toe used to be, but it actually blanches to a deathlike shade of white when he hears this question. The pistol was selected by Devin from a cache of weapons hidden in the crawl space under Devin's parents' mobile home.

"If you ever tell anyone about this stash," Devin hissed at Cliff as he wriggled out from under the trailer, "you'll be dealing with my *dad* then. And believe me," he said, spinning the cylinder on the .38 for effect, "he's not nearly as nice as I am."

Devin's father, Clive Orff, has a reputation all over Faireville for being short-tempered, violent, and irrational; Cliff would rather go to jail than have to stand up to a bare-fisted Clive Orff, let alone facing that psychopath with a gun in his hand.

Cliff's mind races. "I ... um ... I bought the .38 from some guy in the alley behind Jackie Snackie's."

"Can you give us a name? If you can, that's one less charge you'll be on the hook for," the seated cop says.

"I didn't catch his name," Cliff says. "Never saw him again after that."

"Convenient," the female officer huffs. "Can you give us a description?"

"Not really. It was dark."

"Oh, and about those bullets," the female cop says. "You claim that you purchased them at Faireville Hardware and Propane. Can I have a quick look at your PAL?"

"Devin's in the holding cell," Cliff says. "You can go see him if you want to."

"No, no, not your *pal*, your P-A-L ... your Possession and Acquisition Licence. You can't purchase firearms or ammunition without one."

"I, um ... I must have misplaced it."

"Oh, well," the female officer says, shrugging. "I guess we can *definitely* add robbing the Apostrophes Munitions Museum to the list of charges against you. Boy, you are going to be in jail for a long, long time."

But Cliff knows better. *I won't be going to jail, lady. You won't even be able to charge me.* He tries to suppress the grin that is pulling at the corners of his lips.

"Mr. Boswink," the seated officer says, "you are really in serious trouble here. I hope that you understand that. If there is *anything* about these alleged crimes that you haven't told us yet, anything that might *prevent* you from being charged *solely* with these *very serious* crimes, you should tell us now. This is your last chance."

Cliff hears Devin's voice in his head again: *"The cops will try to trick you into changing your story. Make sure that you don't."*

Cliff isn't afraid. He already knows that he will not be going to jail. He won't even be charged. He is protected under the Young Offenders Act, which says that nobody under the age of eighteen can be convicted of an adult crime. Devin told him all about it.

They devised a foolproof plan, in case they got caught, and now Cliff is following it to the letter: Cliff, who is seventeen, and who therefore can't be charged, will take the heat for everything, and Devin, who is nineteen, will therefore not get charged, either. The cops will have no choice but to release them both, and in a few days, Cliff and Devin will meet to divide the contents of the second "missing" bag of cash, which they managed to hide just before the cops arrived.

Cliff smirks, thinking, *Screw you, coppers. We outsmarted you.*

"Is something funny?" the female cop snaps.

"Believe me, Mr. Boswink," the seated officer continues, in a hushed tone of voice, "this isn't anything to grin about. If you are making up this story to protect Mr. Orff, let me assure you that —"

"I'm not making up *anything*! Devin is *innocent*! The criminal mastermind was *me*!" Cliff hollers, pounding the table for dramatic effect.

The force of his blow causes his wheelchair to roll backward, until it bumps into the wall behind the table; this impact shakes his injured foot from its perch on the wheelchair's footrest, and his four-toed foot hits the floor with a slap. This causes Cliff Boswink to scream once again, *"AAAAAAIIIIIIIIIIIEEEEEEEEEEEEEE!"*

The female cop strides over to where Cliff has rolled, lifts his foot back onto the wheelchair's footrest, and pushes him up to the table again, punching the levers to lock down both wheels so that their wheelchair-bound culprit can't roll away again.

The male cop continues, "So, you have nothing to add?"

"I have nothing to add," Cliff says, wincing through the pain. He glares at both officers, thinking, *Screw you, coppers. Screw you.*

"Oh, just one more thing," the seated cop says. "There were two bags of money stolen from the bank's vault, but we've only managed to recover one so far. You wouldn't happen to know what might have happened to the other bag, would you?"

"I dunno," Cliff says. "Maybe those nut jobs in the weird black car took the money."

"You mean the *superheroes?*" the male cop laughs. "Nothing Man and the Purple Zero?"

"Somehow I doubt that *they* took the money," the female cop adds. Cliff folds his arms and purses his lips.

"Okay, then," the male cop says, as he grabs the recorder and rises from the table, "I guess we're finished with you." He glances at the one-way mirror and says, "Steak sandwich time!"

The female cop unlocks the door and holds it open for her partner.

"I'll be outta here before your shift is finished," Cliff mutters.

"What did you say?" the tall, muscular officer says from the doorway.

"I'm protected by the Young Offenders Act," Cliff says, grinning smugly. "I'm under eighteen. So you can't charge me with *anything.*"

"Umm, buddy," she says, "I don't know where you're getting your legal advice, but the Young Offenders Act was repealed back in 2003. And it wouldn't have prevented you from getting charged for this, anyway." She lowers her voice as she steps through the doorway. "It's not like you got caught shoplifting a chocolate bar, son; you attempted *armed robbery.* With *stolen guns.* Believe me, under *any* legislation, you aren't going to be going *anywhere* for a long, long time."

The door closes behind her, and when Cliff hears the locks being clicked shut, he starts crying. And it isn't because of his wounded foot.

It is half-past midnight in the back room of The Sergeant-at-Arms, and Devin Orff is huddled over the darkest, most secluded table he could find, looking as if he's trying to hide behind the half-drained pint glass of beer in front of him.

He is talking into his cellphone, trying to keep his voice quiet enough to avoid being listened to by any of the bar's other shady patrons, but loud enough to be heard over the pounding of the awful heavy metal band who are thrashing haphazardly through a Metallica song on the stage at the other end of the barroom.

"For Chrissakes, Chris, keep looking!" Devin says into the phone. "It should be right inside the grease barrel behind the Faireville Diner ... No, like three doors up Burnoff Street from the bank's rear exit ... Aw, for cryin' out loud, Chris! What the f— No, no, calm down, I didn't mean to yell at you ..."

If Devin was there in the alley with Chris right now, he would punch his younger brother in the face for his pathetic whimpering. *Orffs aren't whiners, damn it!* But Devin can't be seen anywhere near the scene of the crime right now, so he has to be uncharacteristically patient with his annoying sibling.

"Keep looking, buddy, keep looking," Devin says into the phone, feigning patience while the veins in his temples bulge and pulse. "You found it! Excellent! Now reach inside and ... Yes, I *know* it's gross. It's a fucking *grease barrel*, Chris. It's the one place I figured the idiot cops wouldn't want to put their tender little hands. But you're not an idiot cop, are you, Chris. So put your hand inside and ... No, the money *won't* be gross. The bag is waterproof. Now put your hand in, and ..."

Devin covers the receiver of the phone, glares up at the smoke-discoloured tiles on the barroom ceiling, and hollers, "GAWD-*DAMMIT!* WHY DOES HE HAVE TO BE SUCH A LITTLE *PUSSY?*"

A few of the bar's other patrons glance over at Devin.

"Mind your own business," he says.

They do as they are told.

Devin uncovers the phone's receiver and says, "Listen, buddy, I'll give you a hundred bucks to pull that bag outta there, and then stash it in my usual hiding place. A *hundred bucks* for, like, one minute's work. Whaddya say? That's a good deal, isn't ... What? You *got* it? Okay, buddy, go and hide it, and I'll see you soon. Atta boy. Good job, Chris. Good job."

Devin is about to punch the "End" button on the phone, when he thinks of something else.

"Hey, Chris, if you see those two retards who blocked our escape route, tell them that your brother Devin is going to ... What? *What!* The fucking *internet?* Fucking ... *What? Superheroes?* Holy shit. *Superheroes?* Un-fucking-believable. ... They're calling themselves *what?* Nothing Man and the Purple Zero? Well, they will soon be nothing *and* zero," Devin Orff says. "I've got a gun full of bullets with their names on 'em. So, if you see them around town, you tell those two gawd-damned *superheroes* that I am going to personally *super* kill them and string their gawd-damned *super* guts around town as a *super* warning to any other *super* assholes who want to try to get in my way. Okay? Okay. Thanks, buddy. You're *super.*"

After he has hung up on his brother, Devin hisses, "You're a *super* retard."

He takes a long swig from his beer, and then glances around the barroom before calling another number.

"Yeah, it's me," he says. "Yeah, I'm out. Yeah, the idiot took the heat. They're probably gonna peg him for the gun museum robbery, too. I know ... sweet, eh? What a sap. *Young Offenders Act* ... No shit, eh? What a sucker ... Nah, I think I'm gonna lie low for a few days, just in case Cliff changes his mind and squeals ... No, I'll kill him if he does. He knows that. So, no worries, dude, no worries."

He glances around again. Nobody seems to be listening to his conversation. He continues talking under the roar of a sloppy cover of an Anthrax song, played at eardrum-rupturing volume.

"Yeah, I got the cash," Devin continues, stroking the crescent-moon-shaped scar on his chin. "Well, *half* of it, anyway. The cops got the other bag. But it'll be enough." He glances around again. "So you say this product is good? Like *really* good? Addictive, eh? Really *chronic shit*, huh? Okay ... awesome ... Yeah, yeah, cut it with what-ever. Sure, yeah, I don't care what happens to those dumb little stoners ... more money for us, right? Okay, I'll see you soon. You know where and when."

Devin drops the phone into the inside pocket of his jacket, gulps back the rest of his beer, then sits back in the rickety barroom chair with his legs splayed wide.

A waitress sidles up beside him and says, "Hey, stud, ready for another?"

"Nope, gotta go," Devin says, handing the waitress a twenty for the single beer. "Keep the change, baby."

"Thanks, sweetheart," she says.

"Remember my face, baby," Devin says, "'cause I'm gonna have even *more* cash soon. Might even give you a fifty next time, if you're ... y'know ... *nice* to me."

"Looking forward to it," the waitress says, as she tucks the twenty into the pocket on her apron. Then she turns around and walks away, so that Devin can't see her rolling her eyes.

Chapter Eight
Observer X

The five-minute warning buzzer has already sounded, and Bill Brown is running through the hallways of Faireville District High School with his books tucked under his arm, in a race to make it to English class without being late. Bill hates being late.

Earlier this morning, there was a mechanical breakdown at the Krispy Green Pickle Factory, so when Bill arrived there at 6:00 a.m., pulling a freshly picked load of cucumbers in the trailer behind his dad's aging tractor, dozens of other tractors and trailers were backed up outside the factory gates. After patiently waiting for his turn to get inside the loading bay to weigh in, dump his load, and weigh out again, Bill was left with only twenty minutes to get the tractor back to the farm and run to school.

Now he sprints down the hallway, with exactly one minute before the buzzer sounds to signal the beginning of class. *I'm going to make it!* he tells himself. His sneakers squeal against the shining tiled floors as he rounds the last corner. *I'm going to make it!*

And then, right in front of the English classroom door, Bill Brown crashes directly into Elizabeth Murphy.

As Elizabeth tumbles backward, she instinctively throws her arms around Bill to try to prevent her fall; instead, she pulls Bill down with her. Fortunately, the overstuffed bag over Elizabeth's shoulder breaks their fall.

Both of them lie there for a moment, stunned.

Then Elizabeth says, "Bill? Bill, are you okay?"

"*Mmmmmph, mm mm-mmmph*," Bill says.

His speech is muffled because his face is wedged between Elizabeth's breasts, which, despite the rough material of her overalls, feel soft and warm pressed against Bill's cheeks. His hands are shocked (and delighted) to find themselves wrapped around Elizabeth's slender waist, and he realizes that he was right: Elizabeth Murphy is hiding a very fit body beneath her baggy, paint-speckled overalls.

One part of Bill's brain is saying, *Wow ... wow ...*, while another part is screaming, *Retreat! Retreat!* Bill tries to obey the second voice in his head, but he can't seem to pull away; his body is locked against Elizabeth's as if the force of gravity has somehow quadrupled.

At the moment that they hit the floor, Elizabeth hugged Bill even closer to her, and wrapped her legs around him, too. She might have done this as an instinctive self-protective reflex, or it might have happened for some other subconscious reason.

Now Elizabeth relaxes her hold on Bill and unwraps her legs from around him, and Bill raises his head from her chest. He lifts the weight of his body from Elizabeth's, with his palms on the tiled floor like he's doing a push-up.

Elizabeth sees the muscles in Bill's arms trembling.

Bill sees the slight shiver that ripples through Elizabeth's lower lip.

The tile floor is cool under Elizabeth's back and beneath Bill's hands, but the slight space between their bodies radiates heat, like a star about to go supernova.

"Gee, Bill," Elizabeth says, "I thought that maybe we would have had a few dates before getting to this point."

Bill realizes that he is still lying on the floor, in front of the open classroom door, between Elizabeth Murphy's legs. And a long-suppressed memory cuts into Bill's mind.

It is grade three, Valentine's Day.

Elizabeth has just handed a valentine to Bill, with a picture of a kitten saying, "Valentine! You make me PURRRRRRRRRRR!"

"Ooooooh," Virginia Sweet coos, "Bill makes Elizabeth PURRRRRRRRRRR!"

A few of Virginia's Minions start chanting, "Bill and Elizabeth, sittin' in a tree, K-I-S-S-I-N-G!" and "Elizabeth loves Bill! Bill loves Elizabeth!"

Bill flushes red, and he feels like his insides are burning up. Bill is a shy boy, and this sort of attention makes him want to sublimate into the air and disappear.

Now Bill leaps to his feet, as if the force of gravity has somehow just disappeared. Then he extends a hand to Elizabeth, helps her up off the floor, and says, "Are you okay? Did I hurt you?"

"I'm okay," she says. Her heart is pounding. She feels dizzy and light. Her skin is tingling. Her chest aches when she draws a breath to say, "I'm not hurt."

Her blue eyes lock on to his brown eyes.

Bill still has no idea what to do when a female looks at him like this, but he can't look away. Her eyes remind him of the clear sky in the late afternoon before harvest time, and they remind him of swimming out in the deep part of the lake in the middle of August, when the water is warm and waveless.

Bill's heart is pounding, too. He also feels dizzy and light. His skin is tingling just like hers is. He wants to say something, but he doesn't know what.

Now is your chance, Elizabeth! her brain tells her. Or maybe this isn't her brain talking. *Say something! Say something NOW!*

"I normally wouldn't let you touch my breasts until *at least* after the third date," she says, her eyebrows climbing higher, "and you would have to be *in love with me* before I would let you lie between my legs like that. So, at the very least, you owe me three dates, Bill Brown. Just for the breasts."

Elizabeth is amazed that saying these words hasn't caused her to blush the deepest shade of red, but there is something about Bill that makes her feel bold, and maybe even a bit sexy. And, technically speaking, she has never had a *first* date, never mind a third; but Bill doesn't need to know that.

Elizabeth's eyes are still locked on to his. "But I'll settle for just one date," she whispers, "and only if you want to."

Bill suspects that she might be teasing him a little, but he still doesn't know what to say.

He can't speak anyway; he still feels that soft warmth against his cheeks, and he still feels the heat of her body clinging to his skin. He finally manages to say, "Well, Elizabeth Murphy ..." before his breath catches in his throat.

If it were anyone else, Elizabeth would remind him that she prefers to be called "Beth" now, not "Elizabeth" or "Lizzy"; but she likes the sound of Bill's voice, quiet yet deep, gentle yet strong, saying her full, real name.

Elizabeth. Elizabeth Murphy. I am Elizabeth Murphy.

The screech of the buzzer reverberates through the hallway.

"It's a deal," Bill says.

Then Bill and Elizabeth unlock their gazes from each other, and they turn and scramble through the open door, just as Miss Womansfield is about to close it.

Inside, everyone is clustered around Lance Goodfellow's desk at the front corner of the classroom like bees around a hive; nobody has even noticed their late arrival.

Bill lets out a long sigh of relief; if Bobby Bingham had witnessed their collision in the hallway, Bill would have never heard the end of it. Thankfully, Bobby is buzzing around Lance's desk along with the rest of the bees.

Quickly and stealthily, Bill slides into the chair behind his desk before anybody notices the lingering physical result of his contact with Elizabeth. Also thankfully, Marty is in the mass of students gathered in the front corner; otherwise, Marty would probably say something like, "WOW, BILL! IS THAT A ROCKET IN YOUR POCKET?"

Bill is, in fact, the only student sitting at a desk at the beginning of class. Even Elizabeth has wandered up front to see what's going on.

"Okay, class," Miss Womansfield says, "everyone into their seats."

"But, Miss," Marilyn Agnes protests, "have you *seen* this? It's, like, local history unfolding ... It's, like, *amazing!*"

"It is pretty cool, Miss," Kitty McMann says. "I think these guys might be for real."

"Oh, whatever," says Virginia Sweet, who is rarely impressed by anyone other than herself. "Could you fanboys and fangirls puh-*leeze* get away from my desk?"

"Give the lady some *space!*" says one of Virginia's Minions.

"Seriously, Miss Womansfield," Lance says, "you should come take a look at this. It plays right into the presentations we'll be giving about fictional duos ... although *this* duo seems pretty real to me."

"Oh, puh-*leeze*," Virginia reiterates. "This is so *totally* fake."

"Like, *totally!*" a Minion adds.

Lance glances sideways at Virginia; his girlfriend's attitude even gets on *his* nerves sometimes.

"Come and see for yourself, Miss Womansfield," Lance says.

The English teacher's pedagogical instincts tell her that whatever it is her students are looking at might provide her with one of those beautiful "teachable moments" that her professors were always going on about in teachers' college. So she joins the swarm to see what's got their attention. She peers over Lance Goodfellow's shoulder; he's got the latest portable-digital-computer-screen-thingy, upon which he's playing a video from the *NettFun* website.

"Oh, yes," Miss Womansfield says, "someone sent me a link to this earlier this morning. It's that *Nothing Man* video, right?"

"Nothing Man *AND* THE PURPLE ZERO!" Marty Apostrophes cries out from inside the swarm. Marty sticks his head out above the crowd and winks at Bill.

Bill is the only person in the room who hasn't seen the video yet. His jaw drops open. His heart rate, which had slowed almost back to normal after his collision with Elizabeth, now accelerates to race-car-engine RPM.

Oh. My. Gawd! he thinks. *Somebody filmed us?*

At the same moment, Elizabeth Murphy's mood flashes from elation to panic: *But I took that video down this morning! How can they be watching it now? Mr. Gootenbourg is going to fire me for sure!*

Marty continues, "The video should probably be called '*The Purple Zero and Nothing Man,*' don't you think? I mean, come on, the Purple Zero seems to be doing most of the actual fighting."

Bobby Bingham snorts. "Nothing Man is *obviously* the leader. He drives the car! He's *totally* the alpha, *Farty.*"

"Don't call him that, Bobby," Lance says.

"Sorry, Lance," Bobby says. He doesn't apologize to Marty, though.

"Here," Lance says, "I'll restart the video so we can all watch it again from the beginning."

Bill jumps up from his desk and races into the crowd. He has to see this for himself.

Elizabeth also moves closer to the swarm.

Lance pokes the "Play" button on the screen of his device, and on the video screen, the camera's eye focuses on two figures, clad in black and wearing balaclavas, who rush out into a dimly lit alley as an alarm wails in the background.

The camera makes the foreground look brighter, Bill notes, *and the background looks darker than it really was.*

"This is *sooooooo* fake," Virginia says. "It's like Martin Scorsese directed this."

"*Sooooooo* fake," a Minion echoes.

Elizabeth Murphy hovers at the back of the assembled crowd. *Thanks for the compliment, Virginia,* she thinks. *Too bad I'm going to lose my first and only job as a journalist because of this.*

"There's no way the 'Observer X' who uploaded this is just an *observer*," Virginia continues. "He's probably a professional filmmaker, looking for some easy publicity."

"Or *she*," Elizabeth says.

"Yeah," Kitty McMann adds, "or *she*."

"Okay, suffragettes," Virginia says, "don't call the feminist police on me, okay?"

"Yeah!" one of Virginia's Minions adds. "Just because *some of us* like to shave our legs and wear nice clothes, it doesn't mean ..."

"*What?*" Elizabeth and Kitty simultaneously yelp, along with most of the other girls (and a lot of the guys) in the class.

Miss Womansfield, as usual, judiciously intervenes. "Maybe we can talk about all of these issues in a moderated debate, after we've watched the video."

Onscreen, the video camera lens aims up the alley as the Cord 812 roars into view between the walls, effectively cutting off the burglars' escape route.

"Genius move!" Zig Zag Rogers says. "I wonder how they knew these guys were trying to escape from the law? Maybe they've got a police radio scanner in their vehicle."

Zig Zag himself owns a police radio scanner; knowing where the five members of the Faireville Police Force are located at any given moment helps him decide on the best time to visit Burnoff Street to make his weekly purchases.

"For *sure* they've got a scanner," Marty says, a devilish grin stretching across his face. "They knew that the cops were going to the *front* of the bank, so they knew that they had to cut off the escape route at the *back*."

Bill glares at Marty, attempting to convey his thoughts with his expression: *We didn't KNOW we were stopping them from anything! We were trying to escape from the law OURSELVES!*

"These guys must have money, or a wealthy organization supporting them, or something," Rick Rousseau says. "I've never seen a car like that. It's gotta be custom-built for crime-fighting."

"Definitely," Marty says, grinning like the Joker. "Gotta be custom-built."

Onscreen, it appears as if the car has abruptly vanished into the dark.

"Wow!" Dale Bunion says. "It must have cloaking technology, like the Stealth Bomber."

"Totally!" Marty concurs.

Cloaking technology? It was just dark outside! Bill screams to himself. *All we did was shut off the headlights!*

Marcia Montrose, whose dad is in the actual military, says, "The Stealth Bomber has RADAR-jamming technology. It doesn't actually *vanish*. It's black, though, so it's hard to see at night."

Finally, Bill thinks, *somebody with some sense.*

"The Romulan ships on *Star Trek* had cloaking devices, though, sweetie," Dale counters, "and other technologies from *Star Trek* have become reality." He pulls something from his pocket and waves it in the air. "This smart phone is a combination of the communicator *and* the tricorder from *Star Trek*."

"Good point, sweetie," Marcia says.

No! No, it is NOT a good point! All we did was TURN OFF THE HEADLIGHTS! Then, Bill has a second incredulous thought: *When did womanizing, hockey-brawling Dale Bunion and church-attending, ten-o'clock-curfew-abiding Marcia Montrose become "sweeties"?*

Onscreen, one of the balaclava-wearing figures hollers, "Get this car outta here, muthahfuggahs!"

"Whoa!" Miss Womansfield yelps. "Shut it down! I forgot about the language in this clip."

Kitty McMann reasons, "But he said 'fuggah,' Miss W., not 'fucker.'"

Miss Womansfield sighs. The last thing she needs is to be reprimanded by Principal Tappin for allowing profane language in her classroom. Again.

"It's okay, Miss Womansfield," Marcia says. "Nobody will say anything."

Miss Womansfield is relieved. Just last year, Marcia Montrose joined members of her church in picketing the Faireville Apothecary for "promoting immoral promiscuity" by selling condoms, so if Marcia is okay with the language in the video, it's not likely that anyone else will protest.

Onscreen, it appears as if the character they're calling Nothing Man has, in one quick, phantom-like motion, disarmed one of the bandits, shot him in the foot with the robber's own gun to disable him, and vanished into the darkness.

"Unbelievable!" someone says. "He just disappeared into thin air!"

Marty says, "These guys have *definitely* got some sort of cloaking technology."

Dale Bunion, who has never said a kind word to Marty in four years of high school, says, "Right on, bro!"

"It's a camera trick," Virginia Sweet moans.

"*Totally,*" a Minion says. "You can *totally* tell."

It was just DARK! Bill rages internally. *And I was wearing DARK CLOTHING!*

Bill notes that whoever edited this film clip cut out the part where he tried unsuccessfully to start the car and flee the scene, as well as the scene where Devin Orff confronted him about shooting his buddy Cliff Boswink in the foot. *It's pretty skilfully done*, Bill thinks. *You can't even tell that anything was edited out.*

Elizabeth decided to use some "artistic licence" when she removed these parts; it made the heroes look more *heroic*. She also cut a lot of the footage featuring only the two robbers. Why would she want to glorify *criminals*? Thankfully for Elizabeth's own safety, neither of the *alleged* criminal's names made it onto the final cut of Elizabeth's "report."

Onscreen, the uninjured bandit scans the area for Bill, aiming his gun every which way. "Where did he go? Where did he go?"

"He's terrified," Strat Sanderson says. "He knows he's next."

He wasn't terrified, Bill thinks. *We were terrified. He had a gun.*

Onscreen, there is some garbled conversation from the two criminals, then the injured crook starts babbling, "*Nothing man. Nothing man. Nothing man.*"

"He's scared out of his mind," Zig Zag Rogers says.

Marty says, "Wouldn't *you* be?"

"Come out, *nothing man*!" the other robber hollers. "Come out before I start shooting! Come out, *nothing man*! Come out!"

"He knows he's toast," Bobby Bingham says. "You can hear the fear in his voice. I've heard that before, when I've challenged some punk to a fight on the ice."

Virginia says, "Oh, now you're a superhero, too, Bobby?"

Onscreen, the Purple Zero leaps to his feet inside the crime-fighting vehicle, shouting, "HE *IS* NOTHING MAN! AND HE WILL *NEVER* COME OUT! BECAUSE HE HAS *VANISHED* INTO *THIN AIR*! IT'S ONE OF HIS *MANY* SUPERPOWERS!"

Echoing against the walls of the alley, and somehow amplified by the video camera's microphone, Marty's DRAMATIC VOICE is transformed into something else, something that sounds truly super-heroic. And, fortunately for the secret identities of Nothing Man and the Purple Zero, no one recognizes it as the voice of Marty.

"Told you," Dale Bunion says.

"I AM *THE PURPLE ZERO!*" the onscreen voice continues. "WE SPECIALIZE IN FIGHTING DIRTY CRIMINALS LIKE YOU! WE *SPECIALIZE* IN MAKING THE STREETS OF FAIREVILLE SAFE FOR PEOPLE!"

At this point, Elizabeth exercised some more "artistic licence," and she cut the part about kittens, puppies, cows, pigs, frogs, and grasshoppers. To her, that part of the speech just didn't sound very *superheroic*. She also cut out all of the "gayboy" stuff; it wasn't nice for that criminal to say those things, and, as a professional journalist, Elizabeth refused to perpetuate negative stereotypes like that. She figured that the Purple Zero would appreciate these judicious edits.

On the other side of the swarm, Marty Apostrophes hasn't even *noticed* the edits to the video footage; he was in such a state of panic during the whole incident that he doesn't really remember much of anything. The video of their adventurous evening is clearer than Marty's memory of it is.

And I look pretty damned amazing in this next sequence, Marty thinks: the Purple Zero leaps from the hood of the superhero car, knocks the pistol out of the robber's hand, and then dives and springs back up again with a fighting stick in his hands; at least that's what it *looks like*, and Marty already prefers what it *looks like* to what may have *really* happened (which is that he may have accidentally slipped from the hood of the car, accidentally fallen on Devin Orff, and then accidentally broken off an old piece of handrail when he accidentally fell down a second time). "Whoa!" Dale Bunion cries out. "Did you see *that*? He disarmed that robber before the guy could even fire his gun!"

"That guy must have Special Ops training," says Marcia Montrose, whose father is indeed a member of a Special Operations Unit.

"He's probably got karate training, and probably tae kwon do, too," says Kitty McMann, who has studied both martial arts (hence her easy takedown of Bobby Bingham when he tried to force his hands under her tank top).

"He's an ace stick fighter, too," says Zig Zag Rogers, who has no martial arts training, nor any inclination to fight with anyone for any reason, but who has watched a lot of old Bruce Lee kung fu movies while stoned late at night. "I'll bet this Purple Zero dude is also an ace with a set of nunchuks."

"I'll bet he is, too," Marty agrees.

"Shhhhhhh!" hisses Lance Goodfellow. "This next part is *awesome*."

Onscreen, a resonant voice thunders, "Stop that now!" and then Nothing Man seems to materialize out of nowhere.

"Holy crap!" Rick Rousseau yelps. "How the hell did he *do* that? He just reappeared out of *nothing*! He *is* Nothing Man!"

Bill sighs. *For gawd's sake, Rick. All I did was step into the light.*

"Camera trick," says Virginia Sweet.

"It's *not* a camera trick!" Elizabeth yelps.

Virginia turns around in her seat to challenge her. "How would *you* know, Lezzy?"

"Are you a *film director* now, Lezzy?" a Minion giggles.

Elizabeth backs off. She can't reveal that she is Observer X. Not yet.

"You're right, Virginia," Elizabeth says. "I'm no filmmaker. I guess I *wouldn't* know." She doesn't even bother reminding Virginia that she goes by *Beth* now.

Virginia is pleased; she loves being right. Especially in public.

Even though everyone in the room has seen the video before, or actually participated directly in its making, all eyes are riveted on the screen of Lance Goodfellow's device, as if they are watching the events unfold for the very first time.

Onscreen, the crook says, "Says who?"

"Says me," says the superhero in the black cloak. "Says *Nothing Man*."

Practically everyone in the classroom cheers when the criminal hits the ground.

A few of the guys exchange high-fives and repeat the words, "Says *Nothing Man*."

"*AND* THE PURPLE ZERO!" Marty reminds them.

Onscreen, one of the of the superheroes cries, "TO THE *BLACK PHANTOM!*"

And the video ends.

For the remainder of English class, *Hamlet*, as written by William Shakespeare, is put aside yet again, and instead there is a spirited debate about *Real Live Superheroes! Nothing Man and the Purple Zero*, as uploaded by Observer X on October 28.

Chapter Nine

The Prophecy

As the buzzer sounds to end class, Miss Womansfield calls out, "Okay, let's get back on track with our study of *Hamlet* next class. Your presentations comparing Rosencrantz and Guildenstern to the fictional duo of your choice will begin then. Bill and Marty, your presentation on Captain Kirk and Spock will be first. James and Susan, you'll present after them on the Blues Brothers. So be ready!"

Zig Zag Rogers and Strat Sanderson look quizzically at each other for a moment; they are not accustomed to being referred to as "James" or "Susan."

"And don't forget about my annual Halloween party on Friday night!" Virginia Sweet calls out. "I hope you've got your costumes picked out! Remember to bring your invitations … our housekeeper, Consuela, will be checking them at the door. She'll be dressed up as a housekeeper."

Virginia's Minions titter at this joke as they trail out of the classroom behind their leader. Of course, Virginia's Minions have already got their faux-jewel-encrusted invitations, along with all of the guys on the hockey team, and anyone else deemed cool enough to enter the Sweet family's McMansion in Faireville's newest subdivision. Marty, Bill, and Elizabeth were not invited, of course.

As the other students file out into the hallway, Marty fishes inside his backpack and pulls out two books: *Star Trek 101* and *I Am Spock*. He hands the books to Bill and says, "Bloombottom found these on the floor of the Carriage House."

"Where's the third one?" Bill says. "I left all three on the fender of the ... Oh, *crap*."

"Don't worry about it. It'll turn up," Marty says. "But I thought I'd better get these two back to you, anyway; I know that you get all worked up over things like overdue library books."

"Oh, I'm *worked up* right now," Bill hisses, "but not about the library books!"

"Oh, muffin," Marty says, "let's talk about it on the way to math class."

Elizabeth is still lingering at her desk at the back corner of the classroom. Bill wonders if maybe she is waiting for him.

"Hey, Elizabeth," he says, "I've got to talk to Marty about ... our presentation tomorrow, but ... um ... do you want to have lunch with me today?"

Elizabeth gazes back at Bill with a vacant expression.

"Ummm ... this isn't the date ... just lunch," he says. "I still owe you a date. I want to buy you lunch, though, for ... you know. Umm ... okay?"

Elizabeth just nods.

"See you at lunch, then?" Bill asks.

She nods again.

"Are you okay?"

She nods.

"Are you *sure* you're okay?"

Another wordless nod.

"Okay, see you at lunch then." As Bill and Marty push their way through the hallway traffic congestion, Bill mutters to himself, "I hope I didn't give her a concussion."

"What?" Marty says.

"Nothing. Never mind. Listen, Marty, we need to talk about —"

"About how we should give our presentation tomorrow on Nothing Man and the Purple Zero?" Marty says. "Since we *are* Nothing Man and the Purple Zero!"

"We are *not* Nothing Man and the Purple Zero!" Bill hisses.

"We're *superheroes*, buddy," Marty says. "Get used to it."

"*Shhhhhhhhh!* Keep your voice down," Bill says, in a hard yet hushed voice. "We are *not* superheroes. We're lucky we weren't arrested ourselves yesterday."

"Hey, buddy, don't 'shush' me, or I'll start using my DRAMATIC VOICE!" Marty says. "Listen, Bill, we *are* superheroes. Because people *think* we are. It's as simple as that."

"But it's *not* as simple as that," Bill counters. "We don't have any special powers. We don't have any special skills."

"Speak for yourself, pal," Marty says. "We've got the power of surprise, and the power of image. That goes a long way in this world. People respect your power if they believe you've got it." He puts his hand on Bill's shoulder, stops him in the middle of the hallway, and turns his friend to face him. "Hey," Marty says, "do you remember the night of our grade eight graduation?"

"Who could forget?"

"Do you remember Principal Peershakker's final words?"

"Of course I do."

"'Some are born great, some achieve greatness, and some have greatness thrust upon them.' He said that to *us*, Bill. Those were his final words."

"I remember," Bill says. "I remember trying to save him with CPR, too. But I failed, and he died. He died. I failed. Which means that I am the farthest thing from a hero, Marty."

"But you *did* something, Bill!" Marty says. "You *did* something when nobody else did. Everyone else just stood there, but you sprang into action. And that makes you heroic, as far as I'm concerned. I've always thought so, anyway."

Bill just shrugs.

"And I also think that we've just had *greatness thrust upon us*, Bill. And I, for one, am going to do something about it."

"What?" Bill says. "What are you going to do about it?"

"I am going to patrol the streets of Faireville, fighting crime."

"What? Are you out of your —"

"It's a prophecy, Bill. You don't mess with a prophecy."

"A *prophecy*? Don't you think that you're —"

"The Purple Zero will be starting his patrols tonight," Marty says. "And I hope that you, as Nothing Man, will be starting tonight, too, because I'm going to need somebody to drive the Black Phantom. So, meet me at the Carriage House at eight o'clock tonight." Marty turns and resumes walking toward their math classroom. "Or don't."

Bill knows that he should say something like, "Are you serious?", but Bill knows that Marty is serious. Bill has never heard Marty sound so serious about anything in his entire life.

The halls empty as the remaining stragglers rush into their classrooms, but Bill Brown is frozen in place, paralyzed, unsure what to do next.

He only begins to thaw when he feels Elizabeth Murphy standing beside him.

"Hey," she says, moving in front of him, looking up into his brown eyes again.

"Hey," he says back, staring into those blue eyes that remind him of … well, everything good that is blue.

"Look," she giggles, "we *can* meet in the hallway without your face landing between my breasts!"

"And the rest of me landing between your legs," he giggles back.

Elizabeth wonders if she is the first person on Earth to hear Bill Brown giggle. She probably is.

She stops giggling herself, and says, "I didn't mind."

This is probably the sexiest thing that Elizabeth has ever said to a male.

"Neither did I," he says.

This is probably the sexiest thing that Bill has ever said to a female. And they just stand there in the middle of the now-empty hallway, looking at each other. Even when the buzzer sounds, to signal the beginning of the next class, neither of them moves.

"I know who you are, Bill Brown," Elizabeth says.

She bends over to remove a small book from her backpack. The loose material of Elizabeth's orange coveralls pulls tight against her behind and waist; she reminds Bill of a classical sculpture hidden beneath a canvas tarpaulin.

Elizabeth straightens herself to show him the book: *Captain Kirk's Guide to Women.*

"I believe that this is yours," she says. "I found it on Burnoff Street, just after Nothing Man and the Purple Zero stopped those bank robbers."

Bill's eyes widen as he realizes what this means: *She knows.*

"Don't worry," she says, "I won't tell anybody."

Bill takes the book and hides it between the other books tucked under his arm.

"I want to come with you tonight, Bill."

Bill stammers, "You … you … want to come with me? Ummmm … how? I mean … where?"

Elizabeth realizes that she may have inadvertently just said the sexiest thing she's ever said to a male.

She allows Bill to squirm for just a moment longer before saying, "On your mission tonight. On patrol. I want that to be our date."

"What? How did you know about …?"

"I'm an investigative reporter, Bill," she says, lowering her voice to a whisper. "I'm Observer X."

Bill nods. Of course she is. It all adds up.

"And, really, Bill," Elizabeth continues, "Marty is not exactly the quietest guy in the world. I'm surprised half the school doesn't already know your … secret identity."

A tingle rushes through Elizabeth's body. *Secret identity. That is soooooo sexy!*

Their math teacher sticks his head out into the hallway. "You two are late. You know I don't tolerate that. Go to the office and get an Admit Slip."

Without a word to the math teacher, they turn and head for Principal Tappin's office. The door is open when they arrive, but Bill and Elizabeth hover outside rather than entering, because, across from the principal's desk, two boys already occupy the stiff, straight-backed wooden chairs known throughout the school as "The Execution Seats."

The butts of Chris Orff and Davey Batterwall have not been seated long enough to warm the hardwood of their respective Execution Seats, yet already the shining dome of Principal Tappin's forehead is glowing red like an emergency beacon, and the famous veins in his temples are throbbing dangerously.

"You two?" he rumbles. "*Again?*"

Chris Orff shrugs. "The teaching at this school doesn't seem to be serving our particular learning styles very well. I think you, as the principal, should probably do something about that, Mr. Tappin."

Tappin's forehead glows redder, and the veins in his temples throb harder.

"What did you two do *this time?*" he rasps.

"Well," Chris says, "in French class, Mr. Beauregard asked me and

Davey to hand in our book reports. But me and Davey didn't read the book he assigned, so it would have been academically dishonest of us to hand in reports on books we didn't read, don't you think?"

"And *why* didn't you read the book?" Principal Tappin queries, in an interrogator's tone of voice.

"Because the book was in *French*, fer cryin' out loud," Chris laughs.

Davey Batterwall adds, "And also because the book was fuckin' *gay!*"

Principal Tappin leaps to his feet, sending his riveted-leather executive's chair screeching away behind him. He lunges over the desk and hollers (in an uncanny approximation of Marty Apostrophes' DRAMATIC VOICE), "THERE WILL BE NO PROFANITY IN THIS OFFICE! DO YOU UNDERSTAND?"

"Sure, man," Davey says. "Whatever. Don't have a stroke. I was just answering your question, dude."

"YOU WILL REFER TO ME AS *PRINCIPAL TAPPIN!* YOU WILL *NEVER* CALL ME *DUDE!*"

"Okay, *Principal Tappin*," Davey says. "Sorry, *Principal Tappin*. But seriously, *Principal Tappin*, you look like your head is about to explode. Neither me or Orff here know CPR, so you'd better sit down, dude … I mean, *Principal Tappin*."

"'Neither me *nor* Orff,'" Tappin says. "'Neither me *nor* Orff.'"

He *does* feel as if he might actually have a stroke. He just *hates* kids like these two. He pulls his riveted-leather executive's chair back to his desk and sits down. Principal Tappin puts his elbows on the leather pad atop his gleaming, uncluttered, cherrywood desktop, and rubs his temples with his thumbs. *Why? Why? Why?* he wonders. *Why am I here? How? How? How? How did I get stuck dealing with assholes like these two? All I ever wanted to do was coach hockey. I never asked for more than that. I never asked for this.*

Principal Tappin sighs. "Okay, so what happened after you neglected to hand in your book reports?"

"Well," Chris Orff continues, "then Mr. Beauregard wrote the word 'retard' on the board, underlined it three times, and then he put my name and Davey's name on the board underneath. He called us *retards,* Principal Tappin, in front of everybody. He should be fired for that!"

You are retards, Tappin thinks. *Beauregard should be given a medal.*

Then he explains, "*'Retard'* means 'late' *en français.*"

He is greeted with tabula rasa expressions.

"That means 'in French,'" he adds.

"Well, anyway," Chris continues, "I wasn't gonna stand for being called a retard by some little French fag, so I walked right up to the board, and I wrote 'Mr. Beauregard is gay' for everyone in the class to see."

"And then I went up there," Davey boldly adds, "and I wrote, 'Mr. Beauregard sucks cock.'"

Principal Tappin knows that he should fly into one of his legendary rages. He should scream. He should stomp around his office. He should maybe even throw something. But, although this would motivate the boys on his hockey team, he knows that it won't make any difference with these two. So he simply asks, "How long did I suspend you for the last time?"

"Five days," Chris Orff says.

"So it's ten this time," Principal Tappin says. "Go see one of the secretaries for the forms. You parents will have to sign them for you to be readmitted. But you know the routine, don't you?"

Chris Orff and Davey Batterwall give each other high-fives as they strut out of the office.

"Ten-day holiday!" Chris says, almost singing.

"And just in time for Halloween," Davey adds.

"And Devil's Night is tomorrow night!" says Chris. "And now we've got a whole day off school to prepare!"

Chris and Davey notice Elizabeth and Bill hovering outside the principal's office.

"Hey, Lezzie," Chris says. "Still lickin'? Hey, Farmer Bill. How's your boyfriend, Farty Marty?"

Davey thoughtfully adds, "Is there a Gay Pride meeting today?"

Chris drops his shoulder to run into Bill as he passes (as self-proclaimed tough guys tend to do), but he rebounds harmlessly from the taller, sturdier farm boy.

Inside the office, Principal Tappin initials Admit Slips for Elizabeth and Bill, without even giving them a warning.

"So," Elizabeth asks again, as they walk through the still-empty hallways of FDHS, "can I come with you on patrol tonight, or not?"

Bill Brown has never been a man of words; he has always been a man of action.

When Elizabeth was riding her Big Wheel tricycle down the street, and she fell off and skinned her knee, he brought her three things: a Band-Aid for her knee, which was bleeding, a glass of lemonade for her throat, which was raw from crying, and an owl-shaped animal cookie for her heart, because somehow he knew that she loved owls.

When the other girls at school were still teasing Elizabeth about the lisp she'd had as a little girl, and how it made her say "the Pissah of Powah" instead of "the Princess of Power," Bill told the mean girls that, if they didn't stop teasing Elizabeth, he would let everyone in the school know that he had seen them practising French kissing (and some even more advanced techniques) on their dolls in their parents' backyards; Bill, being a quiet boy, observed many things that other citizens of Faireville walked right past.

When the Plexiglas fish tank burst at Elizabeth's "Bon Voyage at Sea" dance, Bill volunteered to help the school's maintenance man mop up the water and expired goldfish. When the janitor grumbled that Elizabeth was "a brainless fool," Bill just said, "And I suppose you've never made a mistake, sir?" Not wanting to lose Bill's help, which would have doubled the length of the cleanup job, the custodian didn't say anything else.

Bill has probably always loved Elizabeth, and he has been trying to show her for as long as he has known her. In grade three, when Virginia's Minions chanted, *"Bill and Elizabeth, sittin' in a tree K-I-S-S-I-N-G!"* and *"Elizabeth loves Bill! Bill loves Elizabeth!"*, Bill flushed red and felt like his insides were burning up, because deep inside him he knew that it was true — at least the *"Bill loves Elizabeth"* part.

But Bill Brown has never been a man of words; he has always been a man of action. As they stroll through the hallway, Bill reaches out and takes Elizabeth's small, warm hand in his.

And then he decides that maybe now is the time for some words, too. "Some are born great, some achieve greatness, and some have greatness thrust upon them," he says.

"Mr. Peershakker's last words," Elizabeth says.

"He said that to *us*. Those were his final words to me, and Marty … and *you*, Elizabeth."

"So I can come with you on patrol tonight?"

"Yes," Bill says. "It's a prophecy, Elizabeth. You don't mess with a prophecy."

And, for the first time since it happened, Bill remembers something from the night that Mr. Peershakker died. After he had tried and tried and tried to get his principal's heart beating and his lungs working again, after the paramedics arrived and pronounced Mr. Peershakker dead, Bill went into shock.

On that cold gymnasium floor, Bill began to shiver; he may have cried a little bit, too. And Elizabeth Murphy saw that he was shivering, and she sat on the floor beside him, and she put her arms around him and warmed him.

Earlier today, his body remembered this moment when, once again, he found himself on a cold floor, feeling the warmth of Elizabeth's body against his. It took until this moment for his brain to catch up with what his body already knew.

Bill Brown grips Elizabeth's hand a little tighter, and he says, "I know who you are, too, Elizabeth Murphy."

Chapter Ten

On Patrol

I t is quiet outside the grand entrance gate of the Apostrophes Estate. The gargoyles that crouch atop the stone pillars glow under the same full moon as the night before, and the spiked tips of the gate's iron bars stand at the ready, like the spears of invisible soldiers awaiting battle.

A lone figure stands hidden in the moon shadow beside the cobblestone driveway. She wears tall, black boots with metal tips on the toes, and lacy long-sleeved gloves that cling to her forearms like dark vines. The rest of her body is encased in a bodysuit that clings to her lean frame, as if she has crawled into the shimmering coat of a black panther. Slung over one shoulder is a tube, like a quiver for arrows.

The gates swing open with a groan, and the Black Phantom rolls out into the clear, starry night, rumbling like a predatory cat.

Like a dancer stepping onto a stage, the woman in black springs onto the driveway and into the headlight beams, which illuminate her figure like twin spotlights. Her straight, crow-black hair is tied back with a single black ribbon, and her face is concealed behind a Roman-style theatre mask, painted silver and black, with catlike eye openings, and a sly expression etched across the mask's mouth.

From the passenger seat inside the cockpit of the Cord 812 Phaeton, Marty Apostrophes cries out, "What's this? A challenger? Our first supervillain? Already?"

Bill brings the car to a halt.

Marty stands up on the floorboard, glaring over the windshield through the grille of his football helmet.

"Come on, *Cat Woman*, or whoever you think you are! It's only our second night on the job! Give us a couple of weeks to fight some *ordinary* villains, okay?"

"I'm not *Cat Woman*, Marty," the lithe figure says. "I'm *Observer X*!"

Marty stammers, "Hey! How do you know my ... my ... Who is this *Marty* that you speak of? I've never heard of him."

Marty pushes his fingers up under his helmet ... no, he hasn't forgotten to pull the turtleneck collar of his purple football sweater up over his face. So how does this so-called Observer X know his real identity?

In three graceful strides, she bounds over to the open car and leaps into the back seat.

Marty segues into his DRAMATIC VOICE (which actually works pretty well when he's being the Purple Zero). "I AM THE PURPLE ZERO! AND THIS IS NOTHING MAN! WHO DARES ENTER THE BLACK PHANTOM WITHOUT OUR APPROVAL?"

Elizabeth Murphy tugs off her mask and says, "It's me, Marty!"

Bill lifts the face shield on his driving helmet and says, "Hi, Elizabeth."

"Hi, Bill," she says.

Mmmmm, she thinks, *he looks so sexy in his black superhero outfit, behind the wheel of this shiny, sleek, curvy, classy black car ...*

Bill turns around in his seat; he is also mesmerized by something that is shiny, sleek, curvy, classy, and clad in black. "I like ... like your ... outfit," he stammers. "I ... *like* it. I ... *really* like it."

"Thanks," Elizabeth says, blinking in a way that makes her real eyes resemble the feline eye-slots on her mask.

She bought the black Lycra bodysuit at the 75 percent off sale at the local Giant Tiger discount store, and the gloves and boots cost her only a small donation to the Salvation Army. She stretches inside her clingy skin of Lycra, and watches Bill's pupils dilate. It was worth spending her first tiny paycheque from *The Faireville Gleaner* on these clothes; she *feels* like a superhero!

"What the hell is *she* doing here?" Marty says.

Bill and Elizabeth don't seem to hear him.

"And, wow ... your hair!" Bill gushes. "Who knew you would look so ... *amazing* with black hair. It's so ... shiny! And ... straight!"

"I actually *combed* it," Elizabeth says. "And the dye job was a last-minute decision. I did it between school and running to the curling rink to cover the Old Timers' Bonspiel for *The Gleaner*."

"I like it," Bill says.

"I figured that if Miss Womansfield can dye her hair black, then so can Observer X." In an uncharacteristic move, Elizabeth flips her straight black mane, causing it to cascade over one shoulder. "You really like it?"

"I *really* like it," Bill says.

"But what the hell is she *doing* here?" Marty says again, with a bit more huff in his voice.

Bill and Elizabeth continue talking as if Marty isn't there.

"So, where did you get the mask?" Bill asks, longing for any excuse to keep looking at her. "It's so ..." (He wants to say "sexy," but Bill can't quite bring himself to say it without blushing.) "It's so *right*. For your costume, I mean."

"I made it in grade eight," she says. "It won a blue ribbon in the art show at the Faireville Agricultural Fair and —"

"WHAT THE *HELL* IS SHE DOING HERE?" Marty thunders.

He feels that he is justified in using his DRAMATIC VOICE this time.

"I invited her," Bill says.

"YOU *INVITED* HER?" Marty cries (dramatically). "SHE'LL BLOW OUR COVER! EVERYONE IN TOWN WILL KNOW THAT WE'RE NOTHING MAN AND THE PURPLE ZERO!"

"If your shouting hasn't informed them already," Bill sighs. "There are countries in Asia that probably heard you."

"I promise that I won't blow your cover, Marty," Elizabeth says. "Because I *am* your cover."

Marty's eyebrows arch so high on his forehead, it looks like they might knock the football helmet from his head. "Say what?"

"I'm your creator, so to speak," Elizabeth says. "I am Observer X."

"Server Rex? Say what?" Marty yelps.

"Elizabeth is the one who filmed us last night," Bill says. "She's Observer X."

"Say what?" Marty says again.

Bill shakes his head. "Observer X, Marty. The pseudonym of the person who uploaded the video. You must have been too busy watching *yourself* in action to notice anything else, eh?"

"Well," Marty says, "who can blame me for that? I *am* pretty fascinating." He turns back to Elizabeth. "Well, thanks for filming us, Elizabeth, but you'd better run along now. We've got superhero work to do."

Elizabeth looks at Bill and blinks. Twice. Three times.

"She's coming with us, Marty," Bill finally says.

"ABSOLUTELY NOT!" Marty roars. "THIS IS DANGEROUS BUSINESS! WE CANNOT BE RESPONSIBLE FOR HER SAFETY! WE ARE THE DYNAMIC *DUO*, NOT THE DYNAMIC *TRIO*." Then, Marty glances down. "Aw, crap," he says, "I'm wearing the wrong shoes. I'll be right back."

Marty leaps out of the Black Phantom and sprints toward the gates of the estate, stopping only to say, "When I get back, *she* had better be gone."

Elizabeth sighs. "He obviously doesn't want me here."

"He'll get over it," Bill says.

"I don't think he'll get over it, Bill. He's in love with you, and he wants *you* to be in love with *him*."

"He's in ... what? Are you crazy?" Bill stammers. "You think Marty is ... Nah! Come on! Just because he's a bit flamboyant doesn't mean that he's ..."

"I've seen the way he looks at you. I think that he feels the same way ... well, the same way that I do."

Bill shakes his head. "Marty and I have been friends for a long time now. I think I know him well enough. He's the same as I am."

"So ... just to be clear ... that means you like girls ... right?"

Bill reaches out and touches the tip of her nose. "I like one girl in particular," he whispers.

At that moment, Elizabeth feels that she absolutely must kiss Bill; it feels as if she might burst into flames if she doesn't. But, just as she leans forward, her reverie is interrupted by Marty's DRAMATIC VOICE.

"WHY IS *SHE* STILL HERE?" he rages as he climbs back into the Cord. "WE ARE THE DYNAMIC *DUO*, NOT THE DYNAMIC *TRIO*! AND THIS IS DANGEROUS BUSINESS! LIVES COULD BE AT STAKE!"

"Marty," Bill sighs, "remember that this is all just pretend, okay? There isn't going to be any real danger, because we're not real superheroes."

"The last time I checked," Marty says, "67,411 people had watched our video. And *they* believe that we *are* superheroes."

"*My* video," Elizabeth corrects. "And it was up to *88,118* the last time *I* checked."

"Not all of them believe that we're superheroes," Bill says. "Read the comments on the websites. Some of them think we're fakes. And, guess what? We are."

"THE PURPLE ZERO IS FOR REAL," Marty says. "I have become my inner hero."

Bill sighs again. "We're just two average guys who happened to stop some escaping robbers. Accidentally. While wearing strange, identity-concealing outfits. While driving an unusual car. While fleeing from the police ourselves. While …"

Bill stops himself. The more he talks, the more ridiculous it all sounds. He feels like turning the Black Phantom around and driving it right back inside the Carriage House. Bill scolds himself, *And when did I start calling the Cord 812 "the Black Phantom"? Am I going crazy, too?*

"If the people *believe* we're superheroes," Marty says, crossing his arms across his chest in a superheroic-looking way, "THEN WE *ARE* SUPERHEROES!"

"I agree with Marty," Elizabeth says.

Marty is surprised. "You do? You agree with me?"

"I do," Elizabeth says. "And this is where I come in, as Observer X. Whenever you guys stop a crime in progress, I'll film it, edit it together, and then post it to the web. And together, we can perpetuate the story that two masked superheroes are fighting crime in Faireville. And the people will feel a bit safer, and the criminals will feel a bit less inclined to commit crimes."

"Actually, that sounds pretty good to me," Marty says. "You'll make us look good in the video, right?"

"Marty," Elizabeth says, "I will make the Purple Zero look *super*."

Marty shrugs (a gesture that is amplified significantly by his huge football shoulder pads), and says, "I guess I can live with that. I always knew that I would be famous for something." Then he raises his fist in the air, and cries, "THE DYNAMIC *TRIO!*"

Elizabeth tugs her black-cat mask over her face, raises her own fist in the air, and echoes, "The Dynamic Trio!"

Bill stares straight ahead through the windshield of the Cord 812. "I must be losing my mind," he grumbles. "I must be losing my mind." Elizabeth leans forward and whispers in his ear, "Come on, Bill. It'll be fun. You can be my Superman, and I'll be your Lois Lane."

After Bill has pulled the driving goggles and face shield down, he allows a blissful grin to spread across his face; there is no need for Marty to know about what is happening between him and Elizabeth just yet.

Bill pictures the small Cord emblem affixed beneath the 812's gleaming grille: beneath a knight's helmet, a simple shield adorned with three red hearts and three silver arrows. *Everything on a coat of arms means something,* Bill muses.

And so, like a helmeted knight leading his troops into battle, he raises his fist in the air and hollers, "The Dynamic Trio!"

The forward-slanted tip of the Cord's coffin nose slices through the cool evening air as Bill's gauntlet-gloved fingers pull the arm on the chrome-plated gear pre-selector box beside the steering wheel. The shimmering side pipes on both sides of the Black Phantom's long cowl roar as Bill stomps on the clutch pedal, and the Cord surges forward in high gear.

In the passenger seat, Marty squints and scans for trouble. In the back seat, Elizabeth removes the quiver-like tube from over her shoulder (a shipping tube from her father's art supply store, to which she attached one of her father's many bungee cords as a strap). She sets the tube down on the floorboard, steadies it between her knees, and reaches inside to remove her film and video cameras, so she can polish the lenses before the crime-fighting action begins. *A good journalist is always prepared,* she thinks.

But Elizabeth's journalistic eyes fall on something more intriguing: on the floor beside her, there is a large, lumpy gym bag.

"What's in the bag, boys?" she calls out over the snarl of the wind and the sustained rumble of the Lycoming aircraft engine.

"What bag?" Bill calls back.

"THOSE ARE THE PURPLE ZERO'S SECRET WEAPONS!" Marty says. "THEY ARE MY *ZERO BOMBS*. TO BE USED IN CASES OF EXTREME EMERGENCY, ONLY!"

"Oh, no," Bill says. "You didn't."

"I tweaked the formula somewhat," Marty says proudly.

Bill shakes his head and says, "Those things don't come out of the bag. Under *any* circumstances."

"You're no fun at all," Marty says.

As the Black Phantom races toward the Gas 'N' Snak, a service station and convenience store on the edge of town, Elizabeth wonders, "Why do you suppose they spell it like that? Would it have been so much trouble to spell the words 'and' or 'snack' correctly? Did they figure that when people pull over to tell them that their sign is spelled wrong, maybe they'll buy some gasoline and potato chips while they're stopped?"

"PULL IN!" Marty hollers. "OH MY GAWD! PULL IN!"

Bill glances down at the recessed fuel gauge in the brushed aluminum dash and shrugs. "We've got lots of gas."

"BECAUSE THERE IS A HOLD-UP GOING ON INSIDE THE GAS 'N' SNAK! AND WE ARE SUPERHEROES!"

Bill glances ahead through the split windshield of the Cord, and his eyes focus through the floor-to-ceiling windows of the Gas 'N' Snak store. Sure enough, there is the fluorescent-lit silhouette of a man who appears to be waving a gun in the face of the clerk behind the counter, whose hands are in the air.

The Lycoming engine screams and the tires screech and smoke as Bill gears down, slams the brakes hard, and fishtails the Cord 812 into the parking lot of the Gas 'N' Snak.

From the back seat of the Black Phantom, Elizabeth already has her video camera rolling as Bill and Marty leap from the cockpit of the car and sprint toward the store.

"TIME TO STOP A CRIME!" Marty cries.

"Or get shot," Bill adds, as he races past Marty and knocks the door of the Gas 'N' Snak open with his shoulder.

The scene inside is not exactly what it appeared to be from a distance.

Behind the cash counter stands a Gas 'N' Snak employee, who is easily identifiable by his lime green golf shirt and lime green cap, both of which are emblazoned with a garish orange and purple Gas 'N' Snak corporate logo; the Gas 'N' Snak guy is shouting and waving a price-code-scanning gun at a prosperous-looking gentleman.

The middle-aged customer is also standing behind the counter, and is shouting just as vehemently, waving his arms in the air. His expensive-looking suit stretches even tighter over his well-fed belly as he sucks in enough breath to holler, "I am not paying *five cents* for a plastic bag! Plastic bags are supposed to be *free!*"

"It's company policy, sir!" the Gas 'N' Snak clerk hollers back. He aims his price-scanning gun across the store; it appears that he is aiming at a cardboard display case full of beef jerky, which resemble dried umbilical cords wrapped in cellophane.

"Beef jerky?" says Mr. Prosperity.

But then Super Clerk aims the price gun higher, at a poster affixed with black electrical tape to the wall above the beef jerky display. Printed on a lime green background, in orange and purple lettering, is the following message:

Gas 'N' Snak™
LOVES PLANET EARTH!!!™

Here at
Gas 'N' Snak™,

we have been charging a *five cent fee per bag*
since 2009, and will continue to do so

**as part of our voluntary commitment to
reduce plastic bag use by 50%**

So, bring a reusable bag to carry your delicious

**Gas 'N' Snak™
Super Snaks™**

and

**LOVE PLANET EARTH!!!™
LIKE WE DO!!!!**

From your friends at
Gas 'N' Snak™

"Gas 'N' Snak", "Super Snaks", and "LOVE PLANET EARTH!!!" are registered
trademarks of Global Consortium Petroleum and Cane Sugar, Incorporated.

"What bullshit!" Mr. Prosperity hollers, after pausing to read the poster. "Gas 'N' Snak doesn't love planet Earth. What Gas 'N' Snak loves is putting an extra five cents in their pocket for something they should be providing for free!"

"Still," Super Clerk shouts back, "you can't put your hand in the till and take money out! Only *I'm* authorized to do that!"

"I'm not paying five cents for a plastic bag!" Mr. Prosperity counters. "It's highway robbery!"

"Well, sir," Super Clerk yells, "stealing from the cash register is *actual* robbery!"

"Five cents is *not* robbery!"

"Look. Either give me back the five cents you took from the till, or give me back the plastic bag and carry your half-dozen Chili 'N' Cheez Super Snaks in your bare hands!"

"This is a *three-thousand-dollar suit*! There's no way I'm carrying my Super Snaks in my *bare hands*!"

"WHAT IS GOING ON HERE!" the Purple Zero thunders.

Both Super Clerk and Mr. Prosperity turn to face Nothing Man and the Purple Zero. They have been so thoroughly engaged in battle that neither of them noticed the two figures with concealed faces storm heroically into the building.

"Halloween isn't for another two nights, boys," says Mr. Prosperity.

"Hey," Super Clerk says, "you're those guys from the internet ... Zero Man and the Perfect Nothing!"

"NOTHING MAN AND THE PURPLE ZERO!" Marty thunders once again.

"Awesome!" Super Clerk says. "You're here just in time. This guy *stole* from the cash register. He's a *burglar*! Arrest him, or something!"

Nothing Man begins, "Well, we don't actually *arrest* people, but we could —"

"Gas 'N' Snak stole five cents from *me*!" Mr. Prosperity says. "I was only taking back what was *mine*!"

Nothing Man glances out into the parking lot, through the floor-to-ceiling windows.

"Umm, is that your car parked out there, sir?"

"Yep."

"Mercedes-Benz CL-class, right?"

"You got it. It's all mine."

"V12 engine," Nothing Man says. "Five hundred horsepower. An outstanding machine."

"Five hundred and *ten* horsepower," Mr. Prosperity says, aiming a smug, tight-lipped grin at Super Clerk. "And it's got rare, custom two-tone pearl white paint. Only six CLs in the world are painted like that."

"Your car doesn't make you better than anyone else," Super Clerk says.

"Actually," Mr. Prosperity oozes, "it does."

"So," Nothing Man says, in that deep, smooth voice that Observer X loves so much, "you're wearing a *three-thousand-dollar* suit, and driving a *hundred-thousand dollar* car ... and you're arguing over paying *five cents* for a plastic bag? With a guy who gets paid minimum wage?"

"I make ten cents an hour *over* minimum wage," Super Clerk says defensively.

"It's the *principle!*" Mr. Prosperity protests. "This ... *bag tax* ... is unfair! *Rebellions* happen over unfair taxes. Read your history!"

"This isn't exactly an historic moment," Nothing Man says, stepping closer. "There isn't going to be any rebellion, is there?"

"I am being a *patriot*," Mr. Prosperity snarls, the volume of his voice rising.

"You're being a *bully*," Nothing Man says, taking another step closer. "Give back the five cents, walk your three-thousand-dollar suit out of here, get into your hundred-thousand-dollar car, and be on your way, sir."

"Or what?"

"OR I WILL BE FORCED TO DEPLOY A *ZERO BOMB!*" the Purple Zero hollers, raising a pair of plastic pop bottles above his shoulder. The bottles are duct-taped together, one bottle filled with a clear liquid and the other with a thick, murky goo.

"No! No! No!" Nothing Man screams. "Don't do it!"

"Shit!" Mr. Prosperity yelps. "Is that a bomb?"

He decides right then that his principles, which are certainly worth five cents, are not necessarily worth his life.

Mr. Prosperity tosses a quarter on the counter, yelping "Keep the change!", and he sprints out of the Gas 'N' Snak, with his prosperous belly wobbling before him. He tumbles into his Mercedes, and just misses hitting the Black Phantom as he speeds away.

As he wrenches the wheel of the Mercedes CL at the first concession road, the tires scream and the five-hundred-*ten*-horsepower engine wails, but even a hundred-thousand-dollar car can't drive itself; Mr. Prosperity cuts the corner too close and scrapes the side of the car against an old telephone pole, leaving about five thousand dollars' worth of custom two-tone pearl white paint behind.

Back on the counter, still inside the contentious five-cent plastic bag, Mr. Prosperity has also left behind his half-dozen Chili 'N' Cheez Super Snaks.

⊚

As the Black Phantom cruises away from Faireville toward the Apostrophes Estate, Nothing Man, the Purple Zero, and Observer X enjoy the rewards from their evening of fighting crime: two Chili 'N' Cheez Super Snaks each, courtesy of Mr. Prosperity, and one Cherry Cola–flavoured Slushee-Pop for each of the three superheroes, as a reward from Super Clerk for their efforts.

In the back seat of the Cord 812, Observer X reviews the footage on the tiny screen of her miniature video camera.

"How's the video, Observer X?" the Purple Zero wonders.

"It sucks," she says, while slurping on her Slushee-Pop. "Even the most creative editing won't save this. In fact, on video it kind of looks like we just terrorized some guy and stole his Super Snaks. I think I should just delete it."

The Purple Zero licks a last gooey strand of artificial-cheese-style-product from the wrapper of his second Chili 'N' Cheez Super Snak and says, "Oh well, we can try again tomorrow night."

"We sure can," Observer X says. She nudges Nothing Man.

Nothing Man steers the Black Phantom up to the gates of the

mansion with one hand, while enjoying a superheroic-sized slurp from the pail-sized Slushee-Pop cup in his other hand.

"Tomorrow night," he says. "Sure! Why not?"

After parking the Black Phantom and hiding away the Zero Bombs in a secluded spot inside the Carriage House, Nothing Man will escort Observer X home; as every crime fighter knows, there is safety in numbers.

Then Nothing Man will walk back to the farm, alone under the light of the full moon, with the juicy warmth of his first kiss from Observer X still tingling on his lips.

Later that night, Bill Brown will have a dream; it will begin the same way as the dream he had the night before, right after he inadvertently became Nothing Man.

He will dream that he is a black falcon, soaring high over the Faireville Bluffs. From the air, he will see a slender black cat, stretching and purring in a pool of moonlight.

He will glide down to the nearest tree, landing on a branch that will allow him to watch the black cat from a distance. And even though he is a falcon, and she is a cat, he will find it impossible to stop watching her.

The sleek black cat will glance up, and she will see him up there in the tree, and her glowing, reflective cat eyes will lock on to his dark falcon eyes.

Her purring will tell him, "I see you."

His squawk will tell her, "I see you, too."

And the sleek black cat will climb the trunk of the tree, and she will slink out onto the branch where the black falcon is perched.

And the falcon will reach out with his black feathered wingtip, and the cat will reach out with her black, silver-fur-tipped paw, and their touch will transform the falcon into Bill, and the cat into Elizabeth.

"Bill Brown," Dream Elizabeth will say, "you make me PURRRRRRRRRRR!"

And Bill's face will not flush red like it did in grade three.

And a chorus of children's voices will swirl around them, singing, "Bill and Elizabeth, sittin' in a tree, K-I-S-S-I-N-G!", and, "Elizabeth loves Bill! Bill loves Elizabeth!"

And Bill's dream will get even better from there.

Chapter Eleven

Thrust

On the Thursday morning after their less-than-epochal crime-fighting sojourn to the Faireville Gas 'N' Snak, Bill and Elizabeth meet once again in the hallway at school.

Elizabeth's hair is still dyed jet black, but her figure is once again concealed inside a pair of her father's paint-speckled coveralls; yet, even hidden inside her alter ego disguise, Bill sees Elizabeth as the sleek, lean, and catlike Observer X.

Bill is wearing his usual bulky plaid lumberjack shirt and baggy, retro jeans, which conceal his size and his labour-muscled limbs; yet, even hidden inside his humble farm boy uniform, Elizabeth sees Bill as the tall, dark, authoritative Nothing Man.

Their heartbeats accelerate as they draw closer to each other.

"Hi, you," he says.

"Hi, you," she says.

Bill is reminded of the dream he had last night.

The sleek black cat's purring told him, "I see you."

And, as the dark-feathered falcon, his squawk told her, "I see you, too."

And here in reality, Elizabeth's hand once again finds its way into Bill's.

As they walk past the lockers of Virginia Sweet and her Minions,

Virginia says, "Nice hair, Lezzy! Are you dressing up for Halloween as the Wicked Witch of the West? All you need is green skin and a pointy hat!"

Elizabeth glances over her shoulder at Virginia as they pass, and fires back, "And you can dress up as the Slutty Bitch of the East, Virginia! Your outfit is already perfect."

"*What* did you say, *Lezzy*?" Virginia says, stepping out from the buzzing cluster of Minions.

Elizabeth stops, lets go of Bill's hand, and spins around to face Virginia. "I think you heard me the first time, Virginia. And stop calling me Lezzy, okay? Grow up."

Virginia huffs and says, "Make me."

"If I have to, I will," Elizabeth says. She pushes her way through the cluster of Minions and thrusts her face forward so she is nose to nose with Virginia Sweet.

Bill braces for some sort of showdown, but all Virginia does is roll her eyes, toss her hair, and say, "Whatever." Virginia isn't going to risk disturbing her fresh manicure, messing up her hair, or injuring her volleyball-spiking wrists in a physical confrontation with this social underling.

"I'm glad that we understand each other, Virginia," Elizabeth says, before turning on the heels of her work boots and walking away.

One of Virginia's Minions huffs, "Loser," while another brays, "What a bitch." The rest of the Minions just mimic Virginia by rolling their eyes, tossing their hair, and also saying, "Whatever."

"Wow," Bill says, as he continues walking with Elizabeth, "that was gutsy."

"You know what, Bill? I *feel* gutsy." And with that said, she stops him in the middle of the hallway, turns him toward her, stands on the tiptoes of her work boots, throws her arms around his neck, and plants a particularly wet and vacuum-intensive kiss on his lips.

When Bill's soul descends back into his body again, he says, "You can be gutsy any time you want to, Elizabeth."

As they turn a corner, they meet up with Susan "Strat" Sanderson and Jimmy "Zig Zag" Rogers.

"Heyyyyyyyy, mannnnn," Zig Zag says to Bill. "Are you rrrready for your prrrresentation in English class this mmmmmorning, mannnnnnnnnn?"

"We go right after you and Marty, Bill," Strat says. Then she lowers her voice to a whisper. "Zig Zag gets so anxious about speaking in public, so he had a little something to, y'know, take the edge off. It seems to be hitting him a lot harder than usual, though."

"Weeeeee're doin' a lllittle … muuuusical number," Zig Zag slurs, gesturing at the robin's-egg-blue Fender Stratocaster that hangs in his girlfriend's hand. "It's gonna beeee … funnnnnnnnnnnnn." His eyes are glassier than ever, and his pupils are so dilated that his irises aren't visible anymore.

"Baby?" Strat says. "Baby, are you okay? You should have waited for your usual dealer to show up instead of …"

Zig Zag begins to wobble on his feet, like a spinning top losing its momentum.

Strat yelps, "Zig Zag? Baby?"

Zig Zag drops to the floor with a cold thud. The trunk of his body twists and bucks, and his limbs thrash as if he's being electrocuted.

Strat drops her namesake guitar on the floor and kneels beside her boyfriend's convulsing body. "Ohmigawd! Ohmigawd! Zig Zag! Baby! Zig Zag!"

Zig Zag's chest heaves, and he makes a sharp, wet, gasping sound, and then bubbly white foam sprays out of his mouth. One more jolt ripples through his body, and he gasps again.

Then he is silent. Zig Zag Rogers lies motionless on the tile floor, arms and legs splayed out at awkward angles.

"He isn't breathing!" Strat screams. "He isn't breathing!"

Bill drops to his knees beside Zig Zag, grabs his shoulders, and shakes him. "Zig Zag! Zig Zag Rogers! Can you hear me, Zig Zag?" He glances up at Elizabeth. "Call 911, right now."

Elizabeth doesn't have a cellphone, so, in the crowd that has already begun to gather in a wide perimeter around Zig Zag's prone body, she turns to one of Virginia's Minions and says, "Give me your phone. Now."

The Minion does as she is told; she understands that this is a Medical Emergency, and that the Rules of Social Hierarchy are thereby suspended.

Elizabeth punches the three numbers: 9-1-1.

With nimble fingers, Bill unbuttons and shrugs off his plaid lumberjack shirt, rolls it up, tilts Zig Zag's head back to clear his airway, and slides the rolled shirt under Zig Zag's neck. Then he places the heel of his left hand in the middle of Zig Zag's chest, slaps his right hand over his left, and begins giving Zig Zag chest compressions.

As he thrusts down hard on Zig Zag's chest, Bill counts off, "One … two … three …"

"Ohmigawd! Ohmigawd!" Strat cries. "Zig Zag! Baby! Zig Zag!"

"Four … five … six …"

When Bill gets to thirty, he begins administering rescue breathing. Bill wipes Zig Zag's mouth, pinches his nose, and seals his own mouth over Zig Zag's, whose chest rises as Bill blows. And then it falls. It rises again with Bill's breath. And then it falls again.

Somewhere in the background, Bill Brown hears Strat Sanderson chanting, "Oh baby oh baby oh baby oh baby oh baby oh baby oh baby …"

Bill switches back to the chest compressions. "One … two … three … *come on, Zig Zag* … four … five … six … *come on, dammit* … seven … eight … nine …"

"Oh baby oh baby oh baby oh baby oh baby oh baby oh baby ..."

"Ten ... eleven ... twelve ..."

As he continues to count off the chest compressions, Principal Peershakker's final words echo in his mind yet again, repeating like a mantra: *Greatness thrust upon you. Greatness thrust upon you. Greatness thrust upon you.*

The mantra continues repeating as Bill leans over to give Zig Zag another set of rescue breaths. Then he does another set of chest compressions. *Greatness ... thrust ... upon you. Greatness ... thrust ... upon you. Greatness ... thrust ... upon you. Thrust ... thrust ... thrust.*

More rescue breathing. Then another set of chest compressions. *Thrust ... thrust ... thrust ...*

Bill counts to thirty again, and as he leans over to administer another round of rescue breathing, a shrieking gasp erupts from deep inside Zig Zag's chest. The dreadlocked teen jolts upright, wide-eyed, gasping, "Crescent ... moon ... chin ... scar ..."

Then he falls back again; Bill's rolled-up shirt cushions Zig Zag's head as it hits the floor.

"Zig Zag, it's me, Bill. Just relax and breathe, buddy. Relax and breathe. There you go. There you go. That's it. That's it."

Between gasps of air, Zig Zag rasps, "Crescent ... moon ... chin ... scar ... crescent ... moon ... chin ... scar ..."

"He's hallucinating," Strat cries, as she lunges for her fallen love. "Oh, baby! Oh, baby!"

Bill stops her. "Let him breathe, Susan. He's not out of the woods yet."

Zig Zag's breathing gradually becomes less panicked, but his inhalations sound like a dull saw blade being dragged across rough bark. On every exhalation, he says, "Crescent moon ... chin scar ... crescent moon ... chin scar."

"He's hallucinating," a sobbing Strat repeats. "I told him not to buy from anyone he didn't know. What the hell did that bastard sell him?"

"Crescent moon ... chin scar. Crescent moon ... chin scar."

When Zig Zag's breathing slows to an almost normal rate, Bill finally feels like he can draw a full, normal breath himself. The air tastes sweet and cool on his dry tongue. He feels his sweaty hair plastered in strands to his forehead. He feels the lactic acid burning in his biceps and triceps. He feels his kneecaps against the hard, cold floor.

"Crescent moon chin scar. Crescent moon chin scar."

Bill's memory flashes back to two nights ago, in the dark alley called Burnoff Street. The force of Bill's punch rolled the balaclava up over his attacker's nose, revealing a crescent-moon-shaped scar, which ran from the corner of his mouth to the bottom of his chin.

Bill's eyes narrow. *Devin Orff.* "He's not hallucinating," Bill says.

"Crescent moon chin scar," Zig Zag says. "The guy ... who sold me that shit ... had a crescent-moon-shaped ... chin scar."

Devin Orff. Definitely.

A sobbing Strat asks, "Is it safe to hug him now?"

"Yes," Bill says. "It's safe to hug him now."

Bill hears the wheels of the stretcher rattling and the boots of the paramedics slapping the floor as they speed toward them. With some effort, Bill lifts himself up onto his feet. His toes and calves tingle, and a sharp pain radiates through his back. He was hunched over on the floor with Zig Zag for a lot longer than he thought.

In a semi-circle around the spot where Zig Zag fell, practically every teacher and student at Faireville District High School has gathered. Bill hadn't noticed any of them until now. He hears their cheering and applause, but he assumes that it is for the arrival of the paramedics, who are now lifting Zig Zag onto the stretcher.

Bill turns and walks away from the sound; for the second time this morning, his soul is not quite inside his body. It takes a touch from Elizabeth Murphy to bring him back again.

"Bill?" she says, brushing his cheek with her fingers. "Bill?"

A tear falls from his right eye. It is absorbed by Elizabeth's black hair. Another falls from his left eye, and her hair catches it as well.

"Is it safe to hug *you* now?" she asks.

Bill nods yes.

Elizabeth's hair will be soaking wet before she lets go of him.

◎

Half an hour later, inside Miss Womansfield's English classroom, everyone is once again clustered around a desk. This time, they are not watching the semi-fictional exploits of Nothing Man and the Purple Zero on Lance Goodfellow's portable-digital-computer-screen-thingy; almost everyone is hovering around Strat Sanderson's desk.

"*Ohmigawd*," Marilyn Agnes says, "is Zig Zag going to be okay?"

"What happened?" Kitty McMann wonders. "Zig Zag was pretty ... *conditioned*. What caused him to react like that?"

Miss Womansfield sees the blanched, glazed-over expression on Strat's face, and asks, "Are *you* okay, Susan?"

Strat's lower lip quivers. "I wanted to go in the ambulance with him, but they wouldn't let me. I'm not his *immediate family.*"

"Do you need to call someone to take you home?" Miss Womansfield asks. "Do you need to talk to the guidance counsellor?"

"My parents are both at work, and they won't get any messages until their lunch break," Strat says, sniffling. "And Principal Tappin already sent me to the Guidance Office, but Mizz Eckburger is out sick today."

Miss Womansfield resists the urge to roll her eyes; Mizz Eckburger is a member of the "3:20 Track Team," one of those teachers who sprint for the parking lot the second the buzzer sounds at the end of the school day. The English teacher finds it deeply ironic that students who miss too many classes are sent to Mizz Eckburger for counselling, given that Mizz Eckburger is only at school about half the time herself.

"Besides," Strat says, "McYuckBurger would just give me a lecture about the *dangers of recreational drugs*, and how Zig Zag should *'Just Say No,'* and all that *blah blah blah*, and I'm not really in the mood for that right now."

Virginia Sweet, who, along with her many other resume-worthy accomplishments, is also the president of the FDHS chapter of DAB (Drugs Are Bad), mutters, "Zig Zag *should* have 'just said no.'"

"Gawd, Virginia," Lance hisses, "this isn't the time or place."

When Bill Brown walks into the room, with one of Elizabeth's arms wrapped around his waist, Strat jumps up to meet him in the doorway, latching on to the side of Bill that isn't already occupied by Elizabeth. Strat presses her face against Bill's shoulder and sobs, "Thank you! Thank you! Thank you! Thank you for saving my Zig Zag! I love him *so* much! Thank you! Thank you! Thank you!"

Bill, in his usual quiet way, just says, "You're welcome, Susan."

Just as the buzzer sounds to begin classes, Marty Apostrophes strolls into the classroom.

"Sorry I'm late," Marty says, "I left a note for our butler to wake me, but he didn't see it until after ..." Marty stops and shakes his head. *Elizabeth Murphy and Strat Sanderson are both hugging Bill. Why are two girls clinging to Bill?*

"Ummmmmm, what's with the love fest?" Marty wonders aloud.

Strat Sanderson looks at Marty from around Bill's shoulder.

"Bill is a *hero*," she says.

Marty glances around the classroom. Other students are nodding in agreement.

Miss Womansfield confirms it. "Bill *is* a hero," she says.

Marty's face flushes red, and his DRAMATIC VOICE is activated in a *particularly* dramatic way. "YOU SON OF A ... YOU'RE TAKING *ALL THE CREDIT*, AND LEAVING *ME* OUT? ARE YOU *KIDDING* ME? THERE WERE *TWO* OF US! NOT JUST *YOU!*"

"Marty," Elizabeth says, "it's not about … um … that thing you think it's about."

"AND *YOU*!" Marty rages. "YOU WEREN'T EVEN PART OF THE TEAM! ALL YOU DID WAS —"

"*Marty*," Elizabeth says, momentarily catching his attention with her wide blue eyes. "This morning, Zig Zag had a convulsion and stopped breathing, and Bill —"

"WHAT DOES THIS HAVE TO DO WITH *ZIG ZAG*? IS HE PART OF THE TEAM NOW, TOO? THE ONLY PEOPLE IN THAT ALLEY WERE *ME, BILL*, AND —"

Elizabeth's eyes are bright, glimmering, almost hypnotic. Marty stops raging for a moment as she says, "Zig Zag had a *convulsion*, Marty. He stopped *breathing*. And Bill used *CPR* to save him. Bill is a *hero* because he *saved Zig Zag's life*."

"BUT, I … HE … YOU …"

It takes a moment for Elizabeth's calm, measured words to penetrate Marty's anger.

"Ohhhhhhhhhhhhhhhh …" he says. "Okay … so this has nothing to do with …" Marty throws his hands up in the air and mugs for everyone in the room. "*Whoops!* Guess I shouldn't have left home without my morning coffee, eh? It makes me *such* a *bitch*."

"Gawd," Bobby Bingham says, "*what* a fag!"

"Shut up, Bobby," Bill says, almost in a whisper.

Maybe it's because two women are flanking Bill, as if he's a muscle-bound warrior on the cover of a sword-and-sorcery novel, or maybe it's because of the cool, post-adrenaline calm in Bill's eyes, or maybe it's just because everyone in the room is looking at Bill and not at Bobby, but, for whatever reason, Bobby Bingham shuts up.

The PA speaker at the front of the classroom crackles, and Principal Tappin's authoritative voice rattles through.

"Attention, all staff and students," Tappin's disembodied voice says. "As of this moment, all classroom activities will be suspended, and all staff and students will move immediately, in an organized and orderly fashion, to Gymnasium A, for a Community Learning Event."

Throughout the entire school, everyone holds their collective breath; in Principal Tappin's militaristic administrative vocabulary, a "Community Learning Event" means that he is going to gather the student population and holler at them in a demeaning way through a loudspeaker, about some minor problem that has likely been caused by only a handful of students, who will skip the "Community Learning Event" and go to Jackie Snackie's instead; yet everyone else will somehow leave the assembly feeling collectively guilty and shameful.

"Attendance," Tappin's spectre-like voice rattles on, "is compulsory for all staff and students. There is an issue of the utmost urgency to discuss."

"This is going to be about what happened to Zig Zag this morning," Strat Sanderson sighs, leaning against Bill. "They're going to use this as an opportunity to holler, *'Drugs are BAD!'* and *'Just say NO!'* And they're going to make Zig Zag into a *lesson* for everybody else." She turns to Miss Womansfield. "This is *not* what I need right now, Miss. Is it okay with you if I just stay behind and play my guitar? It would be therapeutic, I think."

"That's okay with me, Susan," Miss Womansfield says.

"Can Marilyn stay, too, and keep me company?"

"Sure, Susan. Now, everybody else, let's head down to Gymnasium A for the Community Learning Event."

Virginia Sweet is outraged. *So, Strat gets to play her guitar, and Marilyn will probably draw that ridiculous* Punk Mouse and Rebel Kat *cartoon, while the rest of us have to go listen to an anti-drug lecture? How is* that *fair?*

Then something else occurs to Virginia. *Hey, if they're having an anti-drug assembly, why wasn't I, as the president of the FDHS chapter of DAB, asked to speak?*

There is always something to be outraged about when one is as perfect as Virginia Sweet.

◎

It turns out that the assembly has nothing to do with Zig Zag or recreational drug use.

Standing beside Principal Tappin, atop the stage in Gymnasium A, is Carl Crane, the Chief of the Faireville Police Force. He stands in an authoritative pose, just like Principal Tappin; their arms are folded tightly across their chests, and both men stand with their legs apart, as if astride imaginary battlefield stallions.

Principal Tappin lifts the single microphone from its stand, and his amplified voice echoes through the gym.

"Students," he says, "we have gathered you here today because of concerns among members of the community regarding potential illegal actions which could possibly be perpetrated by students of Faireville District High School. To speak to you more about these concerns, I will hand the microphone over to Police Chief Carl Crane."

Sitting cross-legged on the floor beside Bill, Marty wonders, "What the hell did he just say? Why can't the man speak English?"

Onstage, Chief Crane, modulating his voice to sound slightly deeper than the principal's, says, "Thank you, Mr. Tappin."

He pauses to twiddle the tips of his magnificent silver moustache between his thumb and index finger.

"As many of you are aware, tonight is the night before Halloween, which has become unofficially known, in certain circles, as 'Devil's Night.' Traditionally, on this one night, reports of public disturbances, graffiti, vandalism, and arson are higher throughout Faireville than they are for the rest of the year combined."

Chief Crane pauses to let this sink in (and also to twiddle his impressive moustache some more).

From her seat on the floor next to Bill, opposite Marty, Elizabeth leans over and whispers, "It's nice of him to remind all of the potential vandals, arsons, and troublemakers that *tonight is their night to shine.*"

"To curtail this problem this year," Chief Crane continues, "we will be imposing a one-night-only curfew for persons under eighteen years of age."

Some of the students in the crowd groan. Kitty McMann loudly grumbles, "Fascists!"

Principal Tappin snatches the microphone from Chief Crane and rumbles, "Control. Now."

And there is control. Now.

Chief Crane takes the microphone back. "This measure was initiated in a completely democratic way. We asked the Faireville Town Council to approve this cautionary measure, and the motion was unanimously approved. The curfew will begin tonight at twenty-two hundred hours; that's 10:00 p.m. to you civilians."

Elizabeth whispers to Bill, "It's too bad that Chris Orff and Davey Batterwall are missing this speech, eh?"

Bill nods. Yesterday, Bill and Elizabeth watched as Chris and Davey were handed a ten-day vacation from school by Principal Tappin. *"Devil's Night is tomorrow night!"* Chris said. *"And now we've got a whole day off school to prepare!"*

"So," Chief Crane says, his slightly-deeper-than-Principal-Tappin's voice echoing from the walls, "stay inside and behave yourselves tonight."

"*We,* however," Marty whispers, "as Faireville's local superheroes, will be *going out* tonight."

"Are you sure that's such a good idea, Marty?" Bill whispers back.

"You're one up on me," Marty says. "I've got to do *something* heroic tonight, like stopping an arsonist or a vandal, so we'll be even on the superhero scoresheet."

"There's a superhero scoresheet?" Bill wonders. "I doubt that the Superfriends had one."

"Sure they did," Marty says. "Superman had the most points for sure. Aquaman had the fewest, and the Wonder Twins were in the *negatives*, I think. So, I need to stop a crime tonight, so we can be even on the scoresheet." He looks back up at Chief Crane on the stage, but he elbows Bill and whispers, "You can still drive the car, though."

Bill looks up at the stage also, and, though neither Principal Tappin nor Chief Crane are anything like Bill's wise, earnest, soft-spoken elementary school principal, Bill is reminded of Mr. Peershakker anyway.

I couldn't save you, sir, Bill says to his former principal, *but today I saved Zig Zag. His real name is Jimmy Rogers. You would like him, sir. The same way that you liked me, and Marty, and Elizabeth, and all the other kids who were a little bit different.*

"Stay inside and behave yourselves tonight," Chief Crane repeats dramatically, to make sure he is getting his point across to this gymnasium full of potential petty criminals, "because *we will be out there.*"

In Bill's left ear, the Purple Zero says, "And so will we."

"And if you are up to no good," Chief Crane thunders, "we will *catch* you!"

In Bill's right ear, Observer X says, "And so will we."

Police Chief Crane concludes, "We will *catch* you, and we will *stop* you."

Nothing Man looks at the Purple Zero on his left, and at Observer X on his right, and he says, "And so will we."

Chapter Twelve

Devil's Night

In the back seat of the Black Phantom, Observer X tucks the Purple Zero's large, lumpy gym bag under her behind, to make her taller ... and her superior view of the horizon is almost immediately rewarded.

Observer X cries out, "Look! Up there! A crime in progress!"

"*Indeed*," Nothing Man rumbles from behind his face shield.

She points up to the Faireville Bluffs, which stand north of town like Faireville's own Great Wall. There are rolling hills in the fore-ground, but the bluffs themselves present a sheer, vertical rock face.

In the distance, on the crest of the tallest hill, the foundation of a burned-down castle is faintly visible; it once belonged to some lucky natural gas speculator, but since the fire, certain bored local kids have staked a claim on the spot, to make out, smoke pot, and smash beer bottles. On the cliff wall behind this exposed foundation, two figures have climbed as far up the Bluffs as they can manage; they are now spray-painting graffiti on the sullen rock face, in letters taller than themselves.

"When you go looking for trouble," Observer X observes, "you tend to find it."

"Especially on Devil's Night," says the Purple Zero.

"*Indeed*," rasps Nothing Man.

One of the figures on the hilltop is using fire-engine-red spray paint, and has so far written, in fat, uneven block letters:

MR BEAUREGARD IS

The other figure's colour of choice is neon purple, and his unfinished message is:

MISTER BEAUREGARD SU

"OUR FIRST DEVIL'S NIGHT VANDALS!" the Purple Zero proclaims.

"*Indeed*," Nothing Man says, and he steers the Black Phantom from the road. The front-wheel drive pulls the car uphill, plowing through the weeds and debris on the abandoned, overgrown driveway that leads up to the site of the burned-down castle.

As they pull up beside the scorched foundation, not one member of the Dynamic Trio is surprised by who they see standing at the top of the foothills, armed with spray cans and angry sneers.

"Chris Orff and Davey Batterwall," Nothing Man says.

"Chrissy Pissy and Davey Butterball," Observer X adds.

"That's not very nice."

"*They* aren't very nice."

"*Indeed*," Nothing Man again rumbles behind his face shield.

"What's with saying '*indeed*' all the time?" Marty says.

Nothing Man shrugs. "I thought it might make a good superhero catchphrase."

"I like it," says Observer X. "It suits you. It's something a Strong, Silent Type would say."

The Purple Zero shakes his head and says, "Let's just go fight crime now, mm-kay, kiddies?"

At the line where the foothills meet the cliff wall, Chris Orff and Davey Batterwall are in the process of spray-painting nasty things about their French teacher, Mr. Beauregard, on a very visible location on the Faireville Bluffs. Emptied spray cans lie scattered in the weeds like spent cannon shell casings.

Just the day before, Chris and Davey scrawled the same disrespectful things about their French teacher on the chalkboard in his own classroom, in front of twenty-two other students; but inflicting this embarrassment upon Mr. Beauregard wasn't enough for Chris and Davey. Chalk can be *erased*, and the two miscreants wanted to leave a more *permanent* tribute to their French teacher.

Davey stands on his tiptoes to complete the arc of a tall letter C with the neon purple that hisses from his spray can; paint dribbles from his hand and splatters his prominent belly. He stands back to evaluate his handiwork, which now reads:

MISTER BEAUREGARD SUC

Chris is working on a fat, red letter G, so now his graffiti tribute reads:

MR BEAUREGARD IS A G

"This'll teach *le frog* to call us retards, eh?" Chris Orff brays.

"BUT YOU *ARE* RETARDS!" the Purple Zero proclaims, dropping the bag of Zero Bombs on the weedy ground beside him.

Chris and Davey spin around to face the three unexpected interlopers.

"And you're *cowards*," Observer X cries out, her video camera already recording the evidence of Chris and Davey's crime. "There's nothing brave about slandering someone behind his back."

"*Indeed*," adds Nothing Man.

"Actually," the Purple Zero says, glancing over his shoulder at Nothing Man and Observer X, "they're *defaming* Mr. Beauregard, not *slandering* him. *Defamation* is when you *write* a malicious, false, and defamatory statement; *slander* is when you *say* it. Remember from Law class?"

"Indeed," says Nothing Man. "I'm surprised that *you* remember, though, since you barely passed Law."

The Purple Zero shrugs. "Just because I choke on tests, it doesn't mean that I'm not smart." Then he amps up his DRAMATIC VOICE, and hollers, "STEP DOWN, VANDALS! CONSIDER THIS DEFAMATION *FINISHED*!"

Chris Orff does step down. He drops his spray can on the ground and begins loping down the hill toward the Dynamic Trio.

"Hey," he says, "you're the two assholes who got in my brother's way the other night, aren't you? I saw the video. What are you calling yourselves? *Nothing Balls* and *the Perfect Homo*?"

Bill is incredulous. *"Nothing Balls?"*

The Purple Zero turns to Nothing Man and Observer X and says, "See? *That's* slander."

Chris Orff strides closer to Nothing Man, the Purple Zero, and Observer X, unperturbed by the fact that there are three of them and only one of him.

"Well," Chris says, "my brother was released by the police yester-day, and when I spoke to him, he had a message *specifically for you.* He told me to tell you that he's got a gun full of bullets with your names on them, and that he is going to kill you and string your guts around town, as a warning to anyone else who wants to try to get in his way."

Chris now stands directly in front of Nothing Man and the Purple Zero; they can smell the whiskey on his breath (guzzled from a bottle that Chris stole from his father's stash, and has already smashed against the rocks of the burned-out foundation).

"You two are officially on my brother's Bullet List," Chris wheezes, "which means you had better get your asses out of town if you want to live."

Then Chris turns to Observer X, whom he obviously doesn't recog-nize as Elizabeth inside her catlike tights. "And I don't know who you are, sexy, or why you're hanging with these two losers, but you're going to have to give me that video camera." He holds out his hand. "Right now."

Observer X backs away from him. "No way," she says.

With his fists raised, Nothing Man steps toward Chris Orff. "Get away from her."

Chris laughs. "Easy, Tex! I'm not having a fist fight with you. If you can kick my brother's ass, you can *definitely* kick mine. I'm the *nice* kid in our family. I'm the *special* one."

He reaches into his back pocket and pulls out his cellphone.

"But here's what I'm gonna do. I'm gonna call my brother, and when he gets here ..." Chris grins at Nothing Man, and then at the Purple Zero. " ... oh, I suppose he will probably shoot both of you guys right between the eyes. But I'm sure he'll let you beg and cry a bit, first."

He turns to Observer X.

"And you, you sweet little thing, I imagine that Devin will find a way to get that camera away from you. He probably won't shoot you, though. He's gonna *like* you. A lot."

Chris Orff turns and saunters back up the hill to where Davey Batterwall stands before the cliff wall, watching from a distance. Chris punches the buttons on his cellphone and raises it to his ear. When he arrives at the cliff wall, he drops the phone into the back pocket of his jeans and picks up his can of fire-engine-red spray paint.

Both Chris and Davey turn their backs on the Dynamic Trio, raising their spray cans to finish their defamatory vandalism.

"STOP RIGHT THERE!" the Purple Zero hollers.

Chris looks over his shoulder. "You're still here? Seriously, you'd better get lost before Devin gets here."

"DROP THE PAINT CANS!" the Purple Zero cries.

Chris rolls his eyes, and turns to face the wall. "Whatever."

"THIS IS YOUR LAST WARNING!" the Purple Zero hollers,

raising a Zero Bomb above each shoulder. "DROP THE PAINT CANS!"

Chris doesn't even look back this time. "Fuck off."

"Yeah," Davey says. "Fuck off."

The Purple Zero throws the first Zero Bomb. And then the second one. Because the Purple Zero is the least athletic member of the not-very-athletic Dynamic Trio, both Zero Bombs land significantly short of where the two vandals are standing; but, as fate would have it, the breeze is blowing toward the Faireville Bluffs tonight, and the noxious fumes are carried directly into the faces of Chris Orff and Davey Batterwall.

Both vandals drop their spray cans, grip their faces in horror, and scream every expletive they know (which is a lot of expletives; the vocabularies of both Chris and Davey consist mostly of profanities). They cough, they gag, they shout and spit, and they frantically rub their eyes. Through burning, tear-blurred eyes, Davey sees the Purple Zero reaching into the bag for another pair of Zero Bombs, and he screams to Chris, "Run! Run! Run!"

Davey and Chris do run, as fast as their legs will carry them, into the woods that surround the burned-out foundation of the old castle.

"Should we chase them?" Bill wonders.

"Nah," Marty says. "I just stopped an act of vandalism in progress. I think that makes us even on the superhero scorecard."

Elizabeth lowers her camera, and then plays back some of the footage on its miniature screen. "Wow. This video looks great! I'll be able to edit this into something *amazing*!"

"Cool," Marty says. "Hey, who's hungry? I could use a couple of those Chili 'N' Cheez Super Snaks right now."

"Sounds good," Elizabeth says, "but first, I need to do something."

Like a sinewy black cat, Elizabeth sprints up the hill to the place where Chris and Davey have abandoned their graffiti-in-progress. Bill watches her lean, moonlit silhouette as she picks up one of Davey's cans of neon purple paint, and then she stretches to finish the job in her own way. She adds her own slender script to Davey's graffiti, so that it reads:

MISTER BEAUREGARD SUC CEEDS WITH STUDENTS!

"There!" Elizabeth cheers. "Perfect!"

And a snippet of his dream plays in Bill's mind.

He is a black falcon, soaring high over the Faireville Bluffs. From the air, he sees a slender black cat, stretching and purring in a pool of moonlight. And even though he is a falcon, and she is a cat, he will find it impossible to stop watching her.

Now Elizabeth picks up one of the cans of fire-engine-red paint, and she modifies Chris Orff's graffiti to read:

MR BEAUREGARD IS A G REAT TEACHER!

And then Elizabeth's eyes lock on to Bill's. Even from this distance, she can somehow look right into him.

"What do you think?" she says.

And another scene from Bill's dream plays back in his mind; he wonders if Elizabeth can see it, too.

The sleek black cat glances at him, and her glowing, reflective cat eyes lock on to his dark bird eyes.

"It's perfect," Bill says.

When she comes down from the top of the hill, Bill is going to kiss her, deliciously and passionately, for a long, long time. He no longer cares if Marty knows.

In his mind, Bill hears that familiar chorus of children's voices, singing *"Bill and Elizabeth, sittin' in a tree, K-I-S-S-I-N-G!"*

The children's voices are interrupted, though, as a battered, rust-spotted Chevy pickup truck comes roaring up the driveway. It scrunches to a halt in a cloud of dust, bouncing on its squeaking, worn-out springs.

In the truck's dented, rusty box sit Chris Orff and Davey Batterwall, who, even from a distance, smell like a blend of rotten eggs, sour milk, and sewer gas … with just a *hint* of vomit.

The driver's-side door of the truck squeals and rocks on its hinges as it is kicked open by a tall-heeled cowboy boot. Inside the cab, the driver reaches for the gun rack that hangs against the back window, and he grabs the single rifle that hangs there. Then, both boots hit the ground, and Devin Orff stands up tall beside the truck, his eyes narrowed into snakelike slits, his lips scrunched together in a predatory sneer.

The first person he sees is the Purple Zero.

"Prepare to die, scumbag," he rasps, as he stomps toward his target, raising the rifle and aiming it at the Purple Zero's chest.

Nothing Man sprints between Devin Orff and the Purple Zero, spreading his arms wide, shielding his friend from the barrel of the gun.

"Fine, dickhead," Devin Orff snarls, aiming the rifle at Nothing Man instead, "you can be first, then."

Behind his face shield, Bill Brown closes his eyes and holds his breath.

This is it. I am going to die.

Devin's finger squeezes the trigger.

Click.

"What the fuck?" Devin rages.

He squeezes the trigger again.

Click. Click. Click.

"Fuck! Fuck! Fuck!" Devin screams, and he spins toward the truck. "Chris, you little fuck-shit! Were you using this gun?"

"Target practice," the fragrant Chris whimpers. "I was shootin' cans. To get more accurate."

"And you didn't think to put *more fucking bullets* in the fucking gun?" .

"Sorry, Devin!" Chris cries. "I forgot!"

Devin throws the empty gun at the back of the truck. It spirals through the air, and the butt of the rifle strikes Chris in the forehead. Blood spurts from the wound.

"Ow! Ow! Ow!" Chris cries, pressing his palms against the wound.

"*Orffs aren't whiners, damn it!*" Devin shrieks. "If Dad was here, he'd hit ya harder than that!"

"Fuck Dad," Chris says. "And fuck you, too, Devin." He climbs out of the box of the pickup and limps toward the overgrown driveway.

Davey jumps out of the truck and joins his friend.

"You're *so* dead when you get home," Devin hollers after his brother.

"I'm not coming home," Chris says.

"You can stay at my place," Davey says.

"Thanks, buddy," Chris says, as he and Davey disappear over the crest of the weed-covered driveway.

Without warning, Devin Orff spins around and rushes toward the Purple Zero at full speed, slamming his chest with two closed fists.

Marty falls to ground, clutching his chest, gasping for air.

Then Devin turns and punches Nothing Man in the face three times, *Crack! Crack! Crack!*

One of the punches cracks the lenses in the driving goggles. Another punch slams the face shield against Bill's nose, and Bill's blood gushes inside the mask. The third punch causes Bill to lose his balance, and he tumbles to the ground beside Marty.

"You're not so fucking super *now*, are you, *superheroes?*" Devin Orff grunts, as he kicks the already-gasping Marty in the stomach. He pulls back a cowboy boot to kick Bill, too, but he is interrupted by a voice from just behind him.

A female figure in a catlike outfit springs up from behind a crumbling foundation wall. She shouts, "Come *here* and say that, you big, stupid bully!"

"And who the fuck are *you* supposed to be?" Devin says, as he stomps toward Observer X.

A shiver rushes through her body as Devin Orff closes in on her, and the words of Mizz Greener, her grade eight gym teacher, ring in her ears: *"Gawd, Elizabeth! You can't throw to save your life!"*

Elizabeth hurls the jagged chunk of concrete she's been holding, and it hits Devin Orff square in the forehead, in the same spot where the butt of the rifle hit his brother Chris.

Devin Orff tumbles backward against his truck, holding his gushing forehead.

Dazed, angry, with blood running down his face like a crimson waterfall, Devin climbs into the cab and slams the passenger-side door behind him.

"This isn't over, muthahfuggahs!" he shrieks. "This isn't over!"

The engine of the truck begins rumbling and sputtering, and Devin Orff throws the transmission into reverse.

"Meet me tomorrow night at the Badlands," he screams through the open windows, "and we'll finish this, once and for all!"

He stomps on the accelerator and spins the truck around in a wide half-circle, nearly running down Elizabeth with the tailgate of the pickup. The one unshattered tail light glows as he stomps on the brake pedal.

"One on one!" he cries. "One at a time. Fists against fists. Be there."

"Or what?" Elizabeth says.

"Or me and my daddy will go hunting for you," he says. "With our hunting rifles."

He jams the transmission into drive, and says, "No cops, no backup, no nothin'. Just me against you."

Bill tries to stand up, but he is still too dizzy, so from the ground he says, "No guns."

"No guns?" Devin says. "Fine. No guns. I won't need no gun to beat you, you little shit-fuck."

And, with that said, Devin stomps on the accelerator and careens down the narrow old driveway. A plume of smoky dust hangs in the air where the truck roared away.

Marty, whose Purple Zero outfit is covered in mud and dirt, is still labouring to breathe. Bill pulls off his Nothing Man mask. Blood from his nose is splattered all over his face.

"Marty," Bill says, "are you okay?"

Marty rolls over on his side and says, "You saved my life, Bill. You saved my life."

"I didn't save anyone's life, Marty. I got the crap beaten out of me."

"You jumped in front of the gun to save me," Marty says. His voice is soft, and his eyes are glassy. "You saved my life."

"Marty, I think you might have a concussion or something. We had better get you to the emergency —"

"You saved my life," Marty says. "Now I know. You love me, too."

Marty presses his face against Bill's, and kisses him on the lips.

"You love me, too," he repeats, and he moves to kiss Bill again.

Bill scurries backward on the palms of his hands, away from Marty, like a crab evading a predator.

"Whoa! Marty! Whoa!" he yelps. "I think you might have a concussion or something! I think there's something wrong with you."

"THERE IS NOTHING WRONG WITH ME!" Marty cries, climbing onto his feet, his sore lungs struggling for breath. "THERE IS NOTHING WRONG WITH ME, BILL!"

On the ground, Bill stammers, "I … I didn't mean … It's just … I didn't *know* … I didn't think you were …"

"I GET IT, OKAY? YOU DON'T FEEL THE SAME WAY. I GET IT. YOU DON'T HAVE TO ACT SO … *REPULSED!*"

Bill lifts himself up, and the strain of rising from the ground causes his nose to spurt more blood. He sees that some of his blood is on Marty's face now, too.

"Marty, I'm not *repulsed* … I'm just … *surprised*, that's all."

"YOU'RE *SURPRISED*? YOU'RE *SURPRISED*? ARE YOU TELLING ME THAT YOU'RE THE ONLY PERSON IN FAIREVILLE THAT DIDN'T SUSPECT THAT I'M GAY?"

Marty turns to Elizabeth, who is still standing inside the crumbling foundation, with her arms hanging akimbo and her mouth open wide.

"Elizabeth," Marty says, "are you *unaware* that I'm gay?"

"Well, um, no, I suppose I *suspected* that you might be, um …"

Marty turns back to Bill. "DO YOU THINK ANYONE ELSE AT SCHOOL IS *UNAWARE* THAT I'M GAY, BILL? OR IS IT JUST YOU? I GUESS YOU JUST *TURNED A BLIND EYE*, EH?"

"Marty, I … I didn't …"

Marty sniffles. "Will you even be my *friend* now?"

"Marty, we've been through so much …"

"THE ANSWER I WAS LOOKING FOR WAS 'YES,' BILL."

"But that's what I …"

"FORGET IT, BILL. I DON'T *NEED* YOU AS A *FRIEND*. I DON'T *NEED* YOU *AT ALL*."

Marty stomps over to the Cord 812. He climbs into the driver's seat, slams the door closed, and starts the engine.

"Come on, Marty," Bill says, moving to the side of the car. "You don't know how to drive. Let me …"

"I told you, Bill," Marty says, his voice rising, "I DON'T *NEED* YOU! Bloombottom has been letting me practise driving around the grounds. So … I *DON'T* NEED *YOU*!"

"Marty …"

"FUCK OFF, BILL!" he cries. "I. DON'T. NEED. *YOU*."

Marty turns to Elizabeth and says, "You two have fun together, okay?"

And then, just like Marty has seen Bill do so many times, he pre-selects a gear, releases the clutch, and turns the car in a wide circle.

As the long nose of the car swings around, Bill sees the small Cord emblem beneath the gleaming grille: beneath a knight's helmet, a simple shield adorned with three red hearts and three silver arrows. Everything on a coat of arms means something, and, at this moment, the shield of the Cord Corporation seems to perfectly represent the three members of the Dynamic Trio.

And Bill realizes that he may have inadvertently launched his own silver arrow straight into Marty's unarmoured heart.

"Marty," Bill calls out, "I'm sorry!"

But Marty doesn't hear him over the roar of the engine, as the Cord 812 Phaeton speeds down the hill, disappearing into the overgrown foliage.

Chapter Thirteen

The Badlands

Bill's nose is sore from the punches he took last night from Devin Orff, but thankfully it isn't broken; that would have been difficult to explain to his parents at breakfast this morning.

Still, Bill's whole body aches from the previous evening's adventures, and he is *so* tired; it was a long walk home from the Faireville Bluffs, made even longer because he and Elizabeth had to stick to the forest paths and the back streets, to avoid being detected by the Faireville Police Force's Devil's Night Curfew-Enforcement Blitz.

Bill didn't sneak in until after midnight, and he was up again this morning before 5:00 a.m. to deliver a load of apples to the market. Bill would love nothing more right now than to put his head down on his desk and have a long, sweet nap.

From the front of the English classroom, Miss Womansfield says, "Okay, class, finally, after several unexpected delays, it's time for you to present your comparisons between Rosencrantz and Guildenstern and another fictional duo of your choice. Bill Brown and Marty Apostrophes, you're up first."

"Marty is absent from school today, Miss," Bill says, glancing over at the empty seat beside him. "Could we postpone our presentation until he's here?"

After last night's revelation, Bill wonders if he will ever see Marty at school again.

"Sorry, Bill," Miss Womansfield replies, "but, to quote P.T. Barnum, or songs by Queen or Pink Floyd, if you prefer, 'The show must go on!'"

"The show can't go on without Marty," Bill says. "He *is* the show."

Although Bill is usually the one who does most of the actual *research* for team presentations like this one, it's Marty who usually adds the *flair* to the performance. Alone, Bill might not even earn their customary B+.

"Oh, come on, Bill," Miss Womansfield chides, "I remember you saying, just a couple of days ago, that all of your heroes work alone."

"I rescind that comment," Bill says. "I would rather be part of a team."

"Yesterday you saved somebody's life all by yourself," she says, her admiration glimmering through her staid teacher persona, "so I think that you'll be able to handle delivering an English presentation on your own today."

So, Bill Brown stands before his classmates, delivering a monotone recital comparing and contrasting *Star Trek*'s Mr. Spock and Captain Kirk with *Hamlet*'s Rosencrantz and Guildenstern. He's not even halfway through the presentation, and already the eyelids of almost everyone in the room, including Miss Womansfield, are weighing heavy with boredom. As he concludes, it takes a moment before people even realize that Bill has finished speaking. There is eventually a polite smattering of applause.

Zig Zag Rogers and Strat Sanderson are scheduled to present next, but Zig Zag was held overnight at the hospital for observation, so Miss Womansfield allows their presentation to be postponed until Monday.

But I'm *the one who saved Zig Zag yesterday,* Bill muses, *and my assignment didn't get postponed. Are there* any *advantages to this hero business?* Then, Bill remembers Mr. Peershakker's words, that an

Unsung Hero is *"always willing to lend a helping hand, without seeking any reward or affirmation."*

Right on cue, Lance Goodfellow says, "It's okay, Miss Womansfield, Virginia and I will go next! We're ready!"

Virginia's Minions and Lance's hockey buddies are clapping wildly before the Super Couple even makes it to the front of the classroom. The cheering gets even louder when Virginia says, "And I hope everyone is ready for the Halloween party at my place tonight! By invitation only!"

Bill sighs, and he doesn't smile again until much later, when Elizabeth Murphy strides up to the front of the classroom.

"Superman and Lois Lane!" she begins, with even more of her trademark enthusiasm than usual. "Superman is already Superman, and he can do pretty much anything. But somehow, his attraction to Lois Lane makes him even better, makes him even more willing to risk himself to do the right thing."

And Bill Brown feels his energy rising once again. If he is going to make things right with Marty tonight, Bill's Clark Kent is going to need Elizabeth's Lois Lane.

Somehow, Nothing Man and Observer X must convince the Purple Zero to join the Dynamic Trio once again.

Bill Brown has finished his after-dinner chores at the farm, and Elizabeth Murphy has completed her assignment for *The Faireville Gleaner*, to photograph the "Tiny Tots" Halloween Party at the Faireville Community Centre (where a four-year-old boy and his three-year-old brother shared the "Best Costume" prize, because their quick-thinking parents dressed them up as Nothing Man and the Purple Zero).

Now, Elizabeth and Bill stand before the gates of the Apostrophes Estate, where Bill is pressing the button on the intercom panel.

The last red embers of daylight have been choked from the sky by a low layer of cloud. In the dim, diffused moonlight, the gargoyles glare down from their pedestals in a particularly menacing way.

Halloween Night has begun.

Bill paces back and forth before the towering iron gate.

"Relax, Bill," Elizabeth soothes him. "I'm sure Marty's temper has cooled by now. He's got a short fuse, but he always recovers quickly."

"I don't know, Elizabeth," Bill says. "I think it might be different this time."

Bill presses the intercom button again, and then paces back and forth some more. Finally, the thick German accent of Von Kruugen, the butler, hums through the intercom speaker. "Yessssssss?"

"Mr. Von Kruugen, it's Bill Brown. I'm here with Elizabeth Murphy. We're here to see Marty. Could you open the gates and let us in, please?"

"I'm afraid that Master Apostrophes is not available at the moment, sir."

Maybe because it is Halloween night, the tone of Von Kruugen's voice reminds Bill of the Bela Lugosi version of Count Dracula.

"What do you mean, he's not available?"

"Master Apostrophes is not on the grounds of the estate, sir."

"Is that true, Mr. Von Kruugen, or did Marty tell you to say that so you wouldn't have to let us in?"

"I am a professional butler, sir. The security of the grounds is one of my many responsibilities. It is well within my powers of discretion to decide whether or not to open the gates for you. It is not necessary for me to make excuses."

Bill sighs. "I didn't mean to offend you, Mr. Von Kruugen. We just need to see Marty. It's important."

"As I've already said, sir, Master Apostrophes is not on the grounds of the estate. You will have to return when he is present. Good evening."

Bill turns away from the intercom panel, and says to Elizabeth, "Great. Now what should we do?"

Elizabeth squints and strokes her chin, evaluating the situation.

"If I climb up onto your shoulders, I think I can pull myself over the top of that pillar."

"Seriously?" Bill says. "It's a long drop down to the other side."

"That little garden looks freshly tilled," Elizabeth says. "It should provide a soft enough landing. When I was little, I used to jump from the roof of Dad's shop into the bin where they collect the cardboard for recycling."

"Did you shout, '*the Pissah of Powah!*' when you jumped?"

"I sure did," Elizabeth says. "At that moment, I *was* the Princess of Power."

"Do you think you can be the Princess of Power again?"

Elizabeth squints once again at the gargoyle-topped pillar. "This gate isn't much taller than Dad's building. Yes, I can do it."

"What about the security cameras?"

"We'll worry about them after we're inside."

So, Bill leans back against the stone pillar, plants both feet firmly on the ground, and laces his fingers together, forming a cup with his hands that he holds at waist level.

Elizabeth grips Bill's shoulders with both hands, and then lifts her right foot into Bill's interlocked fingers. As she pulls herself up into a standing position, one of her breasts grazes Bill's face, and he is momentarily distracted.

Focus! Bill's brain screams at his body. *Focus! There is a mission to accomplish! Focus on the mission!*

Bill's muscles strain to maintain balance as Elizabeth steps up onto his shoulders and reaches up to grab the edge of the gargoyle's stone platform.

"Almost there ..." she says, as she stands on her tiptoes on Bill's broad shoulders, her fingers just brushing the top of the column. "Almost there ..."

And that's when Elizabeth's toes slip.

She grabs hold of the pillar to break her fall. Instinctively, she wraps her legs around the column as well, trapping Bill's face between the cold stone and the warm inside of her thighs.

"*Mmmmph,*" Bill says. "*Mmmmm … mmmmph.*"

He reaches up, cups his hands under Elizabeth's buttocks, and, with his muscles trembling, he lowers her gently down from the pillar. As her feet touch the cool ground, his hands are still clenched on her behind, and her chest is pressed against his, and, for a moment, both Bill and Elizabeth forget to *focus on the mission.*

From just behind them, a rough, deep voice scratches the air like 80-grit sandpaper. "Okay, lovebirds, break it up!"

Just inside the fence, backlit ominously by diffused moonlight, stands the wrinkled yet imposing figure of Bloombottom the Mechanic.

"You're lucky that I saw you on the video monitors before Von Kruugen did," Bloombottom says, in that raspy, otherworldly voice. "He would have called the police and had you both charged with Public Indecency. Or something worse."

Bill's face flushes, and he releases his grip on Elizabeth's buttocks, but she does not unwrap her arms from around his neck; instead, she pulls Bill closer.

"Fortunately for you," Bloombottom continues, "I am a more sentimental fellow than the butler is."

He pokes a button on the inside of a pedestal, and there is the screeching sound of metal on metal as the grand entrance gate swings open.

"You should come inside, now," Bloombottom says. "Time is running against us."

◉

Inside the Carriage House, Marty's Purple Zero outfit is nowhere to be seen, and the gym bag stuffed full of Zero Bombs has been taken from its hiding spot inside the teardrop-shaped 1937 Talbot-Lago. The Black Phantom, however, remains parked in its usual spot inside the Exotic Car Room.

"Did Marty say where he was going?" Bill asks Bloombottom.

"The only thing he said, in that theatrical voice he uses, is that he had 'A DATE WITH DESTINY!' Whenever Master Apostrophes uses *that voice*, it means that there is going to be some sort of mess to clean up afterward."

A shadow crosses Elizabeth's face. "You don't think that he went to confront Devin Orff, do you?"

"That would be bad," Bill says.

"Oh, my," Bloombottom says, his gruff voice wavering for perhaps the first time ever. "He's involved in a conflict with one of the Orffs? That *is* bad."

"Devin told us to meet him tonight for a showdown at the Badlands," Bill says. "I never thought that Marty would actually *go*. Especially *alone*."

"He must have some of his grandfather's blood in him, after all," Bloombottom says. "I'm calling the police."

He crosses the garage, dials the telephone that is hanging from the wall, and waits a moment before saying, "It's their answering machine. Given that it's Halloween and all, I imagine that they're all out on patrol. I'll call back in a few minutes."

"Bloombottom," Bill says, "if you'll allow me to take the Cord, I'm sure we can catch Marty before he gets to the Badlands. It's a long walk from here."

"Master Apostrophes didn't *walk*," Bloombottom says. "He drove the Crosley Hotshot." Despite the intensity of the situation, Bloombottom cannot resist rolling his eyes about the tiny, silly-looking, underpowered car. "I thought he was just going to practise driving around the grounds, as usual … but then, before I could stop him, he opened the gates and drove away."

"Well, let's go, then!" Elizabeth cries, as she scrambles toward the Cord 812. "There's no time to waste!"

Bloombottom raises a hand to halt her, and says, "You can't take the Cord, I'm afraid."

"What?" Bill yelps. "This isn't the time to *protect the collection*, Bloombottom! Marty is in *real danger*! We've got to *save* him!"

"Oh, I'm not protecting *the collection*," Bloombottom says. "I'm protecting *you*. If Master Apostrophes is confronting one of the Orffs in the middle of the Badlands, the terrain there is far too rugged for the Cord 812's suspension to handle."

Bloombottom gestures across the room at the 1943 Willys Military Jeep.

"Take the Jeep. I've reconditioned the springs and shock absorbers, so it should be able to take even the nastiest bumps. And it's got thick, armour-grade steel and bulletproof glass, too. Just in case."

Elizabeth looks at the Jeep's rear-mounted Browning M1919 machine gun. "Are there bullets in that thing?"

"Well, no," Bloombottom admits. "It doesn't actually work. We took the firing pins out of all of the guns on the estate after the Munitions Museum was robbed. But it may give you, shall we say, a *psychological advantage*."

"I don't think we'll need that," Bill says. "Devin said that there would be no guns."

"Well, then," Bloombottom says, flexing his eyebrows, "I'm sure you can take a fine fellow like Devin Orff at his word. In the past, though, the Orff family has been known to retaliate rather *violently* against their perceived enemies, so you should probably take a moment to change into your superhero costumes, to conceal your identities."

Bill stares at Bloombottom with wide eyes.

"Yes, yes," the ancient mechanic says, grinning slightly. "*Of course* I know about your recent *extracurricular activities*. I may be old, but I know how to use a computer. And when I saw the video, I recognized the *car* ... and then the football uniform that belonged to Marshall Apostrophes ... and then his driving outfit ... and then Marty accidentally called me 'Alfred' yesterday ... and *of course* I put everything together."

Bill's jaw hangs open.

"Who do you think *fixed* the Cord after your first adventure," Bloombottom continues, "when you so carefully parked it in here, but left it in gear, so the transmission lost its vacuum?"

Bill slaps his forehead. "Aw, I should have known! Cords are *infamous* for that problem!"

"And *you* are going to be *infamous*," Bloombottom ominously intones, "if you don't get into your costume and go save your friend!"

Elizabeth pulls her Observer X mask from an oversized pocket, then she unzips her coveralls and shrugs them onto the floor, revealing her shimmering black costume underneath. She snaps the catlike mask over her face and says, "I'm ready."

Bill shakes his head. "I'm not. I left my outfit hidden in the barn at home. And I smashed the goggles last night, anyway. I'll just have to go in my street clothes, I guess."

"No, you won't," Bloombottom says. "Marshall Apostrophes had a *second* driving outfit, which he wore for public events, like the Remembrance Day Parade or the Mayoral Procession. It's not exactly the same, but it'll do the job. I'll fetch it for you while you get the Jeep started."

There is a slim break in the clouds, and moonlight cuts across the red-and-black-streaked clay hills of the Faireville Badlands; all that remains of its once-famous natural gas fields are a couple of dilapidated drilling towers, a few rusted, graffiti-covered storage tanks, and some chunks of abandoned pipe. The landscape is grim, almost post-apocalyptic in its desolation.

Devin Orff's dented, rusty Chevy pickup truck is perched atop the tallest hill in the Badlands, and Devin stands tall in the truck's pock-marked box, scanning the shorter surrounding hills and valleys for his enemies. His index finger runs from the bottom of his chin to the corner of his mouth, following the path of his crescent-moon-shaped scar, which he earned at the bottom of this very hill.

But now I'm on top, Devin muses. *From up here, I can take on any challenger. From up here, I can't lose.*

Many of Devin's personal highs and lows have happened right here. This is the place where he destroyed his best dirt bike. This is the place where some runt mortally injured his two Dobermans, who may have been the only living things that Devin ever really loved. This is the place where he was abandoned by most of the guys in his first gang.

But this is also the place where he first opened that bag of "unrecovered" cash from the bank heist, and this is the spot where he invested it in some "product." This is also the spot where he made his first highly profitable sale to that dreadlocked high school idiot.

Best of all, though, this is the spot where his new, high-rolling life will begin. After tonight, he will buy himself a new pickup truck, with a thousand-watt stereo system in the cab, flames painted on the sides, and neon lights running under the body. And he will get himself some gem-encrusted cowboy boots, a huge gold belt buckle with a big ruby right in the centre, and a platinum chain so thick he could tow a trailer with it.

Devin thinks, *This is my Hill of Triumph.*

But first, he's got a trio of "superheroes" to deal with.

"Come out, come out, *superheroes*!" he cries out, and he listens to his voice echo from the hardened, lifeless clay of the surrounding hills. "Come out, come out, wherever you are!"

Over the crest of a red clay hilltop, the Purple Zero appears, holding a Zero Bomb in each hand.

"I've *already* come out," the Purple Zero says.

"Well, well," Devin brays, pleased by the sound of his echoing voice. "If it isn't *the Purple Dildo!* Where are the other two *Super Zeroes?*"

"They'll be here!" the Purple Zero declares. *They probably won't,* Marty thinks. He cocks one Zero Bomb behind his shoulder, and prepares to launch.

"Now, hold on a second there, buddy," Devin calls out. "We said 'no weapons,' remember?"

"We said 'no guns,'" the Purple Zero counters. "These aren't guns."

"Well, let's expand the agreement, okay? If I can't use my guns, then you can't use your stink bombs. Deal?"

The Purple Zero hesitates for a moment before saying, "Okay. Deal."

"Now, show me that you're a man of your word by dropping them on the ground."

The Purple Zero kneels down and gently sets the two Zero Bombs down on the hilltop; the last thing he needs is for his own weapons to blow up on *him.*

When he rises again, there is a tiny, glowing red dot in the centre of his chest. Across the chasm between the two hills, Devin Orff is aiming a high-powered assault rifle at Marty.

"Unfortunately for you, I'm *not* a man of my word," Devin cackles. "This beauty's equipped with laser sights. Recognize it?"

"I don't know anything about guns," Marty says, with admirable composure under the circumstances. "You said that this was going to be 'One on one ... One at a time ... Fists against fists' ... remember?"

"Well, I changed my mind," Devin Orff says. "Now raise your hands above your head where I can see them, you stupid f—"

Devin Orff's sentence is interrupted by the roar of the Willys Military Jeep as it climbs to the top of a blunt-topped, red clay hill, next to the mound where Marty stands. Nothing Man leaps from the driver's seat and into the back of the Jeep, where he swings the tripod-mounted Browning machine gun around and points it at Devin Orff.

"Drop the gun!" Nothing Man commands.

Observer X is not in the Jeep; she jumped out at the bottom of the hill, to circle around and surprise Devin Orff from behind, if necessary. It would also keep her out of the line of fire if it came down to that, Bill reasoned to himself.

"Drop the gun!" Nothing Man repeats. "Now!"

Devin grins cockily as he continues to aim his rifle at the Purple Zero's chest, and he continues talking as if Nothing Man isn't even there.

"But, seriously," he says, "I'm shocked that you don't recognize this beautiful weapon, 'cause me and my daddy stole it from your own family's gun museum ... *Marty Apostrophes*."

"What?" Marty cries. "How do you know my ... ?"

"Oh, my daddy recognized your granddaddy's football uniform ... didn't you, Daddy?"

From inside the pickup box, the menacing figure of Clive Orff rises like a pale-skinned demon, and he stands up beside his eldest son. Clive also holds a high-powered rifle, equipped with laser sights.

Now there are two bright red dots: one dances in the centre of Marty's chest, and the other hovers directly over Nothing Man's heart.

"Please don't kill us," Marty says.

"Oh, we ain't gonna kill *you*, boy," Clive Orff snarls, "unless you misbehave. You're worth more to us alive ... and to your filthy-rich daddy, too, I suppose."

"We *are* gonna kill your buddy, though," Devin says. "And, when we find that little tart who hit me with the rock, we're gonna kill her *real* good. We'll kill her *twice!*"

Nothing Man has heard the DRAMATIC VOICE enough times; he decides that the time has come to use it himself. "DROP BOTH OF THOSE GUNS! RIGHT NOW! OR I'LL CUT YOU IN HALF WITH THIS MACHINE GUN!"

"Ah, knock it off, ya little faggot," Clive Orff brays. "I know for a fact that that gun ain't got no bullets in it. They disabled all the museum weapons after the robbery. There was even a story about it in *The Faireville Gleaner* ... to make people feel *safe* again."

"THIS GUN HAS *NOT* BEEN DISABLED! IT'S PART OF THE AUTO COLLECTION, NOT THE MUNITIONS MUSEUM. SO, DROP YOUR WEAPONS, OR I *WILL* FIRE."

Clive Orff isn't sure whether to believe this or not. He stares at Nothing Man, with the sights of his rifle aimed at his enemy's chest, and Nothing Man glares back at him, with the Browning machine gun pointed directly at Clive Orff.

It seems like an entire age passes before anyone makes a move.

Finally, Nothing Man glances over at Marty, to make sure that his friend is okay, and that is when Clive Orff jeers, "Fuck off, asshole!" and fires three quick shots at Nothing Man.

The bullets smash against the bulletproof glass of the Jeep's windshield.

Bill drops to his knees inside the Jeep, paralyzed with fear, feeling as if he might throw up.

"Huh," Clive Orff says, glaring at the rifle in his hands as if it has betrayed him. "The sights are a little high on this one. Shoulda fired a few test rounds at home, I guess."

Devin lowers his gun and says, "Holy shit, Dad! Have you lost your mind? That'll have the cops here any second."

"Relax, it's Halloween. They'll think it was firecrackers or something."

While Devin's rifle is lowered, Marty makes a move to get away. In a split second, the glowing red dot from Clive Orff's laser sight glows between Marty's eyes, and Clive's growl echoes from the hills all around them.

"I got the sights on this thing figured out now," Clive says. "This shot'll hit you right in the heart if you take another step."

Marty freezes.

Clive kicks his son in the shin with the heel of his boot. "We don't get no ransom money if you let the hostage get away, you idiot!"

While father and son are distracted, Bill attempts to leap from the Jeep, but this new Nothing Man outfit is a lot heavier than the previous one, and it slows him down.

Devin sees Bill move, and he immediately aims his laser dot at the trunk of Bill's body.

Bill also freezes.

"Now, boys," Clive Orff says, "why don't you put your hands in the air and slowly walk this way. We'll have our guns on you the whole time, so if you make any sudden moves, you're dead."

"NO WAY!" Marty thunders in his DRAMATIC VOICE.

"What did you say, you little —"

"I SAID 'NO WAY'!" Marty repeats. "THE ONLY WAY YOU TWO WORTHLESS LOSERS ARE TAKING *ME* HOSTAGE IS IF YOU LET MY FRIEND GO!"

"There are *two* of us," Clive Orff says, "and we've got *two* guns. There are also *two* of you, but you've got *no* guns. Which equals ... *get your asses movin'! Now!*"

"I SAID, 'NO WAY'!" Marty hollers. "HE GETS TO GO, OR YOU DON'T GET YOUR RANSOM."

"We got two guns!" Clive Orff rasps, his famous temper flaring. "So *move it,* assholes!"

"NO WAY!"

"TWO GUNS!" the elder Orff screams.

"NO WAY!"

"TWO GUNS!"

Subtle variations and permutations of this argument continue, until it seems like another entire age has passed.

"We've got two guns," Clive Orff says for the last time.

"So you've got two guns," says a quiet voice from behind Devin and Clive Orff. "But there are *three* of us. You're outnumbered."

Bill recognizes the voice. *Elizabeth!*

Unfortunately, Devin Orff recognizes the voice, too.

"It's that little bitch that hit me in the head!" he hisses, and the legendary temper that he inherited from his father boils over yet again.

Devin squeezes the trigger of his rifle.

An explosion of gunpowder.

The bullet strikes Bill in the chest.

He tumbles from the Jeep, and his body rolls halfway down the back of the hill.

Devin Orff howls, "Now there are *two* of you!"

Chapter Fourteen

Together We Stand

Devin Orff stomps over to where he heard Elizabeth's voice, and he sweeps the barrel of his rifle back and forth across the slope.

"*Come on out*, you sexy little thing!" he calls out into the darkness. "Now there's two of you, and two of us. *Come out, come out, wherever you are!*"

Elizabeth is crouching in a crevice, where the dim, diffused moonlight cannot reach her. In her black Observer X outfit, she is completely invisible to Devin Orff. It takes all of her strength to prevent herself from crying out loud, but her mind sobs, *Oh Bill, oh Bill, oh Bill* ...

"*MURDERERS!*" Marty screams. "YOU ARE GOING TO PAY FOR THIS, YOU *MURDERERS!*"

"Hey," Clive Orff says, "I ain't murdered anybody ... *yet* ... but I will if you don't *shut the hell up!*"

"Come out right now, *Cat Woman!*" Devin screeches. "Or me and my daddy are gonna put every bullet we've got through your pal Marty!"

"*MURDERERS!*" Marty screams again.

"Now, listen here," Clive Orff hollers back at Marty across the chasm, "these guns are loaded with bullets made by *Apostrophes*

Munitions, which *your family* makes and sells ... so your buddy gettin' shot is *your fault, too!*"

"My ... *my* fault?" Marty stutters. "*My* fault?"

"No bullets, no shooting," Clive Orff says, shrugging. "You just *profited* from the slugs that killed your buddy. A few more shots and you'll be able to add another wing to the *mansion*." He says the word *mansion* with particular bitterness. Then, in a mocking tone, he repeats the words of Marty's grandfather from the recording at the Munitions Museum: "APOSTROPHES MUNITIONS! PROUDLY PROTECTING THE GOOD FROM THE EVIL SINCE NINETEEN-OH-SEVEN!"

Devin Orff continues to scan the slope of his Victory Hill, but all he sees is darkness, and all he hears is silence.

"Okay, bitch," Devin says, smirking, "I'm gonna count down from ten. If you don't show yourself by the time I reach zero, Marty is going to *get a chest full of his own bullets.*"

"Don't worry, sweetie," Daddy Clive brays, "we ain't gonna shoot ya." He glances over at his son. "Pretty girls make *good* hostages. A rich boy and a pretty girl is *just* what we need to profit from this here situation."

Devin starts counting down. "Ten ... nine ... eight ..."

Invisible inside her crevice, Elizabeth holds her breath, trembling, thinking, *I hope I've let enough time pass.*

"Seven ... six ... five ..."

Elizabeth thinks to herself, *Wait until the last possible moment.*

"Four ... three ... two ..."

On the slope of the hill, Elizabeth stands upright, revealing herself in the dim moonlight.

A red laser dot lands immediately in the centre of her chest.

"Okay, *Cat Woman*," Devin Orff says, "climb up here, with your hands in the air. Do anything stupid, and we'll shoot you both."

Elizabeth shouts, "I am *Observer X*!" She figures that if she's going to die tonight, she wants to die as her superhero alter ego.

"Ooh!" Clive Orff hoots. "She's *feisty*! I *like* her!"

"Whatever," Devin snarls. "Her *feist* ain't gonna help her. There's two of them, and two of us … and *we've* got the guns."

A different voice sounds out: "Wrong. There are *three* of us."

To the right side of Devin Orff's Victory Hill, there is a short brown hill that looks like a cigar lying on its side. A figure strides onto its crest. She's wearing a robin's-egg-blue cape, robin's-egg-blue-framed sunglasses, with a robin's-egg-blue Fender Stratocaster guitar slung over her shoulder.

"I am *Sonic Boom*," she says, "and I am here to stop you."

Sonic Boom is joined by a tall, lanky figure with dreadlocks. He is wearing a blue hospital gown, and his face is concealed by a surgical mask.

"Make that *four* of us, man," he says. "I'm the *Blue Cloud*, and I'm here to stop you, too, dudes."

Two more figures join Sonic Boom and the Blue Cloud atop the long, brown hill. They are dressed up like Marilyn Agnes' cartoon characters from the school newspaper.

"Make that *five*? I'm *Punk Mouse*? And I'm here to stop you, too?"

"Make it *six*. I'm *Rebel Kat*! And I am *definitely* here to stop you assholes! Drop those guns, cowards, and let's see what you're really made of!"

Rebel Kat is itching to put her martial arts training to work.

The red laser spots jump from person to person to person. Devin and Clive Orff aren't sure where to aim anymore.

Just to the left of Devin's Victory Hill, there is a bluff that resembles the two humps on a Bactrian camel (or perhaps something else, depending on the observer's level of maturity).

Onto one of the humps climbs a shapely, athletic-looking woman clad in a red latex jumpsuit, festooned with zippers, buckles, and studs. From behind her blood-red mask, she cries, "Make that seven, *losers*. I'm the *Dominatrix*, and I'm here to stop you, too."

The Minions of the Dominatrix surround her atop the hump.

"Make that eight, *losers*," says the Minion in the Sexy Nurse costume.

"Now it's nine, *losers*," says the Sexy French Maid.

The Sexy Secretary makes it ten, and the Sexy Waitress brings the count to eleven.

Onto the other camel's hump stride three young men, dressed in Faireville Blue Flames hockey uniforms; since they don't have turtle-neck collars to pull up over their faces like the Purple Zero does, their helmets don't conceal their identities.

"I'm the *Centre*," Bobby Bingham shouts, "and I'm number twelve!"

Rick Rousseau hollers, "I'm the *Winger*, and I make it thirteen!"

"Fourteen!" Dale Bunion adds, "and I'm the *Defenceman*!"

Several other hockey players join them atop the second hump.

"Fifteen!'

"Sixteen!"

"Seventeen!"

"Eighteen!"

Marcia Montrose stands beside Dale. "I'm *the Disciple*!" she shouts. "And I make it nineteen!"

There is movement at the bottom of the hill where Marty Apostrophes is standing. Marty glances over his shoulder and notices that Bill's body is no longer lying on the slope of the next hill. His heart races. *Bill's alive!* He wishes that he could somehow telepathi-cally send this thought across the chasm between the hills to Elizabeth.

Then Marty sees Lance Goodfellow climbing the slope behind him, until Lance is standing right beside him.

Marty does a double take. Lance is wearing a size-too-small white T-shirt, emblazoned from shoulder to waist with a brightly coloured rainbow decal. He's also sporting a rainbow-coloured clown wig, the kind that obsessive sports fans sometimes wear while watching games.

"I AM *RAINBOW MAN!*" Lance cries out, delivering a stunningly accurate impression of Marty's DRAMATIC VOICE. "AND NOW THERE ARE *TWO* OF YOU, AND *TWENTY* OF US!"

"*Rainbow Man?*" Marty says to Lance.

"Yeah," Lance says, "I was going to make a big, dramatic personal announcement at the Halloween party tonight … but we all got diverted here by Elizabeth, instead."

While Nothing Man and the Purple Zero were engaged in their standoff with Clive and Devin Orff, Observer X sprinted across the Badlands to the swanky, McMansion-filled subdivision where Virginia Sweet and her family live. Initially, Virginia's housekeeper Consuela wouldn't let Elizabeth in without an invitation.

"I forgot it at home," a quick-thinking Elizabeth said. "Why would I be wearing this ridiculous costume if I wasn't invited to a Halloween party?"

That explanation was good enough for Consuela. When Elizabeth came bursting in, Virginia and her Minions, all of Lance's hockey buddies, and everyone else at the party had just gathered around Lance, ready to hear the big announcement that he would not get a chance to make.

As soon as Elizabeth explained what was happening, Strat Sanderson and Zig Zag Rogers immediately agreed to help; they had a personal score to settle with Devin Orff. Social Crusader Kitty McMann was always looking for a noble reason to use her karate training, and Marilyn Agnes would follow her adventurous friend anywhere.

All of the hockey players without girlfriends also immediately agreed to follow Elizabeth to the Badlands; they had only ever seen her wearing her father's paint-speckled coveralls before, so the sight of slender Elizabeth in her clingy, shiny Observer X outfit overwhelmed their supercharged hormones.

This caused a chain reaction; the other members of the Faireville Blue Flames felt obligated by "team spirit" to accompany their teammates on this mission, and Virginia's Minions then volunteered to go along as well; the whole *point* of the Halloween party was to hook up with the guys from the hockey team!

Virginia Sweet muttered something to Elizabeth about "wrecking the party," but she wasn't about to stay home alone while everyone pranced off to the Badlands in their Halloween costumes.

Now Lance looks at Marty, and says, "I guess you're the first to know."

Marty's mouth opens wide. "You mean, you're … ?"

"Yes," Lance says. "I am."

Marty smiles at Lance, and says, "Welcome to the team."

Virginia Sweet overhears them from atop the camel's-hump hilltop, and she glances down at her red latex jumpsuit. "Well, I guess this costume isn't going to have any effect on Lance," she says.

Her Minions sigh and coo in sympathy.

Then the Purple Zero turns to face the Orffs. "IT'S OVER!" he shouts. "YOU'RE OUTNUMBERED TWENTY TO TWO, AND YOU ARE SURROUNDED ON ALL SIDES. YOU HAVEN'T GOT ENOUGH BULLETS IN YOUR GUNS TO KILL US ALL."

"I called the cops from Virginia's place," Rainbow Man says.

"Thanks," Marty says. "Good to know."

"YOU WILL THROW YOUR GUNS DOWN TO THE BOTTOM OF YOUR HILL," the Purple Zero orders. "THEN YOU WILL LIE DOWN ON THE GROUND, WITH YOUR ARMS AND LEGS SPREAD, AND AWAIT THE ARRIVAL OF THE POLICE."

Clive Orff considers gunning down as many of these annoying brats as he's got bullets for, but then something rare happens: his brain overrides his temper. "Too many damn witnesses," he says. Then he utters practically every obscenity in the English language, shakes his head, and says, "I know when I'm beat." He tosses his rifle downhill and lies face down on the hardened red clay. "Come on, boy," he says to Devin.

"Fuck that!" Devin Orff rages. "I'm not going down without a fight!" He spins around and glares at Observer X. "I'm taking you with me, sweetie. I don't care if there's a *hundred* of you. Nobody's gonna stop *me*."

As he raises the rifle, there is a hard, cracking blow to the back of Devin's head, and he tumbles onto the ground in a position similar to his father's. Two strong hands clench his shoulders and roll him over, and the rifle is wrenched from his hands.

Nothing Man stands tall, with one boot on Devin Orff's stomach, and he grimaces as he hurls the gun; it spirals through the air like a spinning helicopter blade, before clattering harmlessly on the hardened clay below.

Devin stutters, "What the ... how the ... I killed you. I *killed* you ...!"

"Obviously you *didn't*," Nothing Man says. "You *bruised* me pretty good, but you didn't *kill* me." He taps the knuckles of his gauntlet against his chest. "If you had ever visited the Apostrophes Munitions Museum ... other than to steal guns, I mean ... you would have seen this driving outfit in one of the display cases."

"Ow!" Devin Orff moans as Nothing Man puts more weight on the boot on Devin's stomach.

Nothing Man ignores him and continues. "Marshall Apostrophes wore this whenever he was driving in public ... you know, in a parade or whatever. As a bullet manufacturer, he had an overwhelming fear of being shot himself, so he had this driving coat made with built-in anti-ballistic armour."

Nothing Man steps off of Devin Orff, raises his fists, and says, "Now get up. If you think I hit you hard after the bank robbery, you have *no idea* how hard I'm going to hit you now."

Devin Orff does not get up.

"Get up and fight me. *One on one. One at a time. Fists against fists.* No guns. Just you and me."

Devin Orff does not get up.

"Yeah. That's what I thought."

Behind Nothing Man, footsteps crunch against the clay. It is Carl Crane, the Chief of the Faireville Police Force. He is flanked on either side by a short, slim male cop, and a tall, muscular female officer. All three have their pistols drawn.

"We'll take it from here," Chief Crane says. "Thanks, Nothing Man."

From across the chasm, Marty hollers, "AND THE PURPLE ZERO!"

Observer X runs over to Nothing Man. She pulls off her mask, lifts the driving helmet from his head, and stands on her tiptoes to kiss him, saying, "You're my hero, Bill Brown."

Bill kisses Elizabeth back, and says, "You're my hero, too, Elizabeth Murphy."

Chapter Fifteen

Bravely Into the Future

After the Showdown at the Faireville Badlands, Nothing Man and the Purple Zero will not be seen or heard from again.

The faded purple football sweater, the shoulder pads, the football pants, and the old-fashioned leather helmet will be placed back into the wooden crate by Marty Apostrophes. Bill Brown will do the same with the long, black, duster-style driving coat, the driving helmet, and the gauntlets. They will nail the crate closed and place it back where it was originally found, in a far corner of the Apostrophes Carriage House. The box will not be opened again until many, many years later.

Real Live Superheroes! Nothing Man and the Purple Zero will be the first and last video that will ever be uploaded by the notorious anonymous reporter known as Observer X.

The catlike Roman-style theatre mask, for which Elizabeth Murphy won a blue ribbon at the Faireville Agricultural Fair and Exposition in grade eight, will be hung up again on the wall in her father's "Creative Space" at the back of his art supply shop, where it will go mostly unnoticed. Elizabeth will keep the gloves and the tights, though; they will nicely complement the second-hand vintage-shop dresses that she will choose to wear instead of her father's coveralls.

But, without Nothing Man, without the Purple Zero, without Observer X, who will be the heroes?

Lance Goodfellow, somewhat predictably, will win the Male Athlete of the Year Award at the Faireville District High School grade twelve graduation ceremony, just like he did in grade eight at Faireville Public School. He will go on to play professional hockey, and he will be one of the top scorers in the league. Lance will become so famous, in fact, that the town sign will be modified to say:

Welcome to

FAIREVILLE

Population 3,511

"The Victorian Era Boomtown"

Hometown of Lance "Hot Stick" Goodfellow

Bobby Bingham will also become a professional hockey player, but he will be hired for his fighting abilities, rather than his playmaking or defensive skills. He will spend most of his career playing on the same line as Lance Goodfellow. After Lance comes out of the closet, Bobby will never say the words "fag," "faggot," "gayboy," or "homo" ever again; in fact, during their hockey games, Bobby will take great pleasure in expediently beating the stuffing out of anyone who addresses Lance Goodfellow using any of these terms.

The other members of the Faireville Blue Flames Triple-A Junior Hockey Team will not go on to play professional hockey, but most of them will excel at other things. Some will be good husbands, good fathers, good bosses, good employees.

Virginia Sweet, also somewhat predictably, will win the Female Athlete of the Year Award at the grade twelve graduation, just like she did in grade eight. Virginia will not pursue athletics after high school, though; rather, she will keep herself fit in order to achieve her goal of attracting a rich professional man, and as soon as he marries her, she will incessantly badger and malign and criticize him, until he gives her half of his money in exchange for a sanity-saving divorce. Virginia will repeat this process six times during her lifetime, and she will have more money in the bank when she dies than all of her ex-husbands combined. She will not, however, have many friends.

Virginia will lose touch with her high school Minions when she finds wealthier, prettier Minions in university. Her high school Minions, for the most part, will benefit from Virginia's absence. They will mostly marry nice, decent men, give birth to nice, decent kids, and generally live out their lives in nice, decent ways.

Marilyn Agnes will become an animator for one of the longest-running animated television shows in TV history. Kitty McMann will be a social worker who helps homeless people make the transition to affordable housing. After his near-death experience, Zig Zag Rogers will eventually wean himself off of recreational drugs, and he will insist on being called "Jimmy" again. He will eventually become a guidance counsellor at Faireville District High School, and his wife, Susan, will be the music teacher; she will still play her robin's-egg-blue Fender Stratocaster on weekends with her bar band, the Wailing She-Kats (who will eventually release an independent album, with cover art by a local painter named Jack-o Murphy).

Under a provision in the current, *real* young offenders' law, Cliff Boswink will be released early from his original sentence, after his testimony helps the prosecution convict his former friend Devin on numerous charges.

Devin Orff and his father, Clive, will never return to Faireville, and the Orff family's several-generations-old reign of terror will finally cease. Father and son will spend their remaining days inside the Gasberg Detention Centre. As an older man, Devin will get a chance at early parole from his consecutive life sentences, which will be denied when he loses his temper and throws a chair at a member of the parole board.

After his father and brother are sent to jail, Chris Orff will live with his friend Davey Batterwall. Perhaps not surprisingly, Davey's parents will exert a more positive influence on Chris than his own father ever did, and Chris will graduate from high school without another suspension, eventually becoming the senior custodian at FDHS.

But who will be the heroes?

Although Marty Apostrophes will never use his DRAMATIC VOICE again as the Purple Zero, he will use it for the many other roles he'll play as a professional stage actor. Marty will perform in some of the greatest theatres in the country, and even in the world.

Marty will become just as famous for being the life partner of hockey superstar Lance Goodfellow; when the cameras zoom in on the hockey players' wives in the seats at games, Marty will always be sure to wave and blow a kiss for all of the hockey fans watching the game on TV. Lance will become so famous as a game-changing superstar that the league will grant him special permission to wear the number zero on his jersey, as a tribute to Marty.

Although the crime-fighting career of Nothing Man will be short-lived, Bill Brown's peacekeeping career will have just begun on that fateful night on Burnoff Street. After graduating from high school, with good grades but no graduation-day awards or accolades, the steady, strong, even-tempered Bill Brown will enrol in Police College.

After serving as a constable with the Ontario Provincial Police, Bill will rise to the rank of Sergeant Major in the Royal Canadian Mounted Police, before finally returning home again to become the Chief of the Faireville Police Force (after the retirement of Carl Crane, whose impressive silver moustache will continue to serve him well as Faireville's ceremonial Town Crier).

Although Observer X's time as an anonymous reporter will also be short-lived, Elizabeth Murphy's career as a journalist will be long and fulfilling. Elizabeth will graduate at the top of her journalism class, and she will write gripping investigative pieces for several newspapers before making the leap to television reporting, where her sparkling personality and incisive interviewing style will make her show, *The Observer with Elizabeth Murphy*, very popular with viewers.

When Elizabeth discovers that she has inherited *The Faireville Gleaner* from Mr. Gootenbourg, she will leave one of the top-rated news programs in the country and return to Faireville, to become the Editor-in-Chief, Publisher, Copy Editor, Advertising Executive, Layout Editor, Office Secretary, Financial Controller, Maintenance Director, and Circulation Manager of one of the last independent local newspapers in the country.

And then, after years of living in different cities but keeping in touch as much as possible, when Elizabeth comes back to run *The Faireville Gleaner*, and Bill comes back to run the Faireville Police Force, their lives will intersect and merge once again, and Bill and Elizabeth will spend the rest of their lives together in Faireville. Their daughter, Kate, will be bubbly and bouncy, with wild hair and an enthusiastic temperament, just like her mother, and their son, Martin, will be tall and strong and hard-working, a man of few words, just like his father.

And when Marty inherits the Apostrophes Estate from his father, he will have absolutely no interest in living there anymore; he would rather have his condo in the city with Lance than a huge, pretentious estate.

So, Marty will give generous retirement packages to Bloombottom, Mildred, and Von Kruugen, and he will use most of his inheritance to convert the estate into a treatment and rehabilitation hospital for the victims of gunshot wounds. Marty will name the institution the Oliver Peershakker Centre, after his late elementary school principal.

Marty will also inherit Apostrophes Munitions, and his first act as president and CEO will be to pay out magnanimous severance packages to its employees. His second act will be to close down the bullet factory for good, and nobody will ever be killed or injured again by a bullet with Marty's last name on it.

To help fund the operation of the Oliver Peershakker Centre into the far future, Marty will sell most of the Apostrophes Estate's assets, including all of the cars in the auto collection, except for two: Marty will keep the Crosley Hotshot for himself, and he will give the Cord 812 Phaeton to Bill and Elizabeth.

Will the former superheroes be tempted to take the Black Phantom out for one last crime-fighting mission? Will they once more relive their former glories as Nothing Man, the Purple Zero, and Observer X?

Maybe they will, and maybe they won't.

Maybe in the future there will be another internet video, with a title like *Real Live Superheroes! Nothing Man and the Purple Zero RIDE AGAIN!*

But probably not; collectively, they will be too busy running a newspaper and enforcing the law and acting onstage and loving their respective spouses and children and friends.

So, who will be the heroes, then?

You. Me. Any of us.

Anyone.

When the circumstances call for it, any one of us can be a hero. A superhero, even.

Greatness can be thrust upon anyone, at any time, on any day.

Fun Facts!

The fictional town of Faireville also appears in the author's previous books, *Cheeseburger Subversive*, *Featherless Bipeds*, and *The Monkeyface Chronicles*. If you've read these other books, you might see a few familiar people and places in this one.

All the facts about the 1937 Cord 812 Phaeton, as well as all of the other cars in the fictional Apostrophes Auto Collection, are true (to the best of the author's knowledge and research, anyway).

Star Trek 101, *I Am Spock*, and *Captain Kirk's Guide to Women* are all real books.

Principal Peershakker's last name is a juggled version of Shakespeare, after the famous English playwright.

Principal Tappin's surname is a juggled version of Patton, after the Second World War general.

Mr. Moreau is named after the fictional "mad scientist" in *The Island of Dr. Moreau*, by H.G. Wells.

Mr. Gootenbourg's last name is a play on Johannes Gutenberg, the inventor of the movable-type printing press.

Zig Zag's nickname comes from a popular brand of cigarette rolling papers.

And, if you were really paying attention, you might have noticed that one of the lawyers in the "Criminal Masterminds" chapter is named Atticus, after the fictional lawyer Atticus Finch in Harper Lee's novel *To Kill a Mockingbird.*

Thanks!

For her tireless work as my literary agent, my thanks to Margaret Hart of the HSW Agency.

Thanks also to Editor Extraordinaire Barry Jowett, superstar copy-editor Andrea Waters, and the entire team at Dancing Cat / Cormorant Books.

For lending their skilled editorial eyes to the pre-submission version of this manuscript, thanks to my former writing students (and future bestselling authors), Julie McArthur and Kristi Ivan.

Thank you Nick Craine, for creating this book's awesome cover!

For generous support during the creation of this book, my sincere thanks to the Toronto Arts Council, the Ontario Arts Council, and the Canada Council for the Arts.

Part of this book was written during my term as Writer-in-Residence at the Richmond Hill Public Library, so my thanks to Li Chen and all of my friends at RHPL!

For their abundant love, support, and encouragement, thanks as always to my wonderful family, especially my parents, Mike and Judy Scarsbrook.

And here's a good quote from Bill Murray: "Be careful who you call your friends. I'd rather have 4 quarters than 100 pennies." It's good to know who my real friends are; my pockets are filled with silver dollars.

And to all of the other unsung heroes in my life ... keep fighting the good fight!

And, of course, this book is for Bluebell.